CW00337247

The Guide to Drama Training

in the UK, 1999/2000

by Sarah Duncan

The Cheverell Press

First published in 1990

This completely revised edition published in November 1998 for 1999/2000
Copyright © Sarah Duncan

British Library Cataloguing in Publication Data
A CIP record for this book is available for the British Library
ISBN 1-872390-20-X

The Cheverell Press
Manor Studios
Manningford Abbots
Pewsey
Wilts SN9 6HS

Typesetting: Geronimo @FirstHand.Net
Cover design: Mark Dunnett and Ed Thomas at Trevor Peters Design, Salisbury

Printed and bound in Great Britain by Redwood Books, Trowbridge, Wilts

The author states that the information contained in this book was checked as
rigorously as was possible before going to press. Neither the author nor publisher can take any responsibility for any changes which may have occurred
since, nor for any other variance of fact from that recorded here in good faith.
The author and The Cheverell Press have used their best efforts in collecting
preparing material for inclusion in this edition of The Guide to Drama Training
in the UK 1999/2000. It does not assume, and hereby disclaims, any liability to
any party for any loss or damage caused by errors and omissions in the Guide to
Drama Training in the UK 1999/2000, whether such errors and omissions result
from negligence, accident or any other cause.

Contents

Introduction:

What sort of course? 4

Raising the money 8

Some points to look for 9

Auditions 12

Specialist Courses 15

Course Directory 16

Section I: Drama School Reports 18

Section II: Degrees in: Drama, Theatre Studies and
Performing Arts 125

Section III: BTEC Awards in Performing Arts 175

Useful Addresses 181

Scholarships, bursaries, charities 182

Glossary of terms used 183

Index 185

Introduction

This book is based on visits to all the main drama schools in 1997 and 1998. During each visit I interviewed the principal or head of drama, had a tour of the facilities and met informally with some final year students. On the basis of these visits I have written a report. Many years ago I did the rounds of drama school auditions and I have tried to cover what I would have liked to have known then. I have tried to be unbiased, but there are undoubtedly some schools where I 'clicked' with the principals, and others where I didn't. Your preferences will not necessarily agree with mine, so there is no substitute for going and looking yourself. Ideally this will be before you apply for an audition.

Auditioning should be as much about you choosing a school as a school choosing you, although it may not feel like that. You could be spending as much as £30,000 in fees so don't accept the first place you are offered. It may be that you are turned down by your first choice schools. Consider auditioning next year rather than going to any school that will take you, especially if you are 18 or under.

Two schools are, in my opinion, a complete waste of time and money. Another three I would not recommend because I suspect that one is financially rocky and the other two are having staffing difficulties. Three others I personally would not go to on grounds of size alone. There are three which I liked very much and would like to see do well, but couldn't honestly recommend at the moment because they lack the status to seriously launch an acting career. A couple of others fall into the same category, but I liked them less as schools. If you discount these schools that still leaves twenty possibles. So how to choose between the schools? This is what I suggest you consider.

What sort of course?

How long should I train for?

Drama schools offer a 'complete' training in one, two or three years. Complete in this case means that you will be prepared for work as a professional actor and launched into the outside world at the end of your course.

Most three year courses follow the same format. The first year is spent in classwork and acting exercises, with little or no performance. The second year adds a few performances, maybe including a tour, plus classwork. The third year concentrates on productions, usually two a term plus a Showcase production of speeches aimed at agents, casting directors, directors and any other potential employer. Two year courses are compromises. They are for people who really need a three year course but cannot raise the money, so they get a shortened version of the three year course. This normally follows the same pattern as the three year course but spends two terms on each phase and not three. The exception is Bristol Old Vic where two year students do Years 1 and 3 from the three year course.

One year courses usually have the same format as the three year courses, but take one term to cover each phase and not a year. These courses are aimed at graduates and mature students who they assume have had considerable previous experience. Please note that the one year courses at Bristol Old Vic and Webber Douglas are not courses as such, but are tailored to the needs of individual students. Some schools, such as the Drama Studio, only run one year post graduate courses. Generally speaking the longer you train for, the more you will benefit. Voice training in particular is a long process and a short course allows little time for any personal exploration. Having done a one year post graduate course myself I know that, although I had a successful career as a professional actor, there were yawning chasms in my training and with hindsight I should have done a two year course (specifically the one at Bristol) or even a three year course. Many graduates do manage to raise the money for three year courses after taking their degrees and they are better actors for it.

Part time courses

There are two choices, firstly schools that offer training in the evenings so that students can work at their usual jobs during the day (for example, the Poor School), and secondly schools that offer training on three full days a week, leaving four working days (the London Centre for Theatre Studies is the only one currently offering this format). It must be emphasised that this is an extremely tiring and stressful way to train, especially as acting training can be demanding without the additional pressures of maintaining a 9 to 5 job.

It may be that your financial situation makes this kind of training the only option. Check out the exact number of hours you will be offered. LCTS for example offers 40 hours training a week, which is as much or more than many full time drama schools. Also compare the fees. None of the part time courses are as cheap as the full time course at Richmond Drama School for example.

Degree or not degree?

There are two choices here. First is to take a degree course in drama or theatre studies. This will not prepare you to become a professional actor and you will have to take another vocational course if you want to break into acting as a career. The second is to take a vocational acting course which may also be a degree.

If you want a career as a professional actor you should choose a course on the basis of what it teaches you and its status in the acting profession. Having a degree rather than a diploma will make no difference to your future employers. Drama school courses which have become degree courses have done so in the hope of increasing their students chances of getting grants from their Local Education Authority. If the school is a publicly funded institution grants are mandatory, if not they are still discretionary. This means that for most schools you are just as likely to get a grant as you would be if it was not a degree course.

There are disadvantages to mandatory status degree courses. Acting training is intensive and best taught in small groups. Students do not need hours of free time to research essays. University degree courses are usually taught in a mixture of lectures attended by hundreds of students and occasional one to one tutorials. Taught hours are low compared to drama schools. But drama school degree courses receive the same level of funding as, say, history degrees. So they need extra money. This can come from increasing student numbers (e.g. Rose Bruford), making the students pay 'top-up' fees (e.g. Central) or finding an outside source of funding (e.g. Guildhall and the City of London).

Discretionary status degree courses have the problem of all the extra paperwork, interference in their course structure and the added costs of the degree course. This was estimated by one school to be at least £30,000.

Vocational acting degree courses vary in the amount of academic written work and written exams you have to do. Some require an essay a term and a dissertation. Others need no written work at all. Some schools run a degree and a diploma course side by side, with the degree students having to put in extra hours each week. Choose what suits you.

The minimum qualifications are as follows: Applicants for the degree course under 21 should have the basic entrance requirements of 5 passes at GCSE and 2 passes at 'A' level or 5 passes in the Scottish Certificate of Education (at least 3 at the Higher Grade) or 4 passes n the Scottish Certificate of Education all at the Higher Grade or an BTEC Higher National Diploma or BTEC National Diploma/Certificate or GNVQ level or International Baccalaureate Diploma.

All vocational drama schools are prepared to waive the minimum requirements according to circumstances, and especially for those applicants over 21.

Finally, the sting in the tail is that it looks as if grants are going to be phased out completely and all students will have to cover their fees and maintenance through taking out loans. All in all, the schools which decided against becoming degrees, such as RADA, Webber Douglas and LAMDA, may have made the right decision.

Non-Vocational Degree Courses

Most degree courses are non-vocational, although many students intend to work as professional performers. Some, such as the courses at Bretton Hall and Dartington, are nearly vocational and students do manage to move into professional theatre without going on a further course. This tends to be those who want to work in specialised performance areas such as community theatre, theatre in education and performance art. Other courses are firmly academic, and it will count against you if you confess to wanting to be an actor or director at interview. You will almost certainly have to take a vocational training course if you want to get into professional theatre. There are many one year post graduate courses which turn academic knowledge and university performance experience into professional entry. Many graduates take longer courses, for example, a third of RADA students have already got degrees.

The one exception to needing a vocational course to move into the profession is Oxbridge graduates. There is a long tradition of Oxbridge graduates going straight into the profession. Recently this has included Emma Thompson, Tilda Swinton, Hugh Laurie and James Wilby. Imogen Stubbs, however, went on to RADA despite her double first from Oxford and taking all the lead roles at OUDS.

BTEC Courses

I have been told by several tutors on BTEC courses that they run vocational training courses, and therefore they should be included in this book as separate entries. I do not include them outside the general listing on p175 for several reasons.

Firstly, most students only get grants for the course that is nearest to them therefore they are not actually choosing from a selection of courses. Secondly, the courses follow the same curriculum and there is limited scope for the individual quirks that make the drama schools so different. Thirdly, while they may train in a vocational way, they are not accepted as vocational courses by the profession. Do agents, casting directors and professional directors come to their productions? No.

That is not to say that they have no value. Drama school principals across the board say that the standard of entrants has risen because more and more applicants have already taken a BTEC course before auditioning. Some courses are excellent. But you will still need to train at a vocational drama school to get into the profession.

Acting teaching methods

There is a story about Lawrence Olivier and Dustin Hoffman working on the set of the film 'Marathon Man'. Having spent days hanging around while Hoffman got into character Olivier took the younger actor aside. "Dear boy," he is alleged to have said. "You'll find it much easier if you try acting."

This sums up the differences between approaches to acting training. Some believe that in acting, truth is everything. Actors must know what their characters feel until it is instinctive. To be able to get to that point they must also know themselves. This is sometimes described by acting students as 'breaking you down and then building you up again.' At some schools it is the centre of the training.

The other extreme is not to teach acting at all. Students are taught the skills (voice, movement and so on) but learn acting through the experience of performing, preferably in a safe environment where they can fail. The assumption is that instinct is everything.

'Method' generally refers to a series of exercises which the actor can go through to discover more about their role, such as "What is my character's objective in this scene? What is their intention?"

Each school has its own approach to acting. The Drama Centre, for example, concentrates on their own method alone. Others look at a range of acting methods and styles. Some will require you to dig deep within yourself before you can be let loose on imaginary characters. At others you can go through the whole course without revealing anything about yourself. The shorter the course the more it will lean to acting by osmosis - there simply is not the time for personal analysis and development.

You should think about which approach you prefer before you start applying for auditions. The unhappy students I met were invariably the ones who had gone to the wrong sort of school for them. Not everybody wants to dredge up their inner selves, or is interested in becoming a commercial type to give the converse.

Raising the money

Whether you get a grant or not depends on a number of factors. Most LEAs only consider three year NCDT accredited courses. (NCDT accredited courses are marked with a *.) Predominantly rural areas are usually more generous; Berkshire, Cambridgeshire, Cumbria, Dorset, and Gloucestershire for example. Some LEAs make you audition for their own panel of expert assessors before choosing who gets grants. An expert member of one of these panels told me that most applicants were hopeless, but they had to give everybody marks above 80% and no negative comments were allowed on the assessment forms. The applicants they thought should get the grants they gave marks above 90%, but the final selection was made by the relevent committee. Off the record they admitted that a student who complained, appealed, or nobbled the committee first would be more likely to get the grants.

Failing a grant you will have to consider raising funds privately, through a career development loan or loans from family and friends. I met a student who worked flat out at two jobs for three years while living on baked beans to raise the money. Others have parents who mortgage their houses.

Some schools have scholarship funds available and there are several full fee scholarships for students on NCDT courses. Charities also give scholarships and bursaries to help students. There are details of scholarships and a list of charities which have given in the past on p182. Do not assume that you will be able to work in term time while you are at full time drama school. All schools advise against it and some flatly do not allow it. For part time schools, see above.

Students can be ingenious in raising funds. One wrote a book about how he raised the money and sold it, all profits going towards his fees. Apart from the usual suggestions about writing letters to all and sundry asking for help (or a £10 note) he suggested car boot sales, sponsorship from friends and family at £1 a week, and donations of non-perishable goods such as toothpaste, loo paper, food tins or stuff to sell at afore mentioned car boot sales.

Do not let the financial side put you off auditioning. Get a place first and then start worrying about the funds.

Some points to look for

Chances of getting in

At some schools the odds on getting in are as poor as 50 to 1. Although discouraging I believe that the worse the odds, the better the training. Look at it this way. Any one involved with education will tell you that some years are 'good' years. Usually a handful of extra talented students raise the overall standard. Conversely a handful of dullards bring down the whole class. I believe that the single most important factor in whether a school works for you is the quality of your fellow students. Obviously you cannot examine the rest of the people who might be taken onto your course. But if they are carefully chosen out of a large pool of applicants it stands to reason that they will be good, and together the standard of that year will be high. Looking at the ratio does not always work of course. For example, the Drama Centre's ratio is 14:1, nothing compared to RADA's 47:1. However, many people will be put off by the Drama Centre's prospectus and philosophy of training, which reduces the number of applicants and lowers the ratio. Exceptions aside, the more people that apply, the better that year will be.

Year size

I am totally prejudiced against large year groups. Acting training is expensive because it has to be taught in small groups. Although large year groups can be divided into smaller groups I believe that the quality of teaching is affected. There are more staff which makes the administration unwieldy. Individual attention becomes harder, if not impossible. It's fine if you are so talented that you will shine regardless of your year size, but what if you are middle of the road? And one cannot help but feel that the numbers are being added for financial reasons. Do you really want to be cannon fodder?

A small student year group means a lot of individual attention and small teaching units which is great, but it may also indicate that the school is having difficulty recruiting students. Another negative is that the school can become very intense and if, for some reason, you do not get on with your contemporaries there are few alternatives. In my opinion the ideal year size is between 20 and 35.

Location

There are four centres of actor employment in the UK: London, Cardiff/Bristol, Scotland (divided between Edinburgh and Glasgow) and 'The North', including Manchester, Leeds, Liverpool. You should train at a school in one of these areas, and preferably the centre where you think you are most likely to be employed. The largest employment centre is London, so if your school is not based there they should put on at least one Showcase production in the West End of London. No London based schools put on showcase productions anywhere else. The Welsh College of Music and Drama puts on their showcase production in Cardiff, London and Manchester.

Facilities

It is easy to be impressed with shiny new buildings and equipment. Always remember that it is the teaching that matters. There should be enough rehearsal rooms and studios so that space is not an issue. The school buildings should be open out of teaching hours so students can do their own work and preparation (for example, searching out new speeches in the library or researching current projects). A canteen (preferably subsidised) is a boon for impoverished students; I would rate a decent canteen over swanky television equipment anyday.

Decent performing spaces are not essential. At the time the drama school I went to did not have a theatre and performances were put on in what had been a Victorian gentleman's drawing room. Four weeks after leaving I was working in a major repertory theatre in a production which transferred to the West End. The difference was frankly not that great although, yes, it would have been nice to have had experience of larger stages at the time of training. More importantly, I would look for a school running a stage management course. This means that final year productions will be staged to professional standards and in fully equipped theatres regardless of whether the school owns its own theatre. Students at schools without stage management courses have to do the work themselves and there is no guarantee that your final work will be shown in a decent theatre space. Stage management work for actors is useful training if your main intention is to work in small scale theatre but frankly a waste of time if your ambitions lie elsewhere.

Television equipment is a very expensive bone of contention. Most schools argue that acting for the camera is not a special form of acting and that the skills can be picked up quickly. Some go further and say that the more real and truthful acting is the better it works on television. Others say that actors need training in camera work and experience of working on location, in studios, in single camera and multi-camera set ups. It is not clear which approach is right; good television and film actors have come from schools with widely different approaches. Most in-house directors working in drama schools come from the theatre and have little television experience. I think that regular classes using cheap video equipment with someone who can actually teach television acting techniques are preferable to the one-off three week television workshop with lots of cameras and an outside director who may have no knowledge of acting techniques at all, let alone the ability to teach them.

Timing

Most drama schools audition between December and June, with applications closing in March (Guildhall only audition 700 so their list is usually closed by the middle of January). Auditions are held throughout those months, with the proviso that auditions held away from the premises, for example overseas, are usually limited to one or two days. The schools with a large number of applicants are trying for a balance within their students so firm places are rarely offered before March. Being on the waiting list does not mean that you have number four on a list and are waiting for three others to drop out but means they are waiting to see where you might fit into the group they are forming.

Quotas

Most schools run informal quota systems. Some are up front, such as the Drama Centre which offers 20 male places to 10 female. Most schools aim for a 50:50 male/female ratio. The more applicants the school has the nearer to 50:50 or even 60:40 the ratio will be. This is because there are more parts written for men, and 70% of acting work is for men. More women apply to drama school however, so the schools which are less well known and therefore have to be less choosy about who they take on tend to have more women. This can mean casting difficulties for final year plays, with the men getting several plum roles while the women share out a few between them.

If you are a very particular type (for example, very short, very tall or very fat) it will be harder for you to get a place than Mr or Ms Average because they will probably only accept one student of that type onto the course. You might be called back for a recall to be compared side by side with others of your type.

The ideal age to apply to drama school is two or three years after you leave school. Schools like students to have some life experience before they start an acting course (or as one principal once memorably said to me 'They're here to act, not lose their virginity'). School leavers are often told to come back next year which is good advice.

Drama schools like graduates (from any subject, not necessarily drama) on three year courses as well as the one year courses. Some schools will not accept students above 30. Others are exclusively for post graduate students, although post graduate also includes mature students without qualifications but with life experience.

Principals

I prefer schools which do not have the founder/owner at the helm because it must stiffle any dissension from the staff or students and it means that they take the profits, whether directly or indirectly in possibly inflated salaries. I know of one school (with charitable status) which supports the principal in an extremely luxu-

rious life style including a yacht in the Caribbean!
Founder principals can also be a problem if they do not know how to let go.
Patricia Yardley at Birmingham has sensibly appointed an administrative and
an artistic successor and is now taking a back seat. Some founders are reluctant
to let go and at a few schools I visited there was a feeling of drift and lack of
purpose among the staff.
There can be an unsettled period when one principal leaves and another comes
in, especially if this is accompanied by a change in direction. Courses and staff
often changeover which means a lack of continutity in teaching for the students.
However, once that unsettled period is over, a lot of good can come out of it so
courses which underwent a changeover two years ago, say, are often at their most
dynamic now.

Leaving early

Most three course fees are paid on a termly basis. If you want to leave before the
end of the course you will have to pay for that term, but no further fees are due.
One year courses usually require you to pay the fees up front so if you decide to
leave then you are not entitled to have any of the money returned to you. One
two year course requires you to pay the fees for the full two years even if you
leave during the first term, which I think is outrageous. Please note that on a
one year course at a different school a student left early and tried to regain some
of the fees through the small claims court. As he had signed an agreement that
no fees were due to be returned if he chose to leave the case was dismissed.

Auditions

Auditions vary, but for most you will be required to prepare two speeches, one
Shakespeare and one modern, and take part in workshops including improvisation, movement, voice and possibly singing. At most auditions you start with the
two speeches and a short interview. This weeds out the no-hopers such as the
ones who do not learn their speeches. The next stage (possibly on another day)
moves onto classwork, interviews and more work on the speeches. There may be
several stages of weeding out on several days. The more applicants, the more
stages. Some schools try and fit it all into one day, others expect students to
come back time and time again.
Go to as many auditions as possible. Your audition technique will improve with
practice, so try and audition later for the schools you really want to go to. You
may even have the added confidence boost of an offer from another school.
Auditions are expensive if you get weeded out at the early stages but cheap if you
make it through to the final rounds. (After all, you will have had the equivalent
of a days training at the school and will probably been given direction on your
speeches which has to be worth £20 to £30.) Most who are weeded out in the

first rounds are too young, or have not bothered to learn their speeches, or do not appear to be committed to acting as a career.

There are several things you can do to improve your chances. Do some simple vocal exercises every day such as tongue twisters and humming or singing scales. Get fit. Give up smoking. Try some movement classes. Yoga is good because it teaches good posture, body control and controlled breathing, but almost anything will do. If there aren't any classes near you then get a video. You will have to do all of the above when you get to drama school so why not start now. Drama schools like to see evidence of a commitment to acting. Watching lots of TV does not count; working backstage at the local repertory theatre does. Most schools (and especially ones that offer a classical training) will also be looking for commitment to theatre acting. Now is not the moment to reveal that you do not see the point of theatre and just want to be on the telly.

Improvisation is a large component of actor training and you will almost have to do some at the audition. This may while your speech is being redirected or it may be in a group with others. Drama schools want team players, so try neither to dominate nor hang back in a corner. Some people are much better at picking up cues and suggestions than others - just watch 'Whose line is it anyway?' to see how some of the performers are almost telepathic. It can be learnt so join a drama group or encourage your friends to play charades for practice. Open up your mind. For example, if you were asked to improvise a customer coming into a hairdressers, why not be a customer whose hair has grown so long that it has to be pulled around in a little cart behind you rather than a lady just after a cut and blow dry.

Audition speeches

Several schools such as Central, Drama Centre and RADA have lists of speeches from which applicants must choose one, so if you're planning to apply to these schools your choice is in part made for you. Otherwise choose speeches which are in your age range and type, roles that you might be cast as. There are books which contain suitable audition speeches but always read the whole play - you might be asked about it.

The two speeches should be contrasting. This means that if one is tragic the other should be comic, if one is angry the other should be happy, if one is reflective the other should be direct speech. Always use monologues, that is, speeches written to be said in one piece, and not several sections cobbled together.

Never use props, do a speech on telephone or expect there to be a particular type of chair, for example. Keep speeches short. Most schools say under three minutes but a few have a two minute limit. Shorter is always better. Say your speech out loud when you are practising it however silly it feels. Include some movement in at least one of the speeches. This does not mean acrobatics necessarily but could include moving from sitting to standing, or lying down, or swirling round.

Speeches should be learnt properly. Get a friend to test you. You have learnt the speech well when your friend feeds you a word or two and you can continue the speech from that point. A frequent comment from schools is how surprised they are that so many people do not bother to learn their speeches properly. You simply will not get past the first round no matter how good an actor you are.

You will almost certainly be re-directed in your speeches. This means that the director will ask you to do the speech again but this time be angry, or do it in the style of a bus conductor or to imagine a poodle is sniffing your legs. This tests a) your imagination, b) how flexible your thought processes are and c) how amenable you are. You can practice this before hand by picking a word at random from a dictionary and doing the speech in the manner of that word however unlikely that word may be.

Shakespeare is harder than modern pieces, but do not be put off. The auditioners are not looking for performances worthy of the RSC, they want to see imagination and the enjoyment of the language. If the speech you have chosen has a particularly good word in it then relish it, even if you are not 100% sure what it means. Listen for the rhythms of the speech and practice saying the difficult bits until they are difficult no more. Go and see a Shakespeare performance or watch the video of Ian McKellens 'Richard III' or Kenneth Branaghs 'Much Ado about Nothing' to see how 400 year old plays can be as electrifying, exciting and funny as any modern film.

Finally remember that they are looking for potential not perfection. It is better to try something brave and extravagant and fail than to be dull. Jump on chairs, dance around the room, let your imagination go wild. Just don't be boring.

Getting help with your speeches

Students often want to know if they should have help with their speeches. The answer is probably no. The school wants to see how your imagination works, not how your drama teacher's does. They want to see what you make of it, not what you can be directed into. It has to be said that most drama schools are extremely disparaging of drama coaches or elocution teachers. One even went so far as to say that they would make more allowances for the applicant who had had help with their speech on the grounds that the help would almost certainly have been worse than no help at all. Drama schools want to see raw talent, and not something that is already polished to perfection.

Once you have been drilled to perform a speech in a particular way it can be difficult to accept direction. Remember that the drama school wants to see how open minded and flexible you can be and may deliberately ask you to perform in a completely different manner.

If you are really stuck and don't know where to begin then a good teacher can be invaluable. Look for someone who has trained at one of the better schools, has worked professionally and has contacts with drama schools. Your drama teacher at school or on your BTEC diploma course may not have been to a vocational course at all. They may be excellent, or they may also know very little about vocational training and the world of the professional actor.

Audition interviews

Your interview is an important part of your audition. Here are some of the questions you are likely to be asked. Why do you want to be an actor? Why do you want to come to this school? What plays have you seen recently? Who is your favourite actor? What is your favourite play? Which area of performance would you most like to work in? Why do you think you need a three year/ two year/one year course? Why did you choose that speech?

Specialist Courses

Stage Management and Technical Theatre

The lack of grants has hit stage management courses hard, with some courses closing and others struggling to be filled. It seems madness because out of all the performing arts courses stage management teaches skills that are in demand in a wide range of industries. Stage managers should look out for a school with good facilites, including a theatre and workshops, a wide range of staged productions at at different venues, and professional placements. Entry is through interviews.

Directors

Directors courses vary widely from being attachments tagged onto an acting course to being full programmes in their own right. When the Gulbenkian report into director training came out the only course it rated was that at the Drama Studio London. Since then a few more have been developed of which the MDra at RSAMD must be the most important. Look for a specifically designed programme of lessons and classes, opportunities to leave with a production ready for presentation and the use of professional actors and not the drama school students. I would also check the quality of the directors running the courses.

Musical Theatre

All drama schools teach singing and dance but if you are an actor who wants to do musical theatre there are a few courses specially designed for you. (Musical theatre dancers and singers usually train at dance colleges which are outside the scope of this book). Look for graded dance classes, individual singing classes and fully staged musical productions in your final year.

Course Directory

3 Year Acting - Mandatory Degree
Arden/26   Central/40   East 15/56   Guildhall/65
Manchester Met/83   Queen Margaret/97   Rose Bruford/105   RSAMD/112
Welsh College/122

3 Year Acting - Discretionary Degree
Drama Centre/48   Guildford/60   Mountview/86

3 Year Acting Diploma
ALRA/19   Arts Ed/29   Birmingham/32   Bristol/35
Cygnet/46   Drama Centre/48   East 15/56   Herts/68
LAMDA/71   OSD/91   RADA/108   Webber/19

2 Year Acting Courses
Bristol/36   Court Theatre/43   LAMDA/72   LISA/80
Redroofs/100   Science of Act/116   Webber/119

1 Year Acting Courses
ALRA/20   ARTTS/22   Arts Ed/30   Birmingham/33
Bristol/36   Court Theatre/43   Drama Studio/52   East 15/57
Guildford/62   Herts/68   LAMDA/72   LAPA/76
LISA/80   Mountview/87   OSD/92   Redroofs/100
Richmond/102   RSAMD/113   Science of Act/116   Webber/119
Welsh College/123

Foundation Acting Courses
LAMDA/73   LCTS/79   OSD/92

Part Time Acting Courses
LCTS/78   Poor School/94   Science of Acting/116

3 Year Actor Musician - Mandatory degree
Rose Bruford/105

3 Year Musical Theatre - Discretionary degree
Guildford/60   Mountview/86

1 Year Musical Theatre
Guildford/62   LAPA/76   Mountview/87

3 Year Stage Management - Mandatory Degree
Arden/27   Central/41   Guildhall/66 Queen Margaret/98
Rose Bruford/106   RSAMD/114   Welsh College/123

3 Year Stage Management - Discretionary Degree
Guildford/62

2 Year Stage Management Courses
Bristol/36   Guildford/63   LAMDA/73   Mountview/88
RADA/109

1 Year Stage Management Courses
ALRA/20   ARTTS/22   Birmingham/33   Court/44
Guildford/63   Mountview/88   Welsh College/123

1 Year Theatre Design
Bristol/37   Court Theatre/44   LAMDA/73   RADA/109

1 Year Wardrobe
Bristol/37   RADA/109

3 Year Directing - Mandatory degree
Rose Bruford/06

3 Year Directing
Science of Acting/116

2 Year Directing Course
Court Theatre/43

1 Year Directing Course
ARTTS/22   Court Theatre/43   Drama Studio/53   LAMDA/73
LAPA/77   Mountview/88   RSAMD/114

Academy of Live and Recorded Arts (ALRA)

Royal Victoria Building, Trinity Road, London SW8 3SX
Tel: 0181 870 6475 Fax: 0181 875 0789
USA Contact: Mark Hanau Tel: Los Angeles (213) 656 2185

Founder and Principal: Sorrel Carson

*   **3 Year Actors Course**
    1 Year Stage Management Course
    1 Year Post Graduate Acting Course

Fees:
3 Year Course: £3,149 per term, £9,447 per annum
1 Year Course: £10,398.75per course
1 Year Stage Management Course: £5828 per course
Scholarships - available, up to £18,000 in fees. No maintenance element.
Approx. 30 hours per week plus evenings and weekends on occasion.
3 Year Course, 33 weeks per year. Stage Management and 1 Year Course, 40 weeks.
Audition fees: Actors: £30. Stage Management: £15
Additional scholarship audition fees: Actors: £30. Stage Management: £15

Wandsworth is just south of the Thames and is a mixture of large, expensive houses plus the shops and restaurants they attract, to less agreeable areas. Over-all it's a nice area to live, with lots of flats to rent at reasonable (for London) rates. Central London is easily accessible by bus, train or car although there is no tube station nearby. Wandsworth is famous for low rates, the open spaces of the common and the prison. The Royal Victoria Building is an enormous Gothic edifice on Wandsworth Common, in one of the better areas (although you have to go through an estate of tower blocks to reach the building). After a period of neglect it was completely renovated into a mixture of office units, very smart apartments and a restaurant. ALRA is the largest single user of the building. The main facilities are the main theatre seating 100, the studio theatre seating 30-50 respectively, the huge Great Hall with a sprung dance floor, the television studio and new radio studio, plus other smaller rooms. The final showcase pro-duction is in the West End for the 3 year students, and at ALRA for the 1 year students.
Sorrel Carson founded the school in 1979, and is still the principal. Her philoso-phy is "acting is reacting. Don't act - I hate the word 'act' but one has to use it - once they start 'acting' then everything goes out of the window, and I don't believe them any more. But once they start to react..."

Auditions

ALRA used to be the school which did not ask for audition speeches. Now, audition speeches are optional, partly because "people think that it can't be a very demanding audition if they don't do pieces". The audition takes a full day, during which time there are classes in voice, movement and improvisation. All the work takes place in groups of about 10, except for interviews which are on a one-to-one basis. They stress that "we are looking for students, but you are looking for the right drama school for you. And if we say no to you, it isn't necessarily that you have no talent, it might be that this is the wrong school for you." In theory they take about 30 students onto the 3 year course each year, and 30 onto the 1 year course. However, "if I see someone with talent even after all the places have been taken, I can't help offering them a place." There are no quotas, although as with most schools, there are fewer male applicants and "talented men are much more difficult to get". If you want a scholarship who have to do another audition in the summer, for another fee, which seems hard.

3 Year Actors Course

The first year is seen as a year of self discovery. The philosophy 'Acting is Reacting' is introduced, together with character and ensemble work and the actor's approach to text. Apart from 'Acting is Reacting', the two most important aspects of becoming an actor are voice and improvisation. "Voice is very important. An actor without a good voice is not a good actor. And improvisation is the basis of good acting." Improvisation and text work are used to study Ibsen, Chekhov and modern writers. The history of theatre is taught in lectures, and Shakespeare is introduced.

There are classes in dance and movement, including classical ballet, mime and the Alexander Technique. Television is an important part of the course and is taught from the start. "We are not concerned with taking a big studio and doing a play and saying that is your television experience. It may not be as exciting as doing big productions, but they do two classes a week and it is the technical side we are interested in. So often youngsters go into television and fall down in rehearsals or shooting because they don't understand the technique, or what the director is asking for in technical terms." The camera is also used as a means of self-appraisal. Radio also starts from the beginning.

In the second year students work on projects which are performed in-house. Term one is Greek tragedy, term two, Shakespeare and term three, Restoration Theatre. Contemporary playwrights are also studied. Voice and movement classes continue, including historical dance, musical theatre and stage fighting. Radio and television classes continue, including single camera and multi-camera techniques, and different styles of television drama.

The third year concentrates on public performances, mainly at ALRA, but occasionally at other venues. The graduation showcase is held in a West End theatre for agents, directors and casting directors. Preparation classes, workshops and lectures are held throughout the year on subjects such as audition technique, Equity, agents, photographs, letters and CVs.

1 Year Post Graduate Actors Course
The course is seen as a transition year to take the student from "university or amateur drama experience to the professional theatre." The first three terms cover similar ground to the first two years of the 3 Year Course, with the proviso that "it takes at least three years to train a voice". Course work includes improvisation, playreading, scene study, radio and television technique, voice production, singing, movement, mime, historical dance, stage fighting, choral speaking and Shakespeare. The fourth term takes place in the summer and concentrates on productions and "preparing for work". The final showcase production takes place at ALRA.

1Year Stage Management Course
The course is designed as a practical apprenticeship which prepares students to enter the professional theatre with a range of practical skills and experience. Students receive a thorough grounding in all areas of stage management, including preparation of prompt books, lighting design and operation, sound preparation and operation, prop making, budgeting and production management. Television floor management and camerawork are also studied. There are attachments in Wardrobe and Scenic Art. Work experience and professional placements are arranged as appropriate. Throughout the course students graduate progressively to ASM and DSM responsibilities.

ALRA has been established for 20 years now. Along with Mountview it has had a reputation for over-crowding. The students I spoke to felt that there were too many people in each year, which meant that it was possible to drift along without anyone (apparently) taking much interest in you. They said that you had to discipline yourself to work hard, and that it was all too easy to just go with the flow. I think if I was a one year student I would be distinctly put out to have my graduation show at ALRA, on the grounds that hardly any agents, casting directors and directors will put themselves out and go to Wandsworth. If it is affordable for the three year students then it should be affordable for the one year students too. Currently I would say it is in a transition phase as Ms Carson hands over more of the day to day business of running the school to the staff.

Advanced Residential Theatre and Television Skillcentre International

Highfield Grange, Bubwith, N. Yorks YO8 6DP
Tel: 01757 288088 Fax: 01757 288253
email: artts@pavilion.co.uk website: http//www.pavilion.co.uk/artts

Principal: John Sichel, Associate Director: Duncan Lewis

1 Year Multi Media Course - Options in Acting, Directing and Production/Operations
10 Week Multi Media Foundation Skills
2 Week Short Course

Fees:
1 Year Course: £6,500 tuition plus £2,800 self catering accomodation (£9,300)
10 week course: £2,500 including self catering accomodation
2 week course: £560 including half board accommodation
Bursaries available, also deferred fee agreement
49 hours per week plus evenings, 40 weeks per year
Interview fee: None

York is in the North East of England, about 200 miles from London. The fast train takes about two hours. It is famous for Roman walls, medieval streets and is one of the most attractive cities in the UK. It has plenty of shops and restaurants, and outside the city is some beautiful countryside. The city has a repertory theatre and an active theatrical tradition that stretches back to the Medieval York Mystery plays, which are presented every four years. The coast is nearby, with Alan Ayckbourn's theatre at Scarborough in easy reach. The only drawback is that it attracts thousands of tourists and can get crowded in the summer months. ARTTS is situated in an award winning converted pig farm (the place abounds with piggy motifs) about 17 miles south of York. The school is entirely residential. Students have their own bedroom with wash hand basin and share a sitting room, dining room, kitchen and utility room between each group. The rooms are pleasant and well designed, but not particularly spacious. The building is on the outskirts of the village with the village shop and pub being at the other end. I personally would want my own transport, although the students did not seem bothered.
The school is well equipped with technical facilities, television studio, recording studio, rehearsal rooms, 200 seat theatre and editing suites which are arranged around a courtyard. Seating is incorporated into the design of the courtyard rather like an amphitheatre so that it can be used for open air performances.

Auditions
"Our selection procedure is very clear. We don't look for qualifications, we don't look for experience, all we look for is enthusiasm and commitment." Applicants fill out a form, and on the basis of that about one in three will be invited for an interview. This will be at ARTTS for UK and European applicants, and over the telephone for other overseas students. Less than half of the interviewees will be offered a place. There is a maximum of 36 places, although they usually operate at less than full capacity. "We are highly selective which is why we are never full - if we just took people who could pay we'd be full all the time". About 15-20 come in October and about 10 in April. Most students are over 21 and are graduates, although there are no strict age limits and many students have been under 21 and in their late 30s. The male/female ratio averages out at about 50:50.

1 Year Multi Media Course
The course trains actors, directors and production/operations technicians. Everybody does the same classes, regardless of their specialisation although "the actors get first call on acting roles, the directors get first choice for directing and so on." The idea is that everybody who leaves will be able to handle a wide range of work within theatre, film, television and radio and, according to ARTTS, most people who leave move from job to job in their first five years after leaving gaining experience before specialising in one particular area. The acting classes cover acting techniques for theatre, film, television, radio, microphone, character creation and development, communication skills, voice, movement (including jazz and modern), singing, improvisation, script and text study, audition and interview techniques. They will also have experience of directing and production such as editing, script writing, production management, design, stage management and camera operation.
One area which is stressed is personal development. "The only judgement we make of people here is DRAMA - Discipline, Respect, Attitude, Motivation and Application. If you have those five right then you are employable. Plenty of people have talent, but unless you can apply yourself to a job you can have all the skills in the world but it's not any good." Students are considered to be apprentices and are judged on professional standards, so no turning up late for class, or being ill, or not doing preparation work. "That's what it's like in the profession. On a film set I could be paying for 50 people and you've let me down, it's just 'Go'. It is as ruthless as that". That the students are resident on site is an important element. Each term the group elects a company manager who runs it as a production unit. "It can be like a pressure cooker, simmering with egos - imagine it! It's horrendous sometimes but they have to find a way of dealing with it."

About one person a year cannot handle it and leaves (probably about the same rate as any other drama school).

The year is divided into four ten week terms split by two week holidays. Hours are long, 9.00 to 6.00 Monday to Friday plus Saturday mornings 9.00 to 1.00. There is invariably work do be done in the evening, such as preparing a film treatment, or writing a script. "We reckon they do two years in one because of the evening work". On the very first day they are thrown into the deep end and expected to produce a television film. The whole course is like that, hands on and practical. Each week there are classes to give them "a staple diet of certain disciplines", namely acting, movement, creative writing, technical sessions across the four disciplines of theatre, film, radio and television, and physical and mental warm-ups every day of the week. "Everything is covered, but the order is changed depending on the group. It's geared very much to the needs of the trainees, not on just the need to get through the timetable". Mornings are spent on class work and the afternoons on the practical application of techniques, whether for theatre, film or television productions. Productions are performed in the theatres at ARTTS. Each year the students devise and write their own production for the Edinburgh Fringe Festival. There are many television and film productions throughout the year. An additional area of interest is ARTTS production which produces training films and corporate videos for major companies as well as drama productions. In their last terms students are able to work on these as professionals.

Short Courses

The ten week course is an introduction to all areas of television, video/film, theatre and radio. All aspects of a live performance from script to stage and screen are covered. The two week course aims to develop a wide range of skills and five an insight into working in the entertainment industry.

When ARTTS first started eight years ago I had my doubts about it's practicality for training actors. It seemed a good idea that a director should know about production and vice versa and over a wide range of disciplines, but on every production I had experience of actors were considered 'the talent' and were emphatically not part of the production team. The idea that an actor might taken equally seriously as a director was unimaginable. However, times have changed. Changes within the film and television industries such as casualisation, the end of the closed shop and the technical improvements to video quality have meant that the business has become much less rigid. People from a variety of backgrounds now make films and videos, write plays and screenplays, direct. An actor such as Peter Howitt can write and direct a major film, 'Sliding Doors' with Gwyneth Paltrow. Emma Thompson wins an Oscar for her screenplay of

'Sense and Sensibility'. Even Quentin Tarentino was first an actor (and sadly persists in casting himself in his films). Nowadays most drama school graduates get their first jobs in television not repertory theatre or set up their own theatre companies. The multi-skilled actor has arrived.

So, if you think you are an actor with a curiosity about the production process, then this is a good course. If you think you just want to act, then this is not a good course, and you should go to one of the other drama schools listed in this book. It also heavily leans towards film and television, and I doubt if any acting graduate from here would be aiming for the Royal Shakespeare Company. Then there is the residential element. The students I spoke to said it could become claustrophobic and that there could be problems, but "you're working too hard to have the time or energy for major rows" said one. An acting student said "I get to do a lot of acting here as well as learning other skills. I think it's good to know that you have all these skills because most actors don't work most of the time, and who knows how things will work out for me? At least on this course I have skills that are in demand. That's why I chose it."

The Arden School of Theatre

Arden Centre, Sale Road, Northenden, Manchester M23 0DD
Tel: 0161 957 1500

Head of Acting: Wyllie Longmore

3 or 4 Year BA/BA (Hons) Acting Studies
3 or 4 Year BA/BA (Hons) Theatre Arts

Fees:
All courses: Mandatory grants, £1000 other
Audition fee: £15

Manchester is one of the biggest and most cosmopolitan cities in the UK and many young people consider it to be the most exciting place to live in Britain. There are four theatres, Granada Television, the Halle Orchestra, one of the largest student populations in Europe and a vibrant night life. It is also the home of Manchester United and Manchester City football clubs and the Old Trafford cricket ground. Accommodation is easy to find. The school was set up in association with the internationally renowned Royal Exchange Theatre Company about seven years ago. Arden is based within City College a few miles out of the centre of Manchester and has access to its facilities including a 250 seat theatre, numerous large dance and rehearsal studios, sound recording studios. There is a large canteen where, disconcertingly, one of the serving staff advised me to keep hold of my handbag at all times.

Auditions
A preliminary audition is held at the Royal Exchange rehearsal rooms in the centre of Manchester. This is a basic interview; applicants who fail at this stage are usually considered too immature. Applicants are then asked to come to a day long workshop at the Arden Centre. For this they are required to prepare some text "They have ten minutes to present anything, which needs to include some words, but could include singing or dancing. We prefer an all-round presentation". They have a list of 'don't do' speeches. Each student has a long interview in front of a panel of three which includes the principal and often the casting director of the Royal Exchange. Currently they are seeing about 160 applicants for 30 places. There are no age limits, although "we tend not to choose the 18 year old". Most students are in their 20s or 30s; they have had a 60 year old on the course.

3 or 4 Year BA/BA (Hons) Acting Degree

The first year is a foundation year where students explore questions such as "What is acting about? What skills do you bring to it? Who are you?" There is very little text work in the first year. "Acting is about far more than learning lines. Practical skills classes include movement, physical theatre, dance, Tai Chi, Alexander technique, phonetics, voice, verse, text study, singing and acting. In this year there are two central projects, one Medieval and one Greek, both performed outside to staff and fellow students.

The second year is more text based. There are modules on Naturalism, Stanislavski as a theorist, Chekhov, challenges to naturalism, Brecht, expressionism, performance arts and comedy. The year ends with the first public performance at the Arden Centre.

The third year concentrates on public performance, always using external directors and designers. Usually each actor performs in four productions, including a Shakespeare in the autumn, four short plays which tour local schools and colleges, and a musical. In the Spring term there is a Show case production for agents, directors and casting agents in both Manchester and London.

Television is covered briefly. They do not have any equipment on site so bring in a team for a workshop. The same applies for radio.

In the third year there are 'preparing for work' blocks. These include practical audition workshops, simulated interviews and seminars with theatre professionals. The relationship with the Royal Exchange does not extend to it taking on Arden graduates, although some have worked there, as have current students in minor roles. However students do go and see productions regularly and meet the directors and actors, who also come to Arden and give seminars. The Royal Exchange casting director also gives advice to students. "They are good advisers and a good professional model. Perhaps you could say we have a godparent and child relationship."

As a degree course there is some written work. Students are expected to keep an acting journal throughout their time at the school and write a self evaluation after each project. In the first year there is one formal essay plus tutorial papers and in the second year two essays of about 2000 words each. There is the option of creating a production portfolio or giving a lecture demonstration. In the third year there is an essay on Shakespeare.

The fourth year is the Honours year. In this year students work by themselves a lot and all their work attracts a written element. They can look at other aspects of theatre, such as directing, issues in contemporary theatre, playwriting. They also undertake placements. Finally they have to write a dissertation, which is either 10,000 words or 5,000 and a practical demonstration.

3 or 4 Year BA/BA (Hons) Technical Theatre Arts

The aims of the course are: to prepare students for a creative working life in which there will be a variety of professional experiences; to offer a course which integrates theoretical, critical and conceptual study with practical application; to offer a course which encourages a breadth of knowledge, curiosity and originality and opportunities for specialism, in order to enable students to meet the intense demands of the theatre and arts entertainment industry. The major areas of the course are contextual studies, design, stage and production management, lighting and sound.

When asked what the school's strengths were Wyllie Longmore told me that "we treat people with respect, we see people individually, we have no preconceptions of them. Maybe we attract more outsiders. I would never say that we produce a stamp of Arden School." The students I spoke to agreed with him. Several felt that they would never have been considered for another drama school. "I don't know what would have happened to me if I hadn't come here. I don't care if I never act professionally, it's been worthwhile just to be here" said one of the older students. "You feel special, important" said another. "We're all really different, but it works." The school is new and relatively unknown, which perhaps reflects the lack of confidence exhibited by the students about becoming professional actors. However, there are good foundations here to build on such as the links with the Royal Exchange. My impression was that there would be no compromising on the standards required, but each student would be judged on their own merits.

The Arts Educational Schools

Cone Ripman House, 14 Bath Road, Chiswick, London W4 1LY
Tel: 0181 987 6666 Fax: 0181 987 6699

Member of the Conference of Drama Schools

Principal: Peter Fowler, Drama School Director: David Robson
Post Graduate Course Director: Adrian James

*   **3 Year Drama Course**
*   **1 Year Post Graduate Acting Company**

Fees:
3 Year Drama Course: £2,575 per term, £7,725 per annum
1 Year Acting Company: £8,000
No scholarships, but some help may be available for existing students.
55 hours per week
Audition fee: £30

Chiswick is a very pleasant part of West London, with good road and tube access into the centre. Students usually live locally. The school is based in a former polytechnic. Class rooms are large, light and airy and there is a large, newly equipped 320 seat theatre on site, a 250 studio theatre plus other facilities such as a large student canteen. Productions are also mounted in the pub theatre virtually next door. The origins of Arts Ed are from two drama schools set up in 1919 and 1922 respectively which were combined in 1939. At the end of the war in 1945 the boarding element of the school specialising in ballet training split off from the rest of the school, and is now no longer part of the Arts Educational Schools London. This consists of three distinct schools, full time academic and vocational education for 8-16 year olds up to GCSE, full time academic and vocational education up to A levels for 16-18 year olds and the two students' courses which are covered here. As a result, there could be 8 year olds as well as 28 year olds learning within the building at any one time. The post graduate one year course is separated from the rest of the school, being based in the former care-taker's house in the middle of the site (although classes take place in the main buildings). This gives a company feel to the year and helps to make them a cohesive group. There is a certain amount of friction between the younger and older elements of the school - "we complain about the noise, and they complain about the bad language" - but nothing major.

Auditions

About 500 apply for 25-30 places on the 3 year course, 15-20 on the post graduate course. About 25 applicants are seen each time. On arrival they are split into three groups and take classes in movement, improvisation and voice work. After lunch they perform two speeches, one classical, one modern - "the usual". People who they are interested in are then asked to stay for an interview. "We don't do recalls because normally you can see there and then who you want to accept anyway, and recalls mean that they have to travel from God knows where and spend a lot of money and I know how short of money people are." They try to have an equal number of men and women. The average age on the three year course is 20 (but they have accepted a 29 year old in the past), the post graduates are mainly in their late 20s, early 30s with no upper limit. The oldest so far was 55.

3 Year Drama Course

The emphasis of the course is on the actor in performance and is Stanislavski based. "We're definitely a Method school, but we don't adhere to it all the way." The work is taken extremely seriously, with 10, 11 or even 12 hour days being the norm. Students are expected to stay researching or working on their projects for a further two to three hours after classes finish at 6.00, and most come in early to get more work done. Every morning starts with an hour long warm-up for everybody on the two courses together. This could be movement, voice or improvisation. The first year is class based, with end of project performances for the staff only. Classes include acting, voice, dance for actors, Alexander technique, vocal development, singing, transformation, improvisation, stage combat and English for foreign language speakers. "We have quite a few foreign students, especially Norwegians. Our reputation there is so high that they can go straight into the state theatres after they have finished here". There is also a Shakespeare project.

In the second year "we tend to open up more. We want people to find more of their physicality and daring, so we bring in all sorts of things, such as commedia and mask. That's also why we do a musical in the second year". Other classes are added such as play reading and sight-reading. Projects include Shaw, Brecht and a modern playwright as well as the musical. Performances are put on for staff and fellow students. At the end of the year productions are taken out to schools to give experience of Theatre in Education. The third year is performance based with performances and rehearsals taking up much of the time. Television technique is covered by regular classes plus workshops. A business course runs for a term and a half, looking at auditions, how to run a business as an actor, presentation and so on. There are two productions each term, usually with five studio performances and four in the main theatre. These are all open to the public. A showcase production for agents, directors and casting directors is held in April, because each summer some of the students leave early to start work.

1 Year Acting Company

The post graduate course is similar in approach from the three year course in the sense that it is Stanislavski and Laban based and very concentrated - scheduled hours are from 9.00 am to 9.00 p.m. "We need somebody who has absolute commitment and has the ability to go straight into it because of the short time; they can't spend time thinking about it. They've go to be prepared to accept criticism and to go with it. We can offer a safe space where people can fail, and this may be their only opportunity to fail." The first term is spent learning an approach to craft and establishing professional working practices, the second looks at adapting the craft to the demands of the text and the application of professional working practices and the third term is entirely performance. They take over the Riverside Studios in Hammersmith for a month and do three plays there in repertoire. The students run it as a professional fringe company and are required to manage all the business side, such as publicity. One of the rooms in their house is set up as an office with a computer, telephone and other equipment that they need.

David Robson and Adrian James are terrifically involved with their respective courses and expect the students to be so too. This is not a course you can drift through; it is hard physical and mental work. As well as long hours the school demands high standards in personal discipline. If you're not punctual when you start, you will be within the first few weeks. Late arrivals in class are simply not allowed in. When I interviewed the students during their lunch break, after 1.50 they all kept one eye on the clock and abruptly vanished at 1.55 - the whole student common room literally emptied within one minute so as to be on time for their 2.00 class. It was impressive, if a bit scary. But the students loved it. It actually brought tears to one post graduate's eyes as she told me how wonderful the school was and how caring the staff. It almost brought tears to my eyes when they told me the hours they put in, but there was not a word of criticism from anyone. It is not a fashionable school, and it has not produced a recent Oscar nominee, and it definitely is not for any one who is not dedicated to being an actor. It produces dedicated, well trained, disciplined actors and offers excellent value for money. One of my favourites and highly recommended if you have the stamina.

The Birmingham School of Speech and Drama

99 John Bright Street, Birmingham B1 1BN
Tel: 0121 643 4376   Fax: 01121 633 0476
email: bssd@bssd.ac.uk   website: http://www.bssd.ac.uk/bssd

Member of the Conference of Drama Schools

Principal: Patricia Yardley, Vice Principal: Michael Gaunt, Chief Executive: Simon Woods

* **3 Year Professional Acting Diploma**
  1 Year Professional Acting Diploma
  1 Year Professional Stage Management

Fees:
3 Year Professional Acting Diploma: £6690 per annum
1 Year Professional Acting Diploma: £6999 per annum
1 Year Professional Stage Management: £6795 per annum
Scholarships: some bursaries to cover fees up to £1000.
33 weeks per year
Audition fees: Actors £25, Birmingham or New York. Stage Management: £12.

Birmingham is in the centre of England, and is Britain's second city. There are good road and rail connections with the rest of the county. In the city there are repertory theatres, concert halls, the National Exhibition Centre, and two television companies, the BBC at Pebble Mill and Central Television. Accommodation is cheap and easily available. The centre of Birmingham has had a huge face lift in the last few years. Money has poured in creating spectacular public spaces and buildings, one of which is the Library Theatre. This is housed within the central library (the largest lending library in Europe) and is used by the school for all its productions. The school was founded in 1936 by the principal's mother. Recently it has moved from premises in the suburb of Edgbaston into the bustling centre. The new building has high ceilings, lots of rehearsal rooms and studios and a subterranean student common room with a vending machine for hot drinks.

Auditions
250 apply for 34 places on the three year course, 200 apply for 24 places on the one year course. Two contrasting speeches are asked for, one classical and one other, plus a lyrical poem. The audition is in two stages. In the morning appli-

cants perform their speeches and are marked out of 20. In the afternoon about 60% are selected to perform their speeches again plus the poem and take part in singing, movement and improvisation workshops. Then they are interviewed by the principal. Again they are marked; over 45 and they are offered a place, 42-45 they are asked to come back on for a recall audition. They pride themselves on giving feedback, so you will be told what to work on if you fail. They try for a male/female ration of 50:50. For the three year course, the minimum is 18 with no maximum, but the majority are in their early 20s. For the one year course the minimum is 21 with no maximum (they have had a 60 year old), but the majority are in their mid to late 20s.

3 Year Professional Acting Diploma
"These are performance based vocational courses. We offer a range of classes to give a framework for continued learning. You can't leave and say 'I've done it all'. You will leave with a range of skills. Acting is a life long learning experience and we are equipping you for that. We want to release your natural ability." The first year is seen as a chance to "find out about what it takes, to interpret, to experiment, to take risks." Each term there is one in-house performance which is seen as a 'work-in-progress'. Classes concentrate on singing, movement and voice.

The second year continues from the first, with classes and increased performance. There are two 'workshop' productions a term (minimal costume and set), of which one will be a musical. These are open to the public and are produced at the Library Theatre. Sometimes one production is a TIE project which they tour to local schools.

During year three there are two 'professional standard' productions a term, all in the Library Theatre, of which one will be a musical. Recently at least one production has been presented as part of the national "Towards the Millennium" Festival. In the final term there is a Showcase production in Birmingham and London for agents, casting directors and directors.

Television is covered by workshops during the second and third years. One workshop is studio based, while the others take place on location using a professional crew and director. Radio is studied throughout the course using professional studios. The school runs its own agency so there are opportunities for students to work professionally while they are at the school, usually in promos, radio commercials and trailers. This is part of their policy to "put students into a professional environment, to train students in real, live theatre. We increasingly use commercial facilities."

There is an optional musical theatre strand. Students who take the option are streamed in singing and dance classes for the first two years and perform a musical workshop production. In the final year they perform a fully staged musical as one of their productions.

1 Year Professional Acting Diploma

The first term aims to provide a grounding of the core skills - voice, acting and movement - through classes and non-public performance. In the second year classes continue and there is the first public performance. In the final term the students rehearse and perform a full staged production in the Library Theatre plus a Showcase production for agents, casting directors and directors in Birmingham and a West End theatre. Also in the third term is a television workshop. Radio is introduced in the second and third terms. Career management preparation is provided throughout the year along with the third year students. The agency represents students both before and after they leave, until they gain another agent.

1 Year Professional Stage Management Diploma

The course is intended for students who seek a career in stage management and related roles in other media. Students may enrol at the start of each term: September, January and April. The course is the combination of two previous longstanding courses, a two year stage management course and a one year post graduate course. The focus is on learning through working on productions with regular classes and specialised workshops. The course covers stage management, properties and scenic construction, Sound and LX, stagecraft, resource, human, physical and financial management and additional classes. Students join with the acting students for basic vocal and movement warm up sessions. There is a period of work experience at the end of the second or beginning of the third term. In the first term students work as assistant stage managers on the school's main productions. This includes working on properties, costume, lighting and sound. They also help with the rigging, setting and striking at the venue during the production period. In the second year they assume the role of deputy stage managers, supervising the ASMs. In the final term they act as Stage Manager for one of the main productions.

In the last ten years Birmingham has changed dramatically from being dull and old fashioned to being modern and dynamic. The same could be said for the Birmingham School of Speech and Drama. The first changes were made when Simon Woods arrived to move the school into new premises in the heart of Birmingham. Now Michael Gaunt has come in to act as vice principal. He changed Guildford School of Acting into a modern and vibrant school, and will presumably do the same job here. Together they should make Birmingham one to watch. Students thought the changes so far were great, especially the new building. They enjoyed the course and they enjoyed Birmingham.

Bristol Old Vic

2 Downside Road, Clifton, Bristol BS8 2XF
Tel: 0117 973 3535 Fax: 0117 923 9371

Member of the Conference of Drama Schools

Principal: Christopher Denys

* **3 Year Acting Diploma**
* **2 Year Acting Diploma**
   1 Year Post Graduate Attachment
* **2 Year Stage Management and Technical Production HND**
   1 Year Theatre Design Course
   1 Year Wardrobe Course

Fees:
All courses: £2450 per term, £7350 per annum
Audition fees: Preliminary Audition £20 London or Bristol, £25 overseas. Weekend School additional £20 (also allow for overnight accomodation in Bristol)

Bristol is 120 miles directly to the west of London, and has a reputation for being a fast growing, dynamic city, great for student life. Bristol University is very lively and has a well known drama department (see page 131); graduates often go onto the Old Vic courses. Bristol also has a repertory theatre and many television, film and radio companies are based here, from Aardman Animation (of Wallace and Gromit fame) to the BBC. The school was founded in 1946. It is on the edge of the wide open spaces of the downs in Clifton, the 'best' part of Bristol, in a pair of large, semi-detached Victorian houses which have been joined together. At the back a new development has given a television studio, dance studio and workshops. There is no theatre and all public productions take place at venues outside the school. Unlike any other drama school except Arden there are direct links with the local repertory company, in Bristol. Final shows are put on at the Theatre Royal, directors and actors take classes from time to time and students may be cast in plays.

Auditions
The first audition lasts for fifteen minutes and consists of performing two speeches, one from a classical verse play (preferably Shakespeare) and one from a modern prose play. The two pieces together should not exceed four minutes. There is a brief interview and applicants may be required to sing, unaccompanied, a short

song of their choice. 300 are asked to return for a weekend school. These start at 6.45 on Friday evening and finish on Saturday at 3.45. During this time they will take 75 minute classes with all the heads of department - voice, movement, acting and so on. About 1000 (it has been up to 2000) applicants are seen for 12 places on the 3 year course, 12 places on the 2 year course and up to 4 places on the post graduate vocational attachment. The age range for the 3 year course is 18 to 30 "but we're very reluctant to take 18 and 19 year olds", the average age is 25, and they have taken a 40 year old. The two year course "we're looking at 25 as the minimum age", with most being between 25-35, although they have taken up to 55, and there are usually people in their 40s on the course. The post graduate attachment has no age limits.

3 Year Acting Diploma
The first year is class based, working on voice and body "the first few weeks are very difficult, especially the ones who have just been hunched over desk for three years, because until they are fit there is not a lot you can do for them. We want to turn out people who have the choice to stand well. For example, the flavour of the moment is Jane Austen and you need to be able to stand up straight, wear period clothes and talk properly. Then if you want you can characterise by altering the posture and the voice." These classes cover voice production, speech, verse speaking, singing, dance, mime, tumbling, combat, acrobatics, microphone and camera techniques. Then there is text based work. "We are, after all, preparing people to make a living by performing texts with may range from Aeschylus through Shakespeare, Sheridan, Wilde, Shaw, Coward etc. to TV sitcoms and hospital, crime or fire-fighting based drama and classic serials." Students are expected to do considerable background reading in their own time, from The Stage newspaper and plays to theatre history and social background. All performances are to the staff only.

The second year is performance based. The first term starts with a tour of the Nativity based on the Mystery plays. "It's a baptism of fire, a member of staff goes with them to drive but ideally do nothing else." This goes out and does 60 to 64 performances at schools, churches and hospitals, ending up with two performances at the Theatre Royal (which are always sold out). During this time they are also taking classes and working on other projects such as "Sheridan and really bad TV scripts - how do you cope? - and lots of Shakespeare because that's the hardest thing". In the second term the project is a TIE tour. The students are split into two groups of six, and work with the same script but different directors to produce two different versions of the same play. Each group does 20 performances each on the standard Equity TIE contract. The third term is the West Country tour to a wide range of about 22 to 24 venues, one and two night stands. During the year they also do a television project which might be single camera on location or a multi camera studio set up. There are also television classes. Another feature is that they record all the 'A' level plays for BBC local radio, in BBC studios with BBC directors. These are broadcast on local radio stations throughout the country.

The final term continues classes, plus productions. They do six main house shows, four lunchtime productions, an in-house musical "primarily for those who are unlikely to be cast professionally in a musical so that they get the feel of it". There is a Showcase production for agents, directors and casting directors in Bristol and at a West End theatre in London. Productions are put on at the professional theatres in Bristol, the New Vic, the Redgrave and the Theatre Royal. Throughout the year there are classes on presentation, marketing yourself and so on. Each week a professional such as a casting director or agent comes in and students perform their two speeches as if for a professional audition. At the end they get notes on how well (or badly) they did and have the opportunity to ask questions.

2 Year Acting Diploma

"It is important to understand that the two year course exists purely for reasons of finance - or, rather, the lack of it. It is not the three year course compressed for those who are capable of working harder." In effect the two year course consists of the first and the third years of the three year course, missing out the performance opportunities of the second year.

1 Year Post Graduate Attachment

The one year post graduate attachment is not a course as such at all, and some years they do not accept any students on to it. What the attachment consists of depends largely on what the individual wants or needs. For example, several previous students have been professional dancers who wanted to move into acting. Therefore they had intensive classes in acting, voice and text study, and very little on movement. The first two terms are of basic training and the last is of preparation for public presentation to employers.

2 Year Stage Management and Technical Production Course

As well as running acting training courses the Old Vic has several well-established courses in production. The two year stage management and technical course (which is validated as a BTEC HND course) offers training for a career in stage management or any technical or organisational area of theatre, television or radio. The last two areas have expanded to reflect the changing nature of the arts and entertainment industry. The first year is a foundation in all the course subjects: stage management, propmaking, lighting, sound and scenic construction. Other subjects include technical drawing, play reading, voice, photography, video, radio, production management, welding, publicity and administration. All students are involved with the productions put on by the school, whether on tour or at the Bristol Old Vic. The second year builds on this foundation and students work in a variety of roles, such as stage manager, propmaker, carpenter, lighting designer, lighting operator, sound designer or sound operator on the school's theatre and touring productions. They also work to broadcast standards in the schools own multicamera studio and digital 16 track recording, mixing and editing equipment. All students spend three weeks on attachment to a professional company.

1 Year Theatre Design Course
A maximum of four students are taken onto the Theatre Design Course, which claims to be the only one set in an all-round theatre school. Entrance is not limited to those with previous training, although the majority do come from degree courses. The first term consists of classes in design, model-making, technical drawing, architectural and costume history and design, carpentry, painting and prop-making techniques. Each student carries out a complete production design. The second term involves designing public productions under supervision, seeing the whole design process from the first discussions with the directors to models, working drawings, construction, painting and the realisation of their work on stage. The third term involves designing for the final "showcase" productions at the Theatre Royal and New Vic Studio. Alongside this each student is help individually to prepare a CV and portfolio and given guidance in and experience of interviews for employment. The year culminates with an end of year exhibition at the Bristol Old Vic and a central London venue.

1 Year Wardrobe Course
The wardrobe course is an intensive vocation and highly practical course covering all aspects of theatre wardrobe work. This includes pattern-cutting, costume making, fabric printing, dyeing, millinery, corset making, history of costume, hiring and buying to budget, wig care, basic make-up and organisation. The students work to design briefs and make and dress all the schools public performances (about ten to twelve each year). There are exhibitions of the students work in London and Bristol at the end of the year. Four students are accepted onto this course.

For one of the major drama schools, Bristol Old Vic is tiny, with a maximum of some 80 students at any one time across all the areas of study. Being in Bristol rather than London makes hardly any difference to one's career prospects and is probably a more pleasant experience. Because of it's location, permanent staff are exactly that; unlike the London schools they can not teach at a different institution on different days of the week. This gives continuity and makes co-ordination between the various departments easier. (However they are all practising professionals and it is expected that they will go off and take professional jobs from time to time). Another advantage of the Bristol location is that the television series 'Casualty' is filmed there and is ever hungry for new actors. The quantity and range of the productions is exceptional in the second year, although the thought of all those schools and village halls might put some off. I had expected there to be a great sense of camaraderie between the students because of the smallness of the school and the shared experiences of touring, but apparently not. "Not in my group anyway" said one student glumly, who felt that there had been too much touring. Another felt "because they always emphasise what's going to happen when we leave, you can feel a bit, it's everyone for themselves. We're encouraged to be individuals, but it means sometimes that you look on the others as the competition." Camaraderie or lack of it aside, they thought the training was excellent and that the school provided lots of support and help at the beginning of a career. One of my favourites, and the two year course is particularly good for those who have had a lot of performing experience but want the techniques and the career development.

The Central School of Speech and Drama

Embassy Theatre, 64 Eton Avenue, London NW3 3HY
Tel: 0171 722 8183 Fax: 0171 722 4132

Member of the Conference of Drama Schools

Principal: Robert Fowler, Head of Performance: Anthony Castro

* **3 Year BA Acting**
* **3 Year BA (Hons) Theatre Practice**

BA (Hons) Drama and Education, p133
BA (Hons) World Theatre at the South Bank University, p 168

Fees:

3 Year BA Acting: Mandatory grants plus extra £950 'top-up' fee,
3 Year BA (Hons) Theatre Practice:
Somerset Scholarships available to Haringey residents under 25.
Audition fees: London £25, Overseas audition £65

Swiss Cottage is just north of Regent's Park and south of Hampstead, both very smart areas of London. The school is conveniently situated a few minutes walk from the tube station and students live all over London. The school was founded in 1906 and moved to the Embassy Theatre in 1956. The school has developed three strands of training: for actors and stage managers, for speech therapists and for teachers (many of the voice teachers you find in drama schools are products of Central). It became a publicly funded institution in the 1980s, similar to a polytechnic and now offers some 16 main courses, from BTEC diplomas to MAs. Overall there are now about 750 students in the school of whom some 150 are actors or stage managers on the BA Acting and BA (Hons) Theatre Practice Course. Throughout the 1990s buildings have been refurbished and new ones built. Facilities include the Victorian Embassy Theatre (built 1899), a new studio theatre, lecture theatres, design studios, workshop facilities, a library, a very nice student canteen as well as rehearsal rooms and offices. More building work is planned.

Auditions

About 600 plus audition for 32 places a year. The minimum age is 18 with no upper age limit although they are less likely to accept applicants over 25. Most students are between 18 and 21 and straight from school. The school publishes a list of recommended speeches. "That doesn't mean you can't do anything else, but we are saying that we know these to be speeches that work, broadly speaking, for 17 and 18 year olds." Applicants prepare two Shakespeare speeches and one modern piece. The first audition takes place in groups of 8-10. One of the Shakespeare speeches and the modern speech are performed in front of the group and a panel with at least two members of staff. Then there is a group interview. Students are asked to write a general statement about acting and taken on a tour of the building by current students "to give them a chance to ask the questions they feel are too trivial to ask the tutors". Meanwhile the tutors decide who they want to see in the afternoon. About 48 come in the morning "and if we keep twelve then that's a good day. It can happen that only one or two are kept on". Applicants are asked to do a speech and it is worked on. "The tutors will have identified an area they want to look at". There are two final recall sessions, each seeing between 30-50 applicants. "The odds are shorter but there's a chill in the air as people start to see the standard of other people's work". Those asked to come may have been given a task, such as finding a different speech, or re-working an old speech in a new way. These sessions are run as a mixture of class work, with improvisation, movement and speech work.   Again applicants are 'weeded out' at lunch time.

3 Year BA Acting
"This is a text oriented course in the sense that 90% of plays are text based rather than movement or devised pieces. Central has a strong tradition of voice work, so it is only sensible of us to go down that path." The course is fundamentally practical, with character work, improvisation, classes plus projects each term. There are lots of cross over areas, "for example, zoo study, an animal observation exercise, comes under movement but could as easily come under character study". London Zoo is conveniently just around the corner. Singing classes are taken throughout the first two years; second year singing is called 'musical theatre', and one of the final productions is a musical. There are no public performances in the first and second years.

Television is covered by a short, workshop programme. Radio is covered in the third year. The final year is production based, with nine shows being presented plus agent showcases. All productions are put on at the Embassy Theatre.

This is not an Honours degree programme (unlike that at Guildhall for example). There is no assessed writing element, no essays or dissertation although students are required to keep a working journal which is monitored by tutors "sometimes they are scrapbooks of pictures, sometimes they are mighty tomes". "We try to grown on what students present and help them improve that, to increase their confidence, to become stronger and more adept. It is about us enabling students to become something and not about us teaching students how to become something".

3 Year BA Hons Theatre Practice

The Theatre Practice degree covers a wide range of vocational skills, with students choosing one area as their primary study from: set design, scenic art, scenic construction, technical stage management, costume design, costume construction, prop-making, puppetry, stage management, production lighting, lighting design, production sound, sound design. The first year is a foundation year of introductory skills across a wide range of theatre production as well as projects to develop their specific area of theatre practice. The second year increases the amount of time spent as a member of a production team, while still attending classes, lectures, seminars and workshops to develop further skills and contextual studies. The third year is production based and requires students to work with a high degree of independence.

Central is going through an interesting patch at the moment. It obviously has had a very good reputation, and the voice training has always been excellent, but at some point in the 1980s it started to go astray. When I first visited in 1989 the students were busy being cool and trendy, and it remains the only visit where I came back to re-interview students because I felt that the ones I had spoken to had been either on something or doing a very good impression of it. Well, that's certainly changed and so has much else. Presumably in an attempt to shake things up a new head of performance was appointed, not an actor or director, but a musical director, the very talented, very driven and very young (for such an appointment) Anthony Castro. The 'old guard' one assumes did not like it and left in droves with much shaking of their heads - many of them can now be found at some of the smaller new schools. The students I spoke to complained about the shake ups, the changes in staff, the lack of continuity. They worried that the course had been marginalised within the school as a whole. "There's no money" was apparently a common refrain from the staff. They definitely felt that their training had been affected by it and one even said that she was glad she was leaving in a few months. But, like any other institution, drama schools can become entrenched and old fashioned so shake ups from time to time are beneficial. Anyway, by the time you read this it should have settled down. Tony Castro undoubtedly has the highest standards himself and demands them of other people so the next few years could be good ones at Central. They'll certainly be interesting.

The Court Theatre Training Company

The Courtyard, 10 York Way, King's Cross, London N1 9AA
Tel/Fax: 0171 833 0870

Artistic Director: June Abbott

2 Year Actors Course
1 Year Post Graduate Actors Course
2 Year Directors Course
1 Year Post Graduate Directors Course
1 Year Post Graduate Theatre Design Course
1 Year Post Graduate Stage Management Course

Fees:
2 Year Courses: £4785 per annum, 1 Year Post Graduate Courses: £5985
Islington scholarship for Islington residents for fees on two year course. Working scholarship: full fees covered for front of house work six days a week. Cleaning scholarship: half fees covered for one days cleaning plus overall care each day.
42 hours per week plus evenings when performing, 36 weeks per year
Audition fees: £25

The Courtyard Theatre is situated just by King's Cross Station, and is easily accessible from virtually any part of London and the home counties. It is situated around a courtyard, with the theatre and main rehearsal studio taking up one side, and offices, theatre foyer and wardrobe around the other two sides. June Abbott had been advising would-be drama school entrants as a director for many years when she decided that there was a need for a different type of actor training, one which was based around a theatre company to provide on the job training.

Auditions
Two contrasting pieces are required, one modern (after 1960) and one Shakespeare. Neither piece is to exceed three minutes. The session starts with a group workshop, then pieces are seen individually by the principal and two of the current company. There is also an interview. Entry to the courses is in January, April and September, depending on the availability of places. Post graduate entry is in September only. Ensemble playing is an essential part of the course, and therefore company members are chosen who integrate well within the group. There are about ten actors in the company at any one time. Most students are over 25, and they have had one or two 60 year olds.

2 and 1 Year Acting Courses

The idea behind the training is that actors traditionally learnt their craft on-the-job while working in repertory theatre, sometimes starting as a stage manager and not an actor. This system has ceased to exist, but the Court Theatre Company aims to combine that system with a range of classes. "The whole premise is that you learn from older students." Broadly speaking each morning is classes, each afternoon is spent in rehearsal and the last four weeks of each term are productions. This gives a hands-on training combined with considerable acting experience in fringe theatre, together with practical knowledge of the technical and administrative sides of running a theatre (although there are also a stage management course, directors course and theatre design course). "When they know themselves and their 'dark corners' then can they begin to tackle their characters. Equal emphasis is placed on developing the technical skills, especially the voice and the body - the actor's instruments." Classes include acting, text analysis, play analysis, improvisation, voice, movement, dance, movement analysis, dance, audition and career skills. Other, occasional, classes include stage combat, film and television techniques, radio techniques, theatre studies, text and choreography. All the classes are based around the plays in production. Because of the structure students train, rehearse and perform together, irrespective of the duration of the course they are taking, and what level they are at. "Students work their way up in terms of parts. By the time they leave they have a working CV." Choice of plays "leans towards the classics, including European and Russian theatre, plus adaptations and new writings. We always use outside directors for the company, and we don't use 'drama school' directors."

As well as the productions throughout the year there is a final showcase production for agents, casting directors and directors. All productions are reviewed by the press "sometimes they don't realise that they're students. We're basically seen as a fringe theatre."

2 and 1 Year Directors Courses

There are two directors' courses, one for two years, the other for one. They are seen as apprenticeships and are almost entirely practical. The course is structured to suit each individual. Apart from directing classes are given in acting, design, technical, the play, administration and projects. The two year course students in the penultimate term choose a new play and work with the writer (if possible) and professional actors to present a week of public performances at the Courtyard theatre. In the final term the trainee director is enabled to set up a fully professional company, under the director's own company name, for a two to four week run at the Courtyard Theatre. The one year course director creates and directs a professional self contained company, rehearsing and performing over two to four weeks at the Courtyard as a Court Theatre Company director.

Theatre Design Course

The Theatre Design course looks at the whole process of production design and focuses on the relationship between the director and designer. Designers may specialise in set, lighting or costume design. The course covers design development (e.g. analysis of text and visual research) underpinning knowledge (e.g. theatre history, principles of scenic construction), design skills (eg costing and budgeting, technical drawings), technical (e.g. lighting, sound, basic property making). There is an option for a further terms Stage Management Course. When I visited the set in the theatre was fabulous, easily the best I saw out all the drama school theatres.

Stage Management Course

The stage management course is not intended to compete with the existing, traditional courses, but to train students in the needs of the smaller scale company. This means that, while covering the traditional areas of training the emphasis has shifted to the skills of design, costume, sound, lighting and prop-making plus a wider range of other skills "more suited to a more co-operative style of working where the stage manager is more often also the electrician, designer and prop maker as well". They claim that 100% of their students gain employment within a few weeks of completing the course; this could of course be with all the companies formed by the graduating directors.

The idea of training actors while working is an intriguing one, although not as close to the old rep system as perhaps portrayed. The old repertory system worked by having only one or two new actors working alongside a whole cast of experienced actors, whereas the new actor works alongside someone who has been in training for perhaps as little as a year more. However, it is true that most drama school productions last for just a few nights and are produced to audiences mainly composed of fellow students, friends and relatives. Here productions last for four weeks and are all open to the general public. Productions are taken on tour both in the UK and abroad, with exchanges to Rome and Paris. When the theatre is not being used by the Courts own productions it is a fringe theatre venue, so students are exposed to other professional companies, actors and directors. The students I spoke to reported that it was very hard work. As well as the demanding production and class schedule they were expected to "muck in", which meant working on front of house duties as well as cleaning the premises. (The principal claimed to have got a cleaner in, and I notice that there are now scholarships for those who clean and do FOH, see above). Their complaints were that there seemed to be little continuity with the teaching staff, and that at times it appeared disorganised. Overall they had enjoyed the course, were pleased they had been on it and would recommend it to others. "Where else would I have been able to do so much acting?" was one comment. One final point is that it is cheap, and decidedly value for money.

Cygnet Training Theatre Company

New Theatre, Friars Gate, Exeter EX2 4AZ
Tel: 01392 277189/425777

Member of the Conference of Drama Schools

Principal: Monica Shallis

* **3 Year Professional Acting Course**

Fees:
3 Year Professional Acting Course: £2,000 per term, £6,000 per annum
Audition fee: £25, plus optional £10 for a written assessment of the audition if
you are not offered a place.

Exeter is the major city in the South West of England but it still retains the feel
of a bustling market town. It is surrounded by the beautiful Devon countryside,
including Dartmoor, and is a few miles from the South coast. Despite being
university town there is not much by way of night life. "You won't find a club
that's open after 1.30". There are several theatres including the Northcott Repertory Theatre which has close links with Cygnet. The company was founded in
1980 and was the first to offer training within a theatre company. They are
based in a former church which has been developed into a 150 seat studio theatre, several large rehearsal rooms, student common room and various offices
and workshops.

Auditions
Applicants are asked to prepare two contrasting pieces, preferably one Shakespeare and one modern. They usually audition three to five people per session,
with a session a month throughout the year. The session takes about half a day
and consists of sight-reading, a song, a few exercises and a bit of improvisation
plus performing the speeches. They are seen by two of three members of staff
and any members of the existing company who want to come in. After an interview they are given four or five lines to learn and are then directed in them.
Then there is a workshop with exercises and improvisation with the company.
Very occasionally they will recall, usually when there are two suitable people of
a very similar type. Between six and eight are taken on each year. The age range
is between 18 - 35, although they have taken on people who are older. Most are
in their 20s.

3 Year Professional Acting Course

The spring and summer terms follow the same patterneach year. The first eight weeks is spent on classes in the morning on the basic techniques of acting, dance, movement and voice and the afternoon is spent rehearsing for the current production. In the first year students play small parts and perhaps act as ASM. Gradually the roles get larger, with the lead roles going to third year students. "We teach according to Michael Chekhov's work. He looked at what really fine actors do by instinct and asked 'is it possible to teach it?' He developed these wonderful exercises which are a very strong part of the training here. It's like Stanislavski but brought further on into the 20th century. Peter Brook is our patron and a lot of his work has gone into the way we teach here." The small numbers make individual attention possible. The students reported that "sometimes you discover that a class has been put on just for you, for your problem". The last four weeks are spent in final rehearsals and productions. Productions are put on at the studio theatre and taken on tour to other venues which vary from the professional repertory companies at Exeter and Plymouth, to the gardens of local National Trust properties, to tiny village halls on Dartmoor.

The summer term is entirely production based, with the company in virtually continuous performance or rehearsal. Again venues vary, but include the Exeter Festival where they will also perform short recitals and readings, and workshops. (I am deeply envious of their 8-night stand at the Minack Theatre in Cornwall, an open air theatre literally carved out of a cliff.) When not required for rehearsals or performances students are expected to be self-motivated and work by themselves "You can often tell those who are going to succeed by who uses a free afternoon to research a new speech or write for auditions instead of spending time just nattering in the coffee bar."

Each year they take one of the productions to either the Edinburgh Festival or to a London theatre (some years they do both, depending on the production). They also perform a Showcase production in London in year.

During the training they will make at least one television film and one radio play. "We are not a television course, but we think it is important that they should have had the experience." Similarly, musical theatre is not studied as such (although everybody takes singing and dance classes) but over the three years they will have one two or three plays where singing and dance are vital. "So the opportunities are there for them to take on that side".

During the third year there are sessions about getting work, writing CVs and so on. "We have an assessment evening each term to which local directors and casting directors are invited as assessors. By the end of the training they have a large number of people they can write to saying 'by the way, you saw me in..'. Our people are used to performing a lot, and many do get their first jobs in the local repertory theatres."

The company style of training is not for everybody; Cygnet admit that one or two students drop out or are asked to leave each year. "People don't understand that they are coming into a company where professional standards are expected from day one; they turn up late, they won't do the work and they come in for a bit of a shock". The students said that you had to be able to be part of a company, that you needed to be flexible. "You have to be there or you're letting everyone else down". They liked the mix of class work in the mornings, rehearsal in the afternoons because "it means you can get a chance to try out things you've done in class straight away." The men particularly liked the practical approach. "I'm not a great one for talking about it, and I'm not one for paperwork, I just like to get up there and do it" said one. They stressed that at times it could be hard work. "Sometimes you have a 6.00am call and then get home at 1.30am after the production" but as a result of the experience they felt very confident in their abilities to deal with audiences in all kinds of venues and all kinds of productions. One joked "We're known as the Happy Shopper of drama schools, cheap and own brand. But I'm pleased I came here and not elsewhere."

Drama Centre London

176 Prince of Wales Road, Chalk Farm, London NW5 3PT
Tel: 0171 267 1177 Fax: 0171 485 7129
email: info@dcl.drama.ac.uk

Member of the Conference of Drama Schools

Principal: Christopher Fettes

*   **3 Year BA (Hons) Acting Course**
*   **3 Year Acting Diploma Course**

Fees:
All courses: £6,500 per annum
45 hours per week, 36 weeks per year
Audition fee: £25

The school is based in a converted Methodist chapel in the Chalk Farm area of London, which is beside Camden and is close to Regent's Park and central London. There is a studio theatre, rehearsal studios and a canteen in the basement. Getting into Central London is easy by tube. Most students find accommodation locally.

Auditions
Applicants are given a list of six classical speeches from which they must choose one, plus one modern speech of their choice. They perform their speeches and are interviewed by a panel of six or seven. This may include work on their speeches and some improvisation. The panel is made up of all the heads of department (e.g. voice, movement, acting) and two current students. "It is a terrible situation where your future is in the hands of one person, where sometimes that person isn't even a member of the school, whereas if you face the committee at least you know it's going to be a matter of debate." About 400 people apply for 30 places, 20 male and 10 female (reflecting the ratio of work available in the profession). The majority are in their early 20s, with a maximum age of 30. "Most people's capacity for sustained growth or major change falls off rapidly after the age of twenty five."

3 Year Acting Degree and Diploma Courses
The school has a strong central philosophy based on the workings of Stanislavski (acting method), Laban (movement) and Theatre Workshop (acting through

improvisation and research). They follow a methodological approach rather than the pragmatic approach which many schools favour. They have the most intellectual approach to theatre of any of the other drama schools; it was always the course most likely to achieve degree status. "We don't train people just to do beer commercials or The Bill. People here are treated as artists." Much of the work is Euro-centric in terms of plays produced, teaching staff and teaching methods and traditions. The list of recent final year productions shows no Ayckbourn or Godber but includes Anouilh, Camus, Kundera, Ostrovsky, Schnitzler, Sophocles, de Vega, and Wedekind - "nothing that would be remarkable in Berlin or Munich or Paris". The two acting courses are basically identical, the difference being that the degree course is formally assessed on both practical and theoretical work throughout each term, and at the ends of each term and each academic year.

Training follows a progression from class work and acting exercises performed for staff only in the first year to the final term where productions are show to the public "not in any sense as finished productions, but because the participation of an audience is necessary at that stage for further progress." Classes include acting study, character analysis (taught by the legendary Yat Malmgren), movement, classical ballet, commedia dell'arte, voice and speech, music and singing and play analysis.

Productions or "rehearsal exercises" in the first two years are confined to naturalistic theatre at first. They look for good writing for actors, for example Odets. Comedy is introduced in the second year, such as a Moliere play, as well as Shakespeare. There is a certain amount of flexibility depending on the needs of the group. Not everybody is allowed to continue to the third year, according to the students.

The function of the third year is to "stretch the student to the fullest extent, and far beyond the point that would be expected of him on entering the profession." There are two productions a term and in the summer term an agents show consisting of duologues.

They do a series of classes on preparation for the profession, including sight reading, audition pieces, setting up your own company and advice from a wide range of professionals such as casting directors, agents, union officials and accountants.

Also in the third year are classes in television and radio; acting for the camera is taught as part of the acting department from the start. Musical theatre is not covered although there is a good music department.

Students said that they had chosen to come here because it appeared to be a) serious about acting and b) not an easy option, both of which they felt to be true. It was described as a wonderful course. "I feel privileged to have trained here"said one. They enjoyed the wide range of plays and the feeling that they were part of a European/International outlook. They stressed that you had to have the ability to work by oneself, and the ability to work on oneself.

The Drama Centre must have more myths attached to it than any other school, one of them being that nudity is obligatory. They assured me that it was not required, but added that most had got their kit off at some stage. "You want to, it's part of getting rid of inhibitions, and once you've done it you stop having any hang ups about it." They agreed with another myth, and said that paranoia was rife. "The school gets through a lot of students. We started with 37 in our year, quite a few dropped out and others were got rid of - 6 weren't allowed to carry on to do the third year - so there are now just 19 of us." I thought the students were by far the brightest, funniest, talented bunch that I met. They acted out classes and funny incidents for my benefit, showing an impressive ability to switch from one mood to another. They were interested in acting and theatre, they supported each other "you learn to get on with everybody here, and be more tolerant of other people's foibles and quirks". The Drama Centre is unique among British drama schools. It is intellectual and European in its approach. It is intense, It takes acting (and itself) ver seriously. It is not for everybody but be in no doubt that it does produce some of the finest actors.

The Drama Studio London

Grange Court, 1 Grange Road, London W5 5QN
Tel: 0181 579 3897 Fax: 0181 566 2035
email: Admin@dramastl.demon.co.uk

Founder and Principal: Peter Layton, Deputy Director: Chris Pickles

*   **1 Year Post Graduate Acting Course**
     1 Year Directing Course
     8 Week Preparatory term
     Summer courses

Fees:
1 Year Acting Course (3 terms): £9,400, 1 Year Acting Course (4 terms): £11,400
1 year Directors Course: £11,400 4 week Summer acting courses: £900 each
Young Actors Summer Course (5 days): £75
42 hrs per week, plus weekends and evenings as required. 35 weeks training per
year (+ 8 weeks if including the preparatory term)
Audition fees: All one year courses: £30. US and Canadian residents US $75.00
Summer Acting Courses (Pre-Professional and Advanced): £10

Ealing is to the west of Central London. It is well served by road and public
transport, with both tube and British Rail links into the centre. Ealing itself is a
thriving area, with plenty of shops and restaurants. It has become a much smarter
area over the last 20 years, and rents can be high, but most students should be
able to find affordable accommodation, especially towards South Ealing. Ealing
Common and Walpole Park are in walking distance. Grange Court is a large,
detached Victorian house near the centre of Ealing. Recently a studio theatre
was built in the garden. The school has video and sound equipment, but does not
have dedicated television or radio studios.
The Drama Studio London was founded by Peter Layton in 1966. He realised
that there was a need for something beyond the standard three year training for
school leavers which was at the time all that was available. Many of the other
drama schools were actively hostile to the concept that you could train an actor
within one year, which is one reason why DSL has not been invited to join the
Conference of Drama Schools. The success of DSL over the last 30 years has led
to many more one year courses being offered.

Auditions
"We are looking for people who, in our judgement, have the imagination, flair
and talent to, within one year of starting the course, be employed within the

profession." They see about 10-15 people each time. "The one thing we can't give anybody is imagination; we can teach technical skills, but we can't teach imagination. And for the imagination to flow the audition process must be as relaxed as possible." The session starts with an informal chat about the course "to let them see what they are letting themselves in for and what we can offer them", then a warm-up to get rid of any tensions, followed by an improvisation session to see the actors working in groups. Then audition speeches are performed within the group. Then a break for lunch, while they decide who they want to stay on. "About 90% of the reasons why we don't take someone is that they are not ready for a one year course, they need a two year course. Sometimes we feel the need to come back with another piece." Those who stay for the afternoon have an individual interview lasting about 30 minutes. They take about 45-55 students each year, of whom a quarter might be non-UK "but it varies from year to year". Minimum age is 21. Students should either have a degree, or equivalent "which could be simply three years of life experience after school". Most students are in their mid to late 20s.

Admission to the directors course is by interview and some practical exercises. Applicants are expected to have had some directing experience and knowledge of theatre history and dramatic literature.

1 Year Actors Course

"We are a non-methodological school. We enable the students to find their way through the various techniques of and skills of the craft of acting with as many different tools as possible. Not "this is the way", but "this is a way". Throughout the year are classes in the basics of voice, movement and acting. Musical theatre is not covered. "We leave that to the specialists". The first term consists of two scene study projects, followed by a Christmas production which is taken to local schools. The second term concentrates on language, and in particular, Shakespeare. A long-standing member of the faculty is Patrick Tucker, a well known and inspiring Shakespearean director who works using "cue scripts". The method is based on the fact that contemporary actors did not receive the complete play (which were hand written in those days), but received cue scripts made up of the actor's line and the appropriate cues. There were also no directors or rehearsals as we know them. Therefore, all the information required by an actor is contained within the words. "It is endlessly inspiring, we see students who couldn't put one iambic in front of the other working so imaginatively with the language by the end of the middle term". The third and final term begins with Restoration and 19th and early 20th century playwrights. There are two main productions this term, both of which are open to the public although the main "Showcase" production does not take place until the following October and consists of scenes and speeches in a West End Theatre for an invited audience of agents, directors and casting directors.

Throughout the year there are two on-going, addition strands; television and "The Work Programme". DSL recognises that much of an actor's future income will come from television in one form or another, so television classes aim to give students the basic techniques and the knowledge of different styles and the demands on the actor, for example the change from the ordinariness of soaps to the instant energy required for commercials.

The Work Programme actively trains the actor to find work. "There is no point in training any actor to do the job if they don't know how to get the job when they get out there." Throughout the year there are mock interviews, mock auditions and classes on getting work. In the third term there is one week devoted to 'work' where students go on placements such as shadowing directors, agents and casting directors.

The eight week preparatory term in the summer is an addition to the one year course, and covers classes in voice, acting and movement. There are no performances. For some students, taking this course is a condition of their acceptance on the main course. Sometimes it is recommended to overseas students to help bridge any cultural or linguistic difficulties.

1 Year Directors Course
The course runs alongside the Acting Course, and the directors are expected to take part in some of the acting, voice and movement classes in the first two terms. Students also study practical elements (such as blocking, statements of intent, design), technical elements (such as lighting and sound) and text analysis. Practical directing sessions are held throughout the year. Students also undertake research assignments and act as assistant directors to the Acting Course directors. In the first term directors show three projects of increasing complexity to the course faculty. In the second and third term there are classes and seminars on the practical, legal and financial aspects of mounting productions. There are two second term projects, one an adaptation of an item of non-theatrical origin, followed by a one-act play. The third term projects consist of another one act play and a full length play. The aim is that directors should leave with a suitable production for a small scale fringe presentation. All second and third term projects are given critiques by a panel of professional directors. All students have a fixed budget for the year, and are expected to submit production budgets and expenses for each project.

There is also a short course in television and video directing, and other workshops and seminars.

Summer Acting Courses
The Pre-Professional and Advanced Courses may be taken in sequence if wished. Each four week course provides classes in acting, voice, singing, movement,

dance, Shakespeare, verse speaking, stage combat and acting for television. There are also theatre and studio visits, and lectures and seminars by visiting directors, actors and teachers. Nine hours a week are spent in rehearsal for a workshop production.

The Young Actors' Summer Course is intended for 9-13 year olds with a primary objection of having fun, while giving them an insight into the professional world of theatre.

One of the interesting features of DSL is that each year is completely new, so in effect it re-invents itself according to the needs of that particular group of students. The group becomes close-knit, which might be a problem if in that particular year you did not fit in. However, it did not seem to have happened to the students I met, who were having a great time, "Brilliant" being the most widely used adjective to describe the course. Several people commented that it had given them tremendous confidence to go out and get work, and all were optimistic. The work on Shakespearean cue-scripts was a highlight, together with the work programme. There are undoubted advantages in being at a drama school which is exclusively for older students, especially when most have raised the funds themselves. "Everybody really wants to work" said one. It is a very pragmatic course, which may disappoint those who believe that acting is an art form, and others may find the concentration on getting work makes the course too commercial. But most people who want a one year course are actors in a hurry to make up for lost time. They want to get out there and start working. This course is an excellent foundation for a career as a working actor.

The directors course is a proper course, and not just a 'tag-along with the actors course' that some seem to be. In the Gulbenkian report on training for directors it was the only course that had a positive review. It has a good mixture between the practical and theoretical elements and competition for places keeps the standards high. That all directors leave with a production ready for commercial presentation is the icing on the cake.

East 15 Acting School

Hatfields, Rectory Lane, Loughton, Essex IG10 3RY
Tel: 0181 508 5983 Fax: 0181 508 7521
email: east15.acting@ukonline.co.uk

Member of the Conference of Drama Schools

Artistic Director and Founder: Margaret Walker

3 Year BA Acting
3 Year Acting Diploma
1 Year Post Graduate Acting Diploma

Fees:
3 Year BA Acting: Mandatory grants for part of the fees, £4,560 per annum for
remainder, £7100 per annum overseas/other
3 Year Acting Diploma: £7,100 per annum
1 Year Post Graduate Diploma: £7450 per annum
31 weeks per year
Audition fee: £25 Auditions held in: London, Los Angeles, New York, Sydney,
Toronto, Tel Aviv, Scandinavia, New Zealand.

The school is situated near Epping Forest about 12 miles north east of Central
London. There is a tube connection to London (which takes forever) and it is
close to the M25 and M11. The University of East London, which validates the
degree, is just down the road. In theory the students could use the facilities. In
practice it could be on another planet as far as they were concerned. Accommodation locally should not be a problem. Hatfields itself is a beautiful Georgian
house. Within the grounds is the Corbett Theatre complex, including rehearsal
rooms, workshops and a bar as well as the 120 seat theatre itself. At the centre of
the building is a medieval tithe barn which was moved from Sussex and reas-
sembled here. East 15 is not accredited by the NCDT because Margaret Walker
is a critic of their criteria for judging a drama school and believes that to ask for
accreditation is to ask for interference in course structure and content.

Auditions
Auditions take the form of a four or five hour workshop starting with a warm up
and then moving onto sessions in speech, movement, acting (including improvisation) and singing. Three speeches are required, two classical and one modern.
There is usually a panel of three people who are checking up on students' potential in terms of spoken voice, their basic ability to sing, their acting ability and

elementary movement and dance. There are about 30 places available on the BA course, with a further 5-10 from overseas or on the diploma course. Minimum age is 18 for the three year course with no upper limit "the intake seems to be getting younger which is to do with recruitment through UCAS". There is no upper limit and they have taken people over 50, albeit not recently. Most students are in their early 20s. Numbers for the one year course have fluctuated over the last few years; ideally there are 15-20 places for graduates.

3 Year BA Acting and Acting Diploma Courses

The diploma course is the same as the degree course except it does not have the written work and there is less one to one tuition in voice, for example. "It's the BA Acting course without frills and for a couple of thousand less. The main drive and ethos are exactly the same i.e. to train them for work in the professional theatre." The school grew from the work of the Theatre Workshop. It has followed a particular path and while open to other influences, has "kept it's own driving force, improvisation and so on, and we do still use those same things but they have now been channelled and adapted. You can either imprint your own personality on to every single role you play, like Maggie Smith, or you try to get the absolute truth in every character you play who probably will be totally different to yourself, like Alison Steadman, who is ex-East 15. What we want is people who will constantly ask questions of themselves, those people who can get inside of the skin of another character. "

The first year is spent on the basics. These include technical classes in voice, speech, movement (Laban based) and dance (ballet, tap and jazz) but concentrates on discovering oneself leading on to character work. "They first have to learn who they are, and that can be a painful process, like taking layers off an onion. But how can you create another character until you know who you are?" All the teachers in the first two years are East 15 trained and "have the ethos throughout their system" (although they have all worked outside professionally). Character study involves research and improvisation, and may mean staying in character for several days. Texts studied include Shakespeare, Jacobean and late 19th century plays. Scenes from these are presented in-house. Additionally students may take small parts in the third year productions in the Corbett Theatre. Where possible, classes take place outside, both in the grounds and also in nearby Epping Forest.

The second year is a progression from the raw basics through the interim stage to the third year. Ensemble work is important. "The drive of the second year comes from the strength of the ensemble and that is only as strong as each individual within the group and their commitment to the work in hand." Students take part in at least six productions in 'intimate settings', where the audience may be only a few feet away. Other performances take place in as wide a range of settings as possible. During the last term students work on an improvised living history project. This involves researching a particular period and adopting the personality of a historical person, who may be anything from a servant upwards, aiming to create a character firmly based on secure documented evidence. The year finishes with all the characters coming together and interacting. Previously this has involved living in a period house for three days as a family and servants would have done at the turn of the century.

In a change from small spacese the thrid year moves into the Corbett Theatre, starting with a Christmas production seen by over 4000 local children. This is followed by two productions each term and a Showcase Production for agents, casting directors, directors etc. Students who show particular promise in singing or dance are given opportunities to show their talents, in a full musical production in the main theatre or a smaller scale show. Guest directors are brought in; they are often intentionally chosen because they have been trained in a different ethos to East 15. Students also follow a "professionalisation plan" in two phases, once at the start of the year and again at the end. Apart from seminars and one-to-one tutorials all students develop between eight or nine audition speeches.

The second year performances in intimate settings are seen as the start of television training. In the third year there are television workshops run by an outside television director where cameras and monitors are brought in.

1 Year Post Graduate Acting Diploma

The course aims to be a miniaturised version of the three year course. The first term is spent with the first years, the second on their own programme and then joins with the third years for the final term. Each day starts with a physical training session, followed by a daily voice and movement practice session. Other classes and tutorials are arranged according to the available time after rehearsals. Productions are selected according to the needs of the group and may include Shakespeare, Jacobean and Restoration playwrights, Ibsen, Chekhov or Strindburg. Students are expected to work on their own on research, both during term and in the holidays.

East 15 is a remarkable school, based on the driving force of a remarkable woman. It has followed the same path confidently regardless of what else is happening around it and as a result it is has always been slightly out on a limb. Recently the main three year course has been validated as a degree by the University of East London, who seem to be more involved with the school than other universities. In some ways this has been beneficial; they supplied computer equipment and a library, and of course, students are now more likely to get grants. On the other hand they seem to have been wasting a few forests on the paper work and "we're all having to learn Edu-speak. We don't have any problems with it, but now you have to think, debate, discuss and make sure it's all minuted." The students I spoke to had enjoyed their time there. They were amused by what they saw as some of the eccentricities of training but as most had read the prospectus carefully they had known what to expect. One however had not, and had been expecting a more conventional course. She was converted to the method of training, but worried that, although she could act, she might not have enough knowledge to get work. This fear was dismissed by another student. "I think you can pick all that up really quickly. What's been important for me is that I know I'll never have another chance, or the freedom, to do so much research and work on character, and that for me, has been the best bit."

Guildford School of Acting

Millmead Terrace, Guildford, Surrey GU2 5AT
Tel: 01483 560701 Fax: 01483 535431
E-mail: enquiries@gsa.drama.ac.uk   Web-site: http://gsa.drama.ac.uk

Member of the Conference of Drama Schools

Principal: Gordon McDougall, Vice-Principal and Head of Acting: Peter Barlow

* **BA (Hons) Theatre (Acting and Musical Theatre pathways)**
* **3 Year Acting Diploma**
* **3 Year Musical Theatre Diploma**
* **1 Year Post Graduate Acting Diploma**
* **1 Year Post Graduate Musical Theatre Diploma**
* **BA (Hons) Theatre (Production and Design pathway)**
* **2 Year Stage Management Course**
* **1 Year Post Graduate Stage Management Course**

Fees:

3 Year Acting Degree and Diploma course: £7350 per annum
3 Year Musical Theatre Degree and Diploma courses: £7950 per annum
1 Year Post Graduate Acting Diploma: £7560
1 Year Post Graduate Musical Theatre: £8000
Stage Management (all courses) £5700 per annum
Scholarships: Two for existing students plus The Student Support Fund. Also some bursaries.
Approx. 38 hours per week. Degree students have between 8-10 hours of extra written and academic work per week.
Audition fees: Preliminary Audition: £15, Second Audition: £20, Stage Management: Free. Auditions in: Guildford, Manchester, Leeds and New York.

Guildford is a large, pleasant town in 'leafy' Surrey to the south west of London. The area is wealthy, and the shops, restaurants and general ambience of Guildford reflect this. Some streets are cobbled, there are many picturesque buildings and the surrounding countryside is lovely. Rents reflect this; prices are comparable to London, and can be hard to find. The local theatre is the Yvonne Arnaud. London itself is easily accessible by rail or road, taking about 40 minutes. As you might expect from such a nice town, student style nightlife is limited and the town is perhaps a little staid ("boring") for some.
GSA was founded in 1965 and has grown into a large, dynamic drama school. They noticed the increase in musicals being put on in the West End and were

thus one of the first drama schools to specialise in musical theatre courses for actors. This is now a major part of the school. Each expansion sees the acquisition of new buildings; all close together and centred on the River Wey which runs through the heart of Guildford. The next acquisition will see the provision of more studios, a television studio and another performing space. Currently they have plentiful rehearsal and dance studios, a 100 seat proscenium theatre, a flexible, up to 120 seat studio theatre, and two small 'black box' studios seating 50-70. They also use other local theatres and performing spaces, including the 650 seat Yvonne Arnaud theatre. They also have a student cafeteria serving good, cheap food. The degree option has been offered since 1993.

Auditions

Acting preliminary auditions require two speeches, neither to exceed 2 minutes, one from a play written before 1900 and another from a contemporary play. Applicants must prepare a brief song. Musical theatre preliminary auditions require a song from the musical theatre repertoire and a speech not exceeding 2 minutes. The audition consists of an interview and performance of pieces to a panel of three, which will include a working professional (such as an actor, director or choreographer) unconnected with the school. About 30-40% are recalled for a second audition. The second audition lasts a whole day and consists of classes and workshops with the faculty covering movement, acting, voice and, for musical theatre applicants, singing. As well as selecting the students, the idea is to give applicants a chance to experience the way that GSA works. 500-700 apply for 30 places on the 3 year acting course, 30 places on the 3 year musical theatre course and 15 places for post graduates. Minimum age 18 for the 3 year courses. Entrance to the Stage Management courses is by interview. Minimum age, 18.

3 Year Acting and Musical Theatre Degree and Diploma Courses

The degree and diploma courses are the same courses, except that the degree courses have an extra element of research and reading, mainly into the background of the current play that is being worked on. Degree students must also write an essay each term and keep a logbook. In the second year there is an extra class called dramatic theory. In the third year the extra work consists of a dissertation and a written exam.

"Our training philosophy is based on the simple idea that all actors need to be extremely versatile in the 21st century. They are going to work in musicals, radio, television and theatre. They need to be able to move easily between each medium as well as being good, truthful, believable actors. Techniques and skills are absolutely essential, but we don't teach them in isolation. A lot of our classes are team taught, which means that an acting specialist might work with a move-

ment specialist on a story telling project. We try and give our students the broad-
est possible range of skills, while also being able to specialise in musical theatre
or acting."

The first year is a foundation year for all three year courses. Terms one and three
are the same for both acting and musical theatre students and consist of classes
in neutral mask body conditioning, creative movement (based on Laban, Alexander and Feldenkrais techniques), dance (including jazz, tap, ballet and period
dance), character building, action, voice, poetry, choral speaking, stage combat,
physical skills, musical appreciation and singing. Classes are structured around
a central project. In the first term it is story telling and in the third it is English
Naturalistic theatre.   In the second term the acting students add improvisation
and text technique classes, including Shakespearean text, and work towards a
central project in Greek tragedy and comedy.   In the second term musical theatre
students take classes in clown and commedia, text interpretation and character
building, and on vocal and physical skills.   There are additional classes in specific dance and singing techniques.   Students work around their central project
of a strongly text-based musical.

In the second year acting students continue classes throughout the mornings.
The afternoons are spent on project work which included Shakespeare and Jacobean theatre, Restoration theatre, Chekhov and his contemporaries and modern
theatre. At the end of the year is the first public performance.

In the second year of the musical theatre option more emphasis is given to specialised training in singing and dance, while acting classes and stage combat
and physical skills training continue. The afternoons are spent on project work
which cover the whole range of musical theatre. At the end of the year is the first
public performance of a musical.

For both acting and musical theatre students the third year is a series of productions of classical and contemporary works. Students are often pooled so that
musical theatre students can appear in straight plays and acting students can
appear in musicals. Venues range from the school's own studio theatres to other
larger theatre such as the 650 seat Yvonne Arnaud in Guildford. Each year a
production is taken on tour to local schools and there is usually a tour abroad.

Television is covered in a two week project in the second year. The amount of
television within the course will undoubtedly grow when the school has it's own
television studio in the new building. Radio is also introduced in the second
year and is on-going.

A 'showcase' production is shown in both Guildford and London in February. "It
gets it out of the way, and agents get sick of going round all the drama schools at
the end of the year, so we're attracting more people than before. It also means
that students can invite any interested agent down to see them in a production."
GSA have a careers consultant who is an experienced casting director. Regular

talks and tutorials are arranged during the final year, including mock interviews and auditions, plus talks and advice from visiting representatives from many areas of the profession, such as Equity and Spotlight. A new feature is the Graduate Company which acts as a bridge between GSA and the professional world. This is a touring company run as a professional theatre and includes outside actors as well as GSA graduates. All roles are cast by audition, as with any other professional theatre company. This is yet another example of the go-ahead policy of the school.

1 Year Post Graduate Acting and Musical Theatre Diplomas

It is assumed that students who undertake the course have a greater degree of self knowledge and self-development and therefore the course is an intensive training in technique.

For students on the acting pathway classes include voice, singing and music, movement and make up. The first term starts with an ensemble project of devised scenes and then goes on to explore emotional range through the context of Greek tragedy. Naturalistic technique is developed through examining Ibsen, Chekhov and contemporary theatre. The second terms includes a project on Shakespeare and the Jacobeans and a short course in radio and television techniques. Another interesting feature of the one year programme is the use of students as 'patients' in medical role play for the training of doctors. This can lead to work as a professional actor.

Students on the Musical Theatre pathway take classes in musical theatre styles, presentation, acting, voice, movement, singing, dance (including tap, jazz and ballet) and make-up. Projects cover all the different styles of musical performance from opera to rock, concentrating on West End and Broadway shows.

In the third term of both courses public productions are mounted and a show case production is presented in Guildford and a West End theatre. Students have the same careers advice and programme as the three year students.

BA Hons Theatre (Production and Design)

There are currently three pathways: Production and Stage Management, Production and Design (Lighting) and Production and Design (Set and Costumes). A fourth pathway in Television Production is being researched. In the first year students study a common core foundation year consisting of the managerial, practical and technical disciplines of stage management and technical theatre. During the second year students choose project, research and production modules from their chosen pathway. In the third year there is a core production research or design project module which counts towards the final degree assessment. Apart from this, the third year is production based with students taking on a variety of senior production roles such as production manager, lighting designer, set designer or costume designer. A strength of the course is that it offers experience of many different types of venue, from small 'black box' studios to large, professional repertory theatres. Secondments take place during the second and third years of the course and have recently included the National Theatre, the Welsh National Opera, the BBC, and many other regional repertory theatres and touring companies.

2 Year Stage Management Course

The course is designed to train professional Stage Managers and theatre technicians. In the first year all students study a common core foundation year consisting of the managerial, practical and technical disciplines of Stage Management and technical theatre. In the second year they may specialise in stage and company management, lighting, sound, property making and scenic construction. They practise their chosen discipline through working on a wide variety of productions in different theatre spaces.

1 Year Post Graduate Stage Management Course

The course aims to give post-graduate and mature students the opportunity to study the managerial, practical and technical disciplines of stage management. Students share some classes, lectures and exercises with the 2 year stage management students, and work with them as members of the production teams. They also work with the one year acting course on performance projects, television exercises and final term productions. It is not as detailed as the two year course, and many of the graduates use the course as a preparation for becoming directors or running their own touring companies.

GSA has changed dramatically with the introduction of the new principal some three years ago. A change in staff during this period has meant a more modern and fresh approach within the faculty. "The flavour of the classes has changed, the attitudes are different." The students felt the shake up. "You feel everything's happening, it's all exciting" and the whole atmosphere is one of dynamism and forward movement. The musical theatre courses in particular have been extremely successful, so much so that a pair of acting student confessed that they felt side-lined, and less important than the musical theatre students. They certainly seemed a lot quieter and restrained than the musical theatre students who were full of high spirits and absolutely oozed self confidence. Judging by what I saw and heard I think it would be possible for some shy and sensitive actors to find it all a little too bright and confident, and it probably would not be suited to someone who loathed musical theatre because even the straight actors do quite a lot of musical work. For anyone else - especially if they were interested in musical theatre - the answer has to be 'go for it!'

The Guildhall School of Music and Drama

Silk Street, Barbican, London EC2Y 8DT
Tel: 0171 628 2571 Fax: 0171 256 9438
website: http://www.gsmd.ac.uk

Member of the Conference of Drama Schools

Principal: Ian Horsbrugh, Director of Drama: Peter Clough

* **3 Year BA (Hons) Acting**
* **3 Year Professional Acting Diploma**
* **3 Year BA (Hons) Stage Management and Technical Theatre**

Fees:
3 Year BA (Hons) Acting: Mandatory awards, £3,600 per annum overseas/other
3 Year Professional Acting Diploma: £3,600 per annum
3 Year BA (Hons) Stage Management and Technical: Mandatory awards, £3,600 per annum overseas/other
Some bursaries to help with tuition fees and/or maintenance available.
36 weeks per year
Audition fee: £30, stage management free.

The Guildhall School of Music and Drama is situated in part of the Barbican Centre Arts complex in the City of London. On site are cinemas, concert halls, art galleries, restaurants. The Royal Shakespeare Company has its London base here, and shares a wall with Guildhall. Some find the Barbican oppressive; it is a mixture of modernist concrete blocks interspersed with walkways and court-yards, and a central piazza beside lakes and fountains. It's quite easy to lose your way despite ample sign posts and coloured lines on the pavements. Although it's a short walk from the tube I invariably get lost, and it can be hard to find anyone who can give you coherent instructions on how to find the school's entrance so allow time for this is you are coming for an audition. The drama side is a relatively small part of the school, confined to dungeon like rooms at the bottom. There are lots of little practice rooms and as you walk round you hear singers and musicians rehearsing. The facilities are good, with two theatres (one seats 320 and the other 75), a concert hall and a marvellous wardrobe and stage management department although little in the way of television facilities. Students can live in the schools own residential block two minutes walk away, which also houses the student canteen. The school is fortunate that it is finan-cially supported by the Corporation of London and has not had to increase stu-dent numbers or dramatically increase the fees.

Auditions

Guildhall is unusual in that they limit the number of applicants they see at audition. The lists opens in September and closes when 700 have applied, usually by the end of December to the middle of January. Applicants are asked to prepare an unaccompanied song and three pieces, one of which must be Shakespeare or other classical verse text, one must be comedic - "people often come having written their own material and some of these are very funny" - and the third is whatever you like. The preliminary audition starts with 20-30 minutes of warm up and exercises as part of a group of 20. Then applicants are seen individually to perform two of their pieces and have an interview. About 100 people are called back for a two day workshop. During this time they will perform their pieces again for three different panels of two people, and each time there will be work on the pieces. There will be a sight reading test and some kind of singing audition and a one to one interview. Applicants are separated into small groups of 8 for a two hour acting, improvisation and movement session. Applicants who want to go on the degree course but do not have any qualifications may be asked to take a short written test. "It's more diagnostic than a hurdle". 24 students are taken on, usually in their early 20s, although there may be the occasional 18 year old. There is no upper age limit.

3 Year Acting Degree and Diploma courses

Students can choose to take either the diploma or the degree course. They are the same course, but the degree course students have a small additional area of research and written work. This comprises one formal essay in the first year and a 5000-8000 research project in the final year.

In the first year the students spend a lot of time "learning to work as part of a group, what it is to be an actor, what it is to be in a theatre space, what they are doing, and why, and who for." This includes lots of improvisation work (in the first term there is no text based work at all). Projects include the medieval mystery plays plus background research, a modern play and Chekhov. When not working on projects they have technical classes based in vocal and physical work. Patsy Rodenburg who is probably the best voice teacher working in the UK is head of the voice department. Working as a company and being a good company member is an important part of the course; Peter Clough referred to it several times during the interview.

The second year continues as the first, but the balance shifts so that more time is spent on rehearsal and less on classes. "The precise amount varies according to the nature of the people on the course". Projects usually cover Brecht, Restoration or 18th Century drama, Shakespeare and a musical, depending on the needs of the group. All the work is performed in-house to staff and fellow students. Also in the second year is a week long television project. Recently the school has increased the involvement with international work, such as bringing a teacher from Moscow to work with the second year students and at the end of second year all the students go to an international drama festival in Italy. They are also taking tours abroad; in the year I visited students had been to Holland, Belgium and Germany. The RSC now leaves its Barbican base for six months a year, and international productions come in which are seen as a resource for the drama school "it would be stupid for us to be in the same building as some of the most world renowned directors and companies without having some contact."

In the third year there are nine public productions, of which each actor will perform in six. One of the productions will be a musical. Because of the music department they "can do large scale musical with resources that even West End theatres can not manage". Sometimes pieces are composed especially for the drama students. There is a programme of career development in the third year, and an interesting attachment system where each student is 'attached' to a working professional actor (sometimes from the RSC). This gives them the chance to get an experienced outside view; however one student I spoke to confessed that although her attachment had been keen to help she somehow never got round to calling her back, which seemed a waste of a good idea. The year finishes with an audition showcase, which is invariably well attended.

3 Year BA (Hons) Stage Management and Technical Theatre

The course gives students a thorough grounding in all aspects of Stage Management and Technical Theatre. By the final year students mount and run all of the schools productions and undertake a professional placement.

Guildhall is considered to be one of the best drama schools in the country, and deservedly so. The ethos is definitely supportive and great stress is laid on being a good company member. Interestingly, although the students thought that the school was very supportive, they suggested that it was sometimes too gentle and caring. "Sometimes I think you need harsh criticism". Similarly, although it was good to be part of a company and to work well with others, they worried that perhaps they had been too well trained. "I don't think we're terribly good at pushing ourselves forward, and I think other schools are better at that, so I'm not sure how it's going to work when we leave." Coincidentally Peter Clough had spoken to me about the need for balance between the actor who was "such a good company member that they kind of disappears themselves and an individual creative selfishness". There was praise for the teaching and they said that the staff were very accessible and open to suggestions from the students. For example, audition classes now started earlier in the year as a result of the students requests. One of the best locations, good facilities, excellent teaching staff, terrific reputation, supportive atmosphere and if you can't get a grant, cheap fees. And because of the limited number of audition places the odds on getting in are better than usual for schools at this level. What more can one say?

Hertfordshire Theatre School

40 Queen Street, Hitchin, Herts SG4 9TS
Tel: 01462 421416

Co-Founders and Principals: John Gardiner and Kirk Foster

3 Year Acting Diploma
1 Year Post Graduate Acting Course

Fees:
3 Year and 1 Year courses: £5,500 per annum
Bursaries for private fee paying students of £2,000 reducing fees to £1,167 per term, £3,500 per annum. Also limited number of part scholarships
36 weeks per year
Audition fee: £25

Hitchin is a pleasant market town about 40 minutes by train to the north of London, surrounded by pleasant countryside and good road links to the rest of the country. Some may find it dull; there is not much in the way of student nightlife for example. Finding local accommodation should not a problem. The school is split between several sites. The main block is a Victorian house near the market square, which houses administration, classrooms and a dance studio. For larger rehearsal spaces and for musical theatre dance work they use the Woodside Campus which has several large rooms. For their theatre they use the Queen Mother Theatre which is a modern, purpose built venue. Both are a few minutes walk from the main building.

Auditions
Applicants are asked to prepare a song and two speeches, one comedy and one serious. Pieces can be from a classical or modern play, and should last no longer than three minutes each. The song may be sung unaccompanied, or with accompaniment from either a tape or a pianist - the school will provide a tape recorder or pianist as required. The audition consists or a group physical warm up followed by a simple jazz routine "just to check there are no physical problems". A vocal warm up comes next, then applicants are seen individually for their song, pieces and interview. In general there are no further recalls. There are about 24 places on the 3 year course and applicants should be between 18 and 30. There are up to 10 places on the one year course, with no specified age range.

3 Year Acting Diploma

The aim of the course is to give students a fully comprehensive range of training to equip them for all the demands of a career in acting and musical theatre. All acting is taught following Stanislavski's principles, but they do not consider themselves to be a 'Method' school. "We follow the students own style. You are who you are, and that's what makes you exciting". Classes cover the main disciplines of acting, dance and voice. Each term studies different projects to expose students to a wide range of styles from the Greeks to modern theatre. Acting projects and musical theatre projects are related, for example, students studying a 1920s play will also be working on a 1920s musical number. Each term there is an additional major production unrelated to the project work. In the Autumn and Spring terms this is a play, in the summer term a musical. In the third year there is a final showcase production for agents, casting directors and directors at a London venue. The school feels that actors should have a wide range of practical skills. These are studied periodically throughout the three year period. Students study mime, mask, circus skills, clowning, horse-riding, swimming/diving, firearms, archery, story-telling, stage fights, radio, voice-overs and TV studio work. Kirk Foster is a published playwright and the school runs a playwriting project; this was so successful for one former student that when I came to the school she was in Hollywood writing a script for a major film company.

The third year concentrates on career development and the getting of work. They hold workshops and classes in a wide range of subjects such as creating a company, audition and interview techniques, voice-overs, commercials, photocalls, Equity membership. Whenever possible the school tries to organise professional work, for example, in training films. They have taken over a small fringe theatre nearby in the centre of Hitchin where they run a professional company. For some students this will be a stepping stone to a career.

1 Year Post Graduate Course

This course is very flexible, working round the needs of each student. "We say 'You've got 36 weeks, what do you want out of it?' And then we construct a timetable around that." This may mean joining in classes across the years of the main three year course, it may mean individual classes in London or elsewhere, it may mean some work experience or placements - one student had a three week placement with BBC Radio Swansea.

There are some obvious negatives about the Hertfordshire Theatre school; it's small, it's relatively new, it's not well known, it's not NCDT accredited, it's not in a location where there is much professional theatre. But given those negatives, it does have a lot going for it. The programme covers many different elements, there is lots of individual attention, they have a theatre with a loyal, local audience. The students I saw were realistic; they acknowledged that it was not, say, RADA or Guildhall but felt that what it did it did well. They like the caring aspects, the feeling that individual training needs were considered, that there was flexibility, that they had opportunities for professional experience and the range of classes and skills. In fact they didn't have a bad word to say about the school. By running, in effect, a two tier system for the fees it offers very good value for money. Not everyone will agree with me but given my preference for small year groups over large ones I feel that potential students should consider it as a definite alternative to some of the big, expensive and flashier schools.

The London Academy of Music and Dramatic Art

Tower House, 226 Cromwell Road, London SW5 0SR
Tel: 0171 373 9883 Fax: 0171 370 4739
E-mail: enquiries@lamda.org.uk

Member of The Conference of Drama Schools

Principal: Peter James, Vice Principal and Head of Drama: Colin Cook

*   **3 Year Acting Course**
        1 Year Post Graduate Acting Course
        2 Year Post Graduate Acting Course
        1 Year Foundation Course
*   **2 Year Stage Management Course**
        1 Year Post Graduate Directors Course
        1 Year Post Graduate Musical Director and Repetiteur's Course
        1 Year Post Graduate Theatre Design Course
        1 Year Post Graduate Theatre Administration Course
        1 Year Post Graduate Movement Instruction Course
        4 week Shakespeare Summer Workshop

Fees:
All 3 Year, 2 Year and 1 Year Acting Courses: £7,350 per annum
All 1 Year Post Graduate Courses (except acting): £5,525
1 Year Foundation Course: £5,000
4 Week Shakespeare Summer Workshop £1250 tuition only, £2,006 tuition plus accommodation
Scholarships are available to help with fees for the three year acting course and two year stage management course plus bursaires for existing students.
33-34 weeks per year (39 for stage managers)
Audition fees: £20 for UK audition, £35 for North America. Auditions in: London, Manchester, Chicago, Los Angeles, New York, Seattle and Toronto.

LAMDA is situated on the Cromwell Road, one of the main thoroughfares going into Central London. To the south is Earls Court, a bustling cosmopolitan centre with a large population of students and back packers, to the north is Kensington which is smarter and more expensive, but no less cosmopolitan or lively. LAMDA is based in a huge Victorian house with numerous studios and rehearsal rooms while across the road is the fully equipped MacOwan Theatre. They use other local halls as additional rehearsal rooms. (It is expected that they shall move to a new site sometime within the next five years - the question is where can they find that can offer them such a good training theatre as the MacOwan plus the space for all the rehearsal rooms and studios required.)

LAMDA is the oldest of all the drama schools, being founded in 1861. Many people know of the school through the LAMDA examinations in various aspects of Speech and Drama. It has made a conscious decision not to be become a degree course, believing that "joining with a university would involve changes to our courses that would compromise their purely vocational character. We think that the intelligence that is required of an academic standard is quite different than that of an actor. Every year we have Oxbridge graduates and the severely dyslexic on the same three year course, and the dyslexia is no more a disadvantage than the degree is an advantage because on the whole it's not what you think about something but how you do it that matters."

Auditions

The preliminary audition consists of doing two pieces, one of which must be Shakespearean verse and the other to contrast with it. These will be performed to two people, followed by an interview with the registrar. For the second audition 10-12 people are recalled per session. Two pieces are required. These may be the same, or they might have been specified by the auditioners. The pieces are performed in front of the faculty including the heads of acting, movement, voice, singing, Alexander and the principal. Applicants also have to learn half of a duologue which they perform with an existing student, sing unaccompanied and sight read. Then the applicants are brought together for a group audition and improvisation. About 1000 people apply for 30 places on the 3 year course, with a further 500 for 36 places on the post graduate acting courses. Minimum ages are 18 for the 3 year and 21 for the post graduate courses. There are no quotas as such, but "we are aware of the danger in taking an overload of girls, finding plays for them to do and work for them afterwards is very difficult." Admission to the foundation course is by interview.

3 Year Acting Course

"We try to nurture the nature of the individual, accepting what the human being is, not rubbing them out and starting again to turn them into something called a LAMDA product." Classes are held in acting, improvisation, voice, movement (including period movement), singing, textual interpretation and analysis, Alexander technique, physical theatre including mime, commedia dell'arte and mask, stage combat, dance including tap, jazz, flamenco and Gaelic, and the history of the industry. In the first year the ratio of class work to performance work is approximately 85% class and 15% performance, in the second year 60% class and 40% performance, and in the third year 85% performance and 15% class.

Television work starts in year two in small groups and is an introduction to how they look, how they can relate to the screen, what they can do. In the third year they do a three week block "which is more like being on location and really tries to address how to act on the screen. We don't have television directors in because television directors are interested in the technology and we're talking about how they act. We try to point out how the screen uses actors and what the actor has to do to be effective. It's a growing course. We want to do more but it's very expensive."

Another new area covers the writing and showmaker aspects of the modern actor, to recognise that "there are companies such as Complicite which have long rehearsal periods where the show is evolved as much by the actor as by anybody else."

Musical theatre is covered in the sense that everybody does singing, both choral and solo, and dance. "We are aiming at a basic level of proficiency for all". The last production is a musical, in which everybody takes part and "anybody who is interested in that area will get a solo."

All productions are in-house for the first two years. The final productions are all at the MacOwan Theatre, including two evenings of scenes and duologues for agents, casting directors and directors. Each year some third year productions are chosen for a six week tour of the Netherlands, Belgium and Germany in the spring which gives good experience of a long run and performing to different audiences in a variety of venues.

2 and 1 Year Acting Courses

The two year and one year post graduate courses have developed from a course which was originally designed in 1956 for US students who had taken a drama degree in the US and were looking for a European, classical acting course. At that time the idea of a one year post graduate course was unheard of, but recently it has become more common. About 10 years ago non-US students were accepted on to the course, and today there are about 40% US and Canadian students. "It is more class based because we expect people who come onto it probably have quite a lot of experience of performing. What they lack is technique to support performance, and not performance experience." The one year course concentrates on European and British classical theatre and covers Greek tragedy, Shakespeare and Jacobean theatre, Restoration, Russian Naturalism and early 20th century playwrights. Classes are given in voice, movement, singing, historic dance, textual interpretation and analysis, Alexander technique, poetry speaking, mask work, tap and flamenco and stage combat. The two year course is new and adds to the mainly classical work of the one year course to include in the second year 20th century drama and its particular techniques (including radio, TV and film). Classes include acting for radio and the screen, modern dance (tap, jazz and ballroom), clowning and illusion. The play content covers English-speaking drama between World Wars I and II, and English speaking drama after World War II. The final term is spent on public productions.

An interesting feature is that as well as doing a 'Showcase' presentation at the MacOwan Theatre, LAMDA has arranged for presentations of duologues by students eligible to work in the US. Duologues rather than monologues are the preferred method of audition in the US and Canada. The presentations take place in New York after the end of the course and are attended by agents and casting directors.

1 Year Foundation Course

The foundation course is for anyone thinking of a career in theatre, whether as an actor, director, stage manager, designer or administrator. Practical classes are given in voice, movement, dance, singing, acting, improvisation, technical aspects of the theatre, the history of English, European and world drama, play readings, verse and prose, play analysis and set term projects. "I think it is no secret that the education in this country does not turn out applicants who are as cultured as they were 15 or 20 years ago. We then generally expected that 18 year olds would have read two or three Shakespeare plays during the course of their education. Now it's possible to go through without having read one. We have kids turning up who may be talented, who may have an aptitude, but who are unread, to say the least of it. That doesn't mean that it is an academic course rather than a vocational course - there's no academic test. It is a general introduction to practical theatre, with as much back stage work as say, voice training, but there will be a lot of play reading and analysis to top up the educational area." Attendance on the course is no guarantee of a place on the three year course, although they do expect to take some on each year.

Post Graduate Diploma Courses

The Post Graduate Diploma courses for Musical Directors/Repetiteurs, Designers, Directors, Administrators and Movement Instructors are limited to one or two places each year per course. Hands on experience is offered in each of the relevant departments. For example, the directors will get experience of working on all aspects of theatrical production from budgeting to performance, including touring.

2 Year Stage Management

The stage management course was established in 1965 and provides a broad training in all aspects of technical theatre, with particular emphasis on stage management. As well as working in the MacOwan Theatre and on tour, all students undertake at least one work placement with a professional theatre or production company. Lectures and practical experience are provided in basic electricity, stage lighting equipment, control systems, lighting design, theatre sound, technical drawing, flying systems, scene painting, propmaking, set design, model making, basic first aid. Students also attend some classes in voice, music and stage combat. An important part of the course is the development of skills such as organisation, scheduling, time management, negotiation and man management. These are of course, transferable skills which can be used in many other professional fields; a Secretary General of the Arts Council was a LAMDA graduate for instance.

Summer Course

The four week summer Shakespeare Workshop is for students over 17. The course aims to demystify Shakespeare "to prevent poetic drama seeming an unscalable mountain; to make the student as comfortable with this kind of drama as he or she is with naturalistic work." Practical classes are given in voice, movement, singing, stage combat, historic dance, Alexander technique, text and scene study. The course includes visits to historic sites, the Royal Shakespeare Company at Stratford-upon-Avon and performances at London theatres showing classical work.

LAMDA is one of the top drama schools in the country. It has good facilities, in a good site, and has a long established reputation. Overall I found the single most striking element of LAMDA was the level of caring shown by everybody, from the principal downwards. "We aim to create an atmosphere that is just about as comfortable as we can make it, so you can do exercises which can be very revealing of the self. You have to have a very safe environment in which they can do that." The principal and the head of drama undoubtedly were concerned for the students well being, discussing their diet like mother hens, explaining how they were trying to raise more money to give more scholarships and bursaries. And the students backed this up. "It's not somewhere that breaks you down" said one. The students seemed very motivated and committed to what they were doing, and it was felt that the school was more open and relaxed than it had been. There also seemed a healthy social life attached to the school; when I visited preparations were being made for what looked like one hell of a party.

The London Academy of Performing Arts

Saint Matthew's Church, Saint Petersburgh Place, London W2 4LA
Tel: 0171 727 0220 Fax: 0171 727 0330

Principal: Cecilia Hocking

1 Year Post Graduate Classical Acting Course
1 Year Post Graduate Classical Acting with Musical Theatre
Option
1 Year Post Graduate Directing Course
1 Semester Classical Acting Course (12 weeks)
Summer Shakespearean Acting Course (4 weeks)

Fees:
All 1 Year Post Graduate Courses: £6,600
1 Semester Classical Acting Course - £2,200
Summer Shakespearean Acting Course - £850
45 hours per week, 33 weeks per year plus some evenings and weekends
Audition fees: Acting and Musical Theatre Course- £50 in person in USA, £25
in person in London, £25 audition on videotape. Directors Course - £10

Bayswater is a smart, centrally located area of London, to the north of Hyde
Park. It has shops and restaurants, including the recently re-vamped Whiteleys
department store. It is very cosmopolitan and you are as likely to hear Greek or
Arabic spoken on the streets as you are English. Just down the road is the ultra
hip Notting Hill area. Despite the expensive and glitzy image, there are still
pockets where the rents are not sky high. I visited the school at it's previous
location, another converted church in Fulham.

Auditions
Two speeches are required, one classical one modern. Applicants are seen individually by a panel consisting of the principal and two or three other teachers.
"We work with them to see how they respond to direction. If they are very
nervous, or if we have doubts we invite them back for a series of workshops to
see how they react with other students. We do try not to recall people, it is the
exception, and we do bear in mind if people have to travel long distances."
Students for the Musical Theatre option are expected to perform a short dance
routine and may be asked for a song from a musical or operetta (to be sung
unaccompanied). Directors are offered places on the basis of an interview with
the principal. Auditions are held in New York as well as in London. Approx. 20
places available per course. Minimum age 21, and most students are 24 +.

1 Year Post Graduate Classical Acting Course

Each term is divided into two performance blocks of six weeks, concentrating on classical texts. "We feel that we have to take the trainee actors on a journey and obviously the greatest journeys are those with the classical texts. They post the greatest stretches, require the greatest leaps of imagination, emotional stretches and also physical demands. We have a co-ordinated programme of classical texts, so that then we feel that they have the ability to cope with modern texts. We do start with a modern text to create the right ensemble feeling, so that the students feel that they can work together. If that bond isn't solid in the first instance then you haven't really got a firm basis for any development."

As well as text study the course covers movement (using the techniques of Rudolph Laban), voice and speech, improvisation and history of theatre. Other lectures and workshops include stage make-up, playreading, audition technique and TV and radio technique. Television workshops come at the end of the training. "Unless actors have a strong technique to expose them to television is a waste of time. So we wait to the end and then we call in a television director who adapts pieces they have previously worked to produce a video, which can then act as a show reel."

One of the interesting elements of the school is an awareness that many young actors now form their own companies. Amidst the more usual round of talks from Spotlight, Equity, a casting director and an agent that form the career development element of the course, they bring in the Independent Theatre Council "to show them how to run their own company". They have in the past had a considerable emphasis on performance within the community, from a schools tour to a tour of country houses for graduates from the school to give the students extended professional experience.

The end of year productions are based at the school, with a Showcase production for agents, directors and casting directors in the West End.

1 Year Post Graduate Classical Acting with Musical Theatre Option

"Experience tells us that there are people who want to sing and dance without having a strong enough acting technique to support it all, which is imperative in musical theatre. So we decided that we had to put the emphasis on the acting first and foremost. We give those actors who have talent extended musical and singing training." Apart from the additional singing and dancing classes the course shares the classes of the acting course. Productions are of musicals with a strong acting element. If the school feels that a student can not keep up to the standard required of the course they may suggest that a student concentrates on the Acting Course only.

1 Year Post Graduate Directors Course

This is a new course which has been designed to "provide the student director with a thorough grounding in the skills and requirements for a life long learning process." As well as attending lectures and classes students will work as assistant directors on student productions and at the end of the course direct "a professional production working with student actors".

1 Semester Classical Acting Course

An intensive course concentrating on practical work on Shakespearean texts. The course includes intensive study of Shakespeare's plays and sonnets, the speaking of Shakespearean verse and prose, the development of vocal resonance, speech agility and vocal projection, physical realisation of character, 16th century Elizabethan dance and Elizabethan sword play and unarmed combat. At the end of the course is a performance in the studio theatre of a condensed version of a Shakespearean play. Applicants are expected to have knowledge of the period and of the main Shakespeare plays. They are asked to prepare two Shakespearean speeches to audition standards.

Summer Shakespearean Acting Course

The course gives a comprehensive introduction to the classical style of theatre centred on the works of Shakespeare. The aim is to give students a classical technique with which to tackle Shakespearean roles and the confidence to present them. One of the major elements is the speaking of Shakespeare today, and there are other workshops in improvisation, acting, history of theatre, movement, voice and speech, stage fighting and fencing. Students are also taken to Stratford-upon-Avon for a 2 night stay to see two plays at the Royal Shakespeare Company (with an option to see a third). Before coming on the course students are asked to prepare a speech of their own choice from a classical play. Minimum age: 17

In the short time between my interviewing the principal and writing this there have been new developments, namely the move to new premises, the dropping of the two year course and the addition of a directing course. Students had enjoyed the course, although one commented that she had wished she had read the prospectus a bit harder before choosing the musical theatre option, on the grounds that, while good, she felt there wasn't enough emphasis on the musical theatre aspect for her "but then they do say it's acting plus musical theatre in the prospectus". They were pleased with small classes and excellent teachers (especially voice) and added that it was a school that went for ensemble playing. "It's not a place for anyone who wants to be a star or get star treatment."

The London Centre for Theatre Studies
The Impact Centre, 12-18 Hoxton Street, London N1 6NG
Tel/Fax: 0171 739 5866

Artistic Director: David Harris

1 Year The Actors Company (3 days per week)
1 Year Foundation Course (1 day plus 3 evenings)
The Actors Studio - Night School and Saturday School

Fees:
Actors Company: £5,600 per annum, Foundation Course: £3,200 per annum
Night School: £375 per term, Saturday School: £375 per term
2 Scholarships available from The Stage and Television Today
The Actors Company: 40 hours,Foundation Course 18 hours, 45 weeks per year
Audition fees: £25 The Actors Company, £20 Foundation Course

The London Centre for Theatre Studies is in Shoreditch, just north of the City of London. In the last five years this area has been discovered by developers and is a mixture of expensive modernist buildings, run down streets and shops awaiting development, and refurbished Victorian areas. One of these is Hoxton Square and the surrounding streets. The combination of cheap yet central London property has attracted many arts and media organisations to the area, including LCTS. The school has one floor of a large building around a central courtyard. This provides space for several very large rehearsal studios -"the skills of communicating to people get forgotten if you're acting in a cupboard" - a student common room and kitchen and offices. David Harris created and ran the Acting Company for Arts Educational Schools; a change of circumstances led him to leave Arts Ed and found his own school. He has gathered round him teachers who used to teach at other drama schools, notably Central and the Poor School, of whom the best known are probably George Hall and Margaret Braund, formerly Director of Acting and Head of Voice respectively at Central for many years.

Auditions
Auditions last for about an hour. Applicants are required to prepare two contrasting speeches, one modern and one classical. They are seen individually, perform their speeches and are interviewed by the Artistic Director.   Students must be over 21, and most are in their late 20s and upwards.

The Actors Company
When David Harris ran the Acting Company for Arts Ed, I was amazed at the hours the students were expected to put in. Using the same tactic he crams in 40

hours a week into three days: Friday, Saturday and Sunday. This leaves students four days off, to enable them to work and earn. Teaching style is based on the work of Stanislavski and Michael Chekhov and the overall aim is "to provide a solid vocational training from which is built an acting ensemble working in repertory". In each of the first three terms actors rehearse and perform a play from one period of theatre. Classes include acting study (including camera work), voice and speech, Alexander technique, voice and singing tutorials, ear training, accents, movement, historical dance, musical theatre, theatre representation, audition technique, make-up, dramatic literature. Improvisation is not included as David Harris feels that "it's about making things up out of your head, whereas an actor is there to interpret the text". Class work supports the production using musical theatre, dance, prose and poetry, literature, dialect as required to give each area of study a practical application and focus to the rehearsal process.

The final term lasts nine weeks and is a full time production period of six days per week. In the last four weeks of the term they take over the Jermyn Street theatre for a repertory season. This finishes with an "Agents Showing" for agents, directors and casting directors etc. They claim to have a good attendance rate; despite the small size and newness of the school this is not unlikely for a school with their contacts.

There are other courses for mature students. The Night School provides a foundation in Voice and text, the acting class and the rehearsal class on three evenings a week. The all day acting class runs every Saturday for twelve weeks. Night and Day school is a one year foundation course on Sundays plus three evenings a week.

It's hard not to be impressed by the dedication and drive of David Harris and his teaching staff. As one student said "they have so much energy and enthusiasm, it makes me exhausted and I'm more than half their age". As a group the students seemed very cohesive and relaxed with one another. They were impressed with the teaching and liked the school hours. David Harris told me that he felt that to train seriously just on evenings was not possible. "I don't want them when they are tired from working, I want them at their best" and the students agreed with this approach. Most worked for three days at another job - "you do need to have one day off a week, it's too much otherwise." "And you have to do a lot of research and reading in your own time" added another. "I could spend the rest of the week just doing work for here". It was also one of the few schools where the students talked about acting. One of the students had started a one year course at a more commercially minded drama school elsewhere but had dropped out. "The difference is that here we're being taught acting."

London and International School of Acting

138 Westbourne Grove, London W11 2RR
Tel: 0171 727 2342 Fax: 0171 221 7210

Founder and Principal: Brian Lidstone

2 Year Acting Course
1 Year Post Graduate Acting Course
6 Months Intensive Acting Course

Fees:
2 Year Acting Course: £5000 per annum 1 Year Post Graduate Acting Course:
£5000
6 Months Intensive Acting Course: £2500
40 hours per week, 40 weeks per year
Audition fee: £20

LISA is based in the Bayswater area of London, which is a smart area immediately to the west of Central London and near Notting Hill with it's famous carnival and the Portobello road. Recently the area has become much smarter, but students should be able to find accommodation locally. LISA rents various premises for rehearsals and productions. When I visited they were in a cavernous community centre resembling a fortress, but I understand that plans were underway for LISA to move into a new arts centre being developed by the local council.

Auditions
Applicants are expected to learn two scenes or speeches of the student's own choice, to contrast mood or style, each to last approximately three minutes. They may also be asked to sing a song unaccompanied. Pieces are followed by an interview. All auditions are on a one-to-one basis.

The Courses
The year runs on a four term basis, each term having 10 weeks with a three week break in between. Students study voice production, speech, singing, phonetics, dialects, choral speaking, poetry, sight reading, memorising technique, audition technique, acting techniques, script analysis, characterisation, mime, improvisation, observation, spontaneity, make-up, fitness, dance, Kata, physical theatre, stage fighting, broadcasting, camera acting as well as performing contemporary and classical plays. One feature of the courses is that students perform in a

variety of public places, such as hospitals and libraries. These may be devised pieces, or poetry readings. Television and radio are covered in short courses with outside directors. Part of the course is devoted to getting work as a professional actor.

I came to see LISA in the middle of rehearsals for a show directed by the principal. I only had the opportunity for the briefest of chats with him, and a quick word with those students not on stage. The students I spoke to were happy with the training, although none of them seemed to have any clear ideas about what they were going to do with themselves when it finished in a few months time. Most of the classes were taken by the principal or another director who, according to the students, had just graduated from the LISA course and had no other outside experience. They seemed content with this, and said he was very good.

Manchester Metropolitan University

Department of Communication Media, School of Television and Theatre
Capitol Building, School Lane, Didsbury, Manchester M20 6HT
Tel: 0161 434 3331 Fax: 0161 247 6390
website: http://www.mmu.ac.uk

Member of the Conference of Drama Schools

Head of Department: Robert Sharp, Course Leader: Niamh Dowling

*   **3 Year BA (Hons) Theatre Arts (Acting)**

Fees:
BA (Hons) Acting: Mandatory grants. £750 per annum home/EU students, £6,000
overseas
Audition fee: None

Manchester is one of the biggest and most cosmopolitan cities in the UK and
many young people consider it to be the most exciting place to live in Britain.
There are four theatres (including the Royal Exchange), Granada Television, the
Halle Orchestra, one of the largest student populations in Europe and a vibrant
night life.   It is also the home of Manchester United and Manchester City football clubs and the Old Trafford cricket ground. Accommodation is easy to find.
As part of the former Manchester Polytechnic the school has access to all their
facilities which are extensive although as the university is four miles away "it
means we don't have to bother with the hierarchy". The School of Theatre itself
is based in a wonderful art deco building, built first as a cinema which then
became the original ATV television studios. A large theatre space with flexible
seating has been created in what used to be a film sound stage and there are
numerous other rehearsal rooms, lecture theatres and studios. The building also
houses the Film and Television part of the BA Design for Communication Media
so, as you might imagine, there are excellent facilities for film and television
work including television studios, editing suites, cinema and aspiring directors.

Auditions
About 1000 applicants for 24-30 places. Applicants are asked to prepare three
speeches, none to exceed two minutes, one speech to be Shakespeare and in
verse, one to be modern, and the third to be a contrast "in terms of mood, not
style" to the first two. The preliminary audition consists of performing two of
the speeches. The third speech is usually only asked for if the panel feel that you
have made bad choices with the first two or if you are a border line case. The

recall audition consists of a day long workshop for groups of 8-10, with work on the pieces, and improvisation, movement, voice and speech sessions plus a short interview. Students are seen by a panel of four to six representatives of all the different departments involved - voice, movement, acting and so on. The minimum age is 18, but the average age of students is in the mid 20s with "a lot in their early 30s - we encourage mature students to apply." The male/female ratio is 50:50.

3 Year BA (Hons) Acting

The first year looks at "the development of the individual through group work, to remove the ego." This is done by studying the "Self" - the natural body, the natural voice, the natural personality - in mask work, chorus and ensemble work. All scene study is based on Stanislavski's work. Classes taken by students include anatomy, dance, phonetics, masks, improvisation, text, body and voice.

The second year "concentrates on examining the apparent tension for the actor between the demands of realistic and epic acting through a series of acting workshops." These include Brecht, Restoration, television, and finish with a full Shakespeare play. The Brecht is based on the work of Grotowski. During the year the students devise their own theatre piece and are encouraged to perform it for specified audiences. One of the features of the course is that there are links with theatre in Eastern Europe, both with directors coming to Manchester and Manchester students going East. The second years tour Poland for two weeks, and there is a link with the theatre in St Petersburg which sends a director each year.

The third year is a performance year, starting with naturalistic plays, such as Chekhov and Ibsen, and finishing with a season of four contemporary plays. There are close relationships with the professional world and these productions are often directed by directors from the Contact and Library Theatre in Manchester and the Bolton Octagon. The summer season is usually directed by London directors. There is a showcase production which is shown at the Royal Exchange and in London just before Easter. Radio classes start in the third year and television work continues - the film and television department have twelve directors who all have to present a piece each year. Musical theatre is not taught although "there is a lot of singing" and there is a heavy physical bias to the training.

During the first and second years students must keep a work book and write an essay each term, relating to that term's project. "It is a way to focus the work and broaden the training." In the third year students undertake an area of research of their choice and produce a dissertation of 8,000 - 10,000 words. This is called the Independent Project and is expected to reflect "the students' own assessment and enquiry in relation to their work and potential employment contexts."

The course is perhaps closest to the Drama Centre in its rigorous approach to text and the exploration of self. It differs in the type of texts used; final productions tend to be of contemporary plays and the school has a reputation of producing strong, modern actors (for example Julie Walters and David Threlfall). Many of the students come from Scotland, Ireland and the North with a sizeable proportion of international students. Students enjoyed the course and felt well equipped to go out into the profession; about half intended to stay in the Manchester area. The one area of criticism concerned support (or rather lack of it) on the academic side "I thought they would help more, but you're left to get on with it" said one (who had just been awarded a first).

Mountview Conservatoire for the Performing Arts

104 Crouch Hill, London N8 9EA
Tel: 0181 340 5885 Fax: 0181 348 1727
email: enquiries@mountview.drama.ac.uk

Member of the Conference of Drama Schools

Principal: Paul Clements, Head of Acting: Brian Astbury, from April 1998, Pat Trueman

* **3 Year BA (Hons) in Performance: Acting Option**
* **3 Year BA (Hons) in Performance: Musical Theatre Option**
* **1 Year Post Graduate Acting Course**
* **1 Year Post Graduate Musical Theatre Course**
  1 Year Directors Course
* **2 Year Stage Management, Technical and Design Studies (degree status to come)**
  1 Year Post Graduate Stage Management, Technical and Design Studies Course

Fees:
3 Year Acting Course: £7575 per annum
3 Year Musical Theatre Course: £8175 per annum
1 Year Post Graduate Acting Course: £10,260 per annum
1 Year Post GraduateMusical Theatre: £11,060 per annum
1 Year Post Graduate Directors and Stage Management Courses: £7695
2 Year Stage Management Course: £7575 per annum
Scholarships: Approx. 7 for tuition fees only each year.
Audition fees: £30 in London; Conducted overseas by representative, £60 or $100.

Mountview is split between two sites, one at Wood Green and the other at Crouch End. Both are in North London, with good access to the centre by public transport from the Wood Green site. Accommodation around either Crouch End or Wood Green is easy to find and cheap (for London). The Crouch Hill site is the original home to Mountview and has been adapted from a Victorian detached house. As well as studio and workshop spaces there are two main theatres, one a proscenium arch seating 108 and the other a studio seating 60. The stage management, technical and design courses are based here. The acting courses are based at the Wood Green site which is a modern complex of rehearsal rooms, radio and television studios, library and a canteen. There are also two annexes containing further rehearsal rooms and studios.

Auditions

Between 500 and 1000 people audition each year. The number of places varies; the theoretical maximums are very high, but they rarely accept that many. On the three year course the theoretical maximum is 75, with generally numbers being in the mid 60s. For the one year course the theoretical maximum is 45, with currently 39 on the course, although it has been as low as 23. About 30 audition each time. Auditions start with a movement warm up, then a vocal warm up, then an introduction from either the principal or the head of acting with the chance to ask questions. Then all have a movement/dance session in which they are taught a very basic set of dance steps, and perform a song to the head of music theatre. Then they go to two of three panels and perform their speeches and work on the text. Some are let go at this stage. The rest stay for another hour or two working with the principal, head of acting and other staff members on their speeches. There are no further recalls. They try for a male/ female ratio of 50:50, but it is usually closer to 40:60. Most students on the three year courses are in the age range of 17-23, and on ht e one year course from 22 up to 30s and 40s. Roughly 60% take the acting option and 40% take the musical theatre option.

3 Year Acting and Musical Theatre courses

"We're constantly readjusting the course, we don't want the course set in stone. We want a course that is flexible and responsive to what is happening around it. It is based on the premise that if they can do the heavy going classics nothing in the modern repertoire holds any fears for them." The first year is common to both the acting and the musical theatre option. Classes are divided equally between acting, voice and singing and movement and dance plus television classes, all fed into projects. During the year the projects include story telling, Brecht, Jacobean and the Greeks.

Acting option:

In the second year the actors cover comedy. "It is terribly important and no drama school manages to do enough of it because of all the other things which they have to cover". Projects include Wilde and Coward, Chekhov, Shakespeare and American playwrights. The year finishes with a devised project and a radio project. There is also a song and dance module throughout which "helps to lighten the tone of all that Shakespeare".

In the third year the actors start with another devised project. "We do a lot of devised work in response to the fact that so many companies have collapsed. We try to turn out actors who are totally capable of running their own company, creating and generating their own work." Then they do a television project. This lasts for three weeks and is shot on location with specially written scripts. They provide tapes to the students so they have something to show casting directors etc. This is followed by three full productions, one of which may be a musical. Finally they perform their 'grads', a Showcase production in a West End Theatre. "I personally would never choose anyone on the basis of a grad, because all it tells you is that some one has been drilled to within an inch of their lives by a very good director. But it's the way it works."

From the second year onwards there is a career development programme, and Mountview have an extremely efficient publicity and marketing department which promotes the school and the students.

"We have an eclectic method of teaching. I don't feel that there is one actor training that caters for everybody. A lot of Stanislavski's wok is outdated now - if he was around he'd be changing it. We have a lot of teachers from the different traditions - Stanislavski, Lecoq, Grotowski. We say to the students, you are getting all these things, choose what works for you. Every actor's has got to put together their own system."

Musical Theatre Option:

In the second year the musical theatre option separates from the acting option. "It is a very practical course aim at turning out people who will be of use to musical theatre as it stands now, and is constantly updated to keep in touch with what is currently happening." It starts with song and dance workshop based on the major styles of the 20th century. Craft classes continue in the three major disciplines, but there is more emphasis on singing than acting, although there are still projects on Shakespeare and Chekhov. The year finishes with a full presentation of a book musical.

In the third year the students do two musicals, one involving the whole year group, a panto, their either another musical or a play. They also have a three week television project, and finally their 'grad' with the acting students.

1 Year Post Graduate Acting Option

The post graduate courses are separated into the acting and musical theatre options from the beginning. Throughout both courses are craft classes in the three disciplines of acting, singing and voice and movement. "A lot of them come from universities and they are totally in their heads. So we give them nothing but physicality for the first five weeks." This is followed by scenes from modern text, projects in Shakespeare and Chekhov, a modern classic play, a restoration project. In the final term are the three week television project and one full play, plus the graduation showcase production in the West End of London. They are investigating putting on more than one full scale public production for this course but "plays are written to be plays, not to give fifteen equal parts".

1 Year Post Graduate Musical Theatre Option

The musical theatre option is similar to the three year course "but condensed". They start with song and dance workshops, followed by Shakespeare and Chekhov, a book musical, Restoration project "we find the enormously florid style is immensely helpful". The final musical production and Graduate Showcase in the West End is performed together with the one year actors. Throughout craft classes in the three disciplines continue and in the final term there is the three week television project.

1 Year Directors Course
Normally two students per year are accepted onto the one year directors course. This aims to give a thorough background in the theoretical, practical and technical aspects of being a director. Over the three terms students gain experience from the point of view of the actor, the designer - set lighting and costume - the stage manager and the director through a combination of classes and practical production work. It is tailored as far as possible to the requirements and previous experience of the individual students. The course finishes with two performance projects using professional actors, the first being a one act play and the second a full production.

2 Year Stage Management, Technical and Design Studies Course
The two year stage management, technical and design studies course (which is destined to become a three year degree course shortly) aims to give the student the widest possible training in a full range of professional skills, with the emphasis on practical work. The course covers practical stage management, set design theory and practice, property making, model making, set construction, scale drawing, scene painting, basic electrics and lighting, sound, computer aided design (CAD), costume history, making and management, theatre organisation and practice, television technique, musical score reading, theatre history and text study. Students can later choose to specialise in set and costume design, stage management or lighting and sound. During the second year students work as stage managers, designers and technicians on a range of public performances and television shoots. As an alternative to working on one of the productions students may undertake a secondment to a professional theatre or workshop. Students have an option to continue for a third, specialist year.

1 Year Post Graduate Stage Managment, Technical and Design Studies Course
This course is highly intensive. The first term is class room based, covering stage management, stage electrics, lighting design, sound and sound design, set design and scene painting, properties, model making, set construction and carpentry, costume, computer aided design (CAD), technical drawing, textual studies, inter-personal and communication skills, research projects. The second and third terms are spent on production assignments, one of which is a two or three week attachment to a professional theatre, film or television company or similar

organisation. In the third term students take on senior production roles reflecting their own special interests, such as set designer, lighting designer, company stage manager. There are also classes in career and professional development, specialist lectures and masterclasses.

Summer Courses

Summer courses are all two weeks in duration. Shakespeare's Text in Action aims to introduce students to a wealth of information about Shakespeare's characters and the emotion, behaviour and imagery contained win this writing. The course often works with the Globe education Centre at the Globe Theatre which provides opportunities to both study and perform at an historic venue.

The Musical Theatre and Acting Courses have a similar format with classes in the mornings and rehearsals in the afternoon, culminating in a performance at the end of the course. Masterclasses are also given by leading professionals.

Also available are evening courses, and Easter and summer workshops.

When I visited Paul Clements had just taken over the principal's position from the school's founder, Peter Coxhead. He had come from being principal at the Welsh College of Music and Drama, where I had been impressed by his individual style, the concern the school had for each student. That concern will be, I believe, a useful addition to Mountview which is a large (if not the largest), professional drama school. Students were concerned about numbers and reported that sometimes one felt lost among everybody else. They claimed that there were 78 students in the current first year. This led to pressure on rooms, rehearsal spaces and queues in the canteen were a norm. When there are so many in the year "you have to shove to the front to get any attention and I'm not very good at that" said one. Their favourite part of the course had been the devised play. The new buildings at Wood Green are stunning and provide a lot of space, but they need every inch. All institutions change when a new principal or head comes in; it will be interesting to see what Paul Clements does. I hope it will include reducing the overall student numbers.

The Oxford School of Drama

Sansomes Farm Studios, Woodstock, Oxford OX20 1ER
Tel: 01993 812883 Fax: 01993 811220

Member of the Conference of Drama Schools

Principal: George Peck

*   **3 Year Acting Course**
      1 Year Acting Course
      6 Month Foundation Course

Fees:
3 Year Acting Course: £5710.50 per annum
1 Year Acting Course: £7,050 for course
6 Months Foundation Course: £2,855.25 for course
School bus: £70 per term
Audition fees: £20

Oxford is known the world over as the home of Oxford University. There are now two universities based there, and they have attracted other teaching establishments such as secretarial and language schools, so there is no shortage of student life in the city. As one would imagine there are museums, art galleries, shops, restaurants and performing spaces including a repertory theatre. London is an hour away by road or train. Woodstock is about 10 miles to the North of Oxford. It is a pleasant small town made famous by being on the edge of the grounds of Blenheim Palace. A few miles on from Woodstock in the middle of fields you come to a set of converted and purpose built buildings, once a farm, that form the Oxford School of Drama. Students live in Oxford and are bussed to the school and back each day in the school's mini-bus. There is a small additional charge for this service.

The school was originally founded as a summer school for teenagers and has from these beginnings grown into a full time drama school. Recently it was invited to join the CDS and the three year course received accreditation from the NCDT. The facilities consist mainly of rehearsal studios, although there are plans underway to build a small studio theatre.

Auditions
Applicants are picked up from Oxford and returned at the end of the day. About 14 people are seen each session. Applicants are asked to prepare two contrasting

speeches, one classical (preferably Shakespeare) and one modern. The session starts with a general improvisation class, then each student is seen individually by the principal and another tutor. There may be recalls to be seen by other members of staff. About 500 people are seen for 14-16 places on the three year course, 12 on the one year course. Students should be over 18 for the three year and over 20 for the one year course. Most students are in their early to mid 20s, with a perhaps a couple in their 30s.

3 Year Acting Course

"It's the greatest gift people can discover here, learn who they are, learn to love themselves, to be able to go out into the profession protected and at the same time satisfied because they are working creatively. I still shudder when I see actors behaving badly or in a slap happy way, not caring about the work they do and not being rigorous with the text."

The three year course has developed from the two year course, mainly to allow more time for productions. Throughout the course classes are taken in movement, voice and speech, music (including singing and musical theatre) and verse and poetry (including Shakespearean verse). The first year is seen as "an exploration of the actor's craft and aims to develop an understanding of the actor as a creator." Acting classes include, for example, truth and theatrical truth, animal studies, mask work, imagination and action, motivation and response. At the end of the year the students present a naturalistic play in-house. The second year builds on the first, looking into greater detail at the demands of texts. Acting classes include advanced character study, style and exaggerated truth, character analysis and limes of action, the actor in performance. There are two presentations each term covering a wide range of theatrical styles. From this point onwards an agent or director comes to the school every term and sees audition speeches.

The third year concentrates on public performance and career preparation. The first two terms are based at Woodstock and public performances take place at a range of venues in Oxford and possibly on tour. For the final term the school moves down to London. "To train here is fine, they are out of the pressures and they can just concentrate, but there's no doubt that an actor, especially when starting out, needs to be in London. This way we can run at least four or five weeks of performances in London so students can make the move under the umbrella of the school. Also, these days an agent is more likely to say 'yes, I'm thinking about it, but I'd like to see you in something else' so we give them the opportunity to be seen in four things. Finally it gives them the opportunity to get the feel of being part of a company." The students perform an agents showcase production each term in the final year. Classes include advanced audition classes, marketing for the actor, professional development, developing range and flexibility.

Television work starts in the second term of the course "when the students are still learning about truth and still rigorously having to be truthful in the space. We bring in the cameras and for a bit they're very untruthful." They do more camera work in short blocks in the second and third years, usually bringing in freelance staff and equipment or going to a local production company. Radio is taught in classes during the second year.

Throughout the course there are masterclasses given by professional directors, actors, casting directors and so on. Students are also able to attend seminars and lectures given by the Cameron Mackintosh Professor of Contemporary Theatre. Those who have held this post include Sir Richard Eyre, Lord Attenborough, Arthur Miller, Peter Shaffer, Michael Codron, Alan Ayckbourn, Sir Ian McKellen and Stephen Sondheim.

1 Year Acting Course

The course is split into two halves. The first two terms are spent in classes and in-house presentations. These include two classical plays, a modern play and a narrative text. Classes include the acting process, body awareness and self expression, physicalisation and character, Shakespearean verse, animal studies, radio and film technique, mask work, and audition classes as well as classes in voice and movement. The third and fourth terms are spent in rehearsal or productions. In each term there is a Showcase production in either London or Oxford or both. The final fourth term, like the final term of the three year course, is spent in London, first in rehearsals then in a repertory season in a London theatre. During these last terms there are professional development classes.

6 Month Foundation Course

The course runs for two terms and is aimed at school leavers who are taking a year out before moving on to further education or finding employment. Topics include acting methods and techniques, musical theatre, stage management, audition techniques, stage fighting, film and television.

Probably the single most outstanding feature about the Oxford School of Drama is the attention given to professional development, whether in classes, the multiple Showcase productions in different terms or the 'London Season' at the end of the three and one year courses. Many students at schools outside London show a marked reluctance to leave their comfortable lives for the unknown perils of the capital - as another principal said "they stay here for a bit, then they drift down to London". To launch a career needs more drive than drift so top marks to OSD for pushing them out of the nest, having provided a good launch pad. Another feature is that they use some unconventional venues, such as the Groucho Club, which must attract a higher turn out. It is in interesting combination, to have the commercial side attended to so thoroughly while the acting teaching itself is concerned with personal development. Students were enthusiastic about the course and didn't seem fussed about the mini-bus ride in and out, as I had thought they would be. They liked living in Oxford and they liked working in the countryside so the transport was necessary. Only one student felt negatively about the course; she had been unhappy with the emphasis on personal discovery and exploration and felt that her self-confidence had been shaken. The other students stressed that this had not been their experience. One could not help but feel that she was a square peg in a round hole and an example of why it is so important to find a school with the right approach for you.

The Poor School

242 Pentonville Road, London N1 9JY
Tel: 0171 837 6030

Principal: Paul Caister

2 Year Acting Course (evenings and weekends)

Fees:
2 Year Acting Course: £1090 per term, £3270 per annum
19 hours per week plus occasional extra evenings and days. In the last two terms there is no Easter break, and there may well be demands on weekday day time. Audition fee: £20

The Poor School is located right by Kings Cross Station and so is easily accessible from virtually any part of London and the home counties. They have the ground floor of a run down Victorian building. Recently they were able to acquire the shop premises at the front of the building and have converted it into a studio theatre seating between 50 and 80. When not in use it provides an extra large studio to add to the two they currently have. The Poor School pioneered the idea of a full acting training crammed into evenings and weekends for those who could not afford to give up work but desperately wanted to train as an actor or for those who simply could not afford the fees charged elsewhere.

Auditions
Two speeches are required, one of which must be from Shakespeare. Neither speech is to exceed two minutes. "You must pick pieces you believe you understand and trust your instincts". Applicants are first seen individually when some may be weeded out, then in small groups of about six people. They work on their pieces within the group as well as doing improvisation, staying for about 3-4 hours. "We see hundreds and hundreds" for 32 places a year, about four men to three women. There are no other quotas aside from maintaining the sex ratio except "hopefully we don't think in types, but the profession does so we might take that into account for very idiosyncratic types". The age range in the past has varied from 18 to 51, but most students are in their early to mid 20s.

2 Year Acting Course
The first four terms are primarily class work, with any performance being strictly in-house. "I hope everybody here follows their own philosophy in teaching. We've all been influenced by people, but we don't try and fulfil a style, we try

and do theatre the way we think is right. The sort of theatre we produce is a little bit more concerned with the true side of acting rather than the more gratuitously flamboyant style of acting." Classes cover movement, voice, acting study, verse and text, dance and singing, animal study. Musical theatre is not covered except in "the sense that singing and dancing is part of the course". Regarding television Paul Caister is "of the view that acting is acting, and there is not a television style, a film style, a stage style. You apply your acting to whichever medium you are in. Mostly it is common sense, nothing that an intelligent person would pick up in a few days. I mean, how long does it take to learn not to rustle the pages on the radio?"

The last two terms are virtually entirely rehearsal and performance, with no Easter break. Six productions take place in this period, each lasting three weeks. Students are expected to stage manage, run the bar and front of house for these productions. The final two nights of training is Agents Night, when students perform scenes in front of an invited audience of agents, directors and casting directors. "We give as much practical advice as is humanly possible, always understanding that it is very hard to gauge. There aren't golden rules and nothing replaces the experience of actually finishing and seeing how you go." Many Poor School graduates seem to be doing well, especially in television, and the school's reputation is growing.

Make no mistake about it, a course such as that offered by the Poor School is extremely hard work. All students I spoke to had started off working full time, but had fairly rapidly given up to cope with the demands of the training. Working full time in the last two terms is virtually impossible. Discipline is required to get to class on time and punctuality is demanded. Paul Caister (described as 'messianic' by one student) works everybody extremely hard to get results. But the students respected this. One said "I knew it would be tough, and it has been." I have always thought that successfully completing a course like this said something about an actor; and it appears from the ever increasing numbers of Poor School students in work that other theatre professionals think the same way.

Queen Margaret College

Corstophine Campus, Edinburgh EH12 8TS
Tel: 0131 317 3247   Fax: 0131 317 3248
email: admissions@qmced.ac.uk   web site: www.qmced.ac.uk

Member of the Conference of Drama Schools

Principal: Joan Stringer, Head of Drama Dept: Ian Brown

* **3 or 4 Year BA (Hons) Acting**
* **3 or 4 Year BA (Hons) Stage Management and Theatre Arts**
BA (Hons) Drama and Theatre Arts p159

Fees:
3/4 Year Courses (4th Year for Honours): Mandatory Grants, £5,950 per annum
for overseas/other
Audition fees: £10 preliminary audition, additional £15 for re-call.

Edinburgh, the capital of Scotland, is a beautiful city surrounded by wonderful
countryside. It is considered to be one of the best places to live in Britain. It is
famous for, among other things, the arts Festivals in the summer. Most of Scotland's television and theatre production companies are based either here or in
Glasgow (an hour away by train). Queen Margaret's College is located on the
outskirts of Edinburgh in a campus setting. Accommodation is either in halls of
residence on site - "rabbit hutches" or in town, which apparently led to problems
for those without cars. The drama department is a slightly anomalous part of the
college which offers degrees in business management, communication, health
and social sciences but no other arts or humanities degree courses. There are
numerous rehearsal rooms and two studio theatres. Other facilities on site include a students' union, bar, cafeteria, squash and tennis courts, a swimming
pool and fully equipped television and radio studios. There are about 1500 students in all, with about 200 in the drama department. However, thanks to Lottery money, from 1999 the entire drama department will move into the Gateway
Theatre, right in the centre of the town. This used to be Edinburgh's repertory
theatre, then became television studios. The site is being completely refurbished
together with new buildings to give some of the best facilities (and very well
located too) for a drama school anywhere in Britain. Under the Scottish system
Ordinary degrees take three years while Honours degrees take four. There are
four degrees in all taught by the drama department of which two are vocational
and two are academic. Of the academic courses, Drama and Theatre Arts was
created to complement the vocational courses, focussing on the five crafts of

directing, writing, literary management, administration and community theatre. In the final year students specialise in one of these areas. The Combined Studies course focusses on the historical, textual and theory side of the drama studies degree and can be studied in conjunction with media studies.

Auditions

About 500 applicants are seen for 20 places. Two speeches are required for the preliminary audition, one Shakespeare, one modern. At the recall the speeches are performed again individually, and then the group comes together for an improvisation session.

3 or 4 Year BA (Hons) Acting

The Acting degree is taught in four subject areas - Acting, voice, text and movement, with the bulk of the work being taken with acting studies. "We are developing the actor's instrument, the voice and body, and also the understanding of text. The development of the acting classes is also a synthesis of what is learnt in the other three areas, so in the first two years you are doing a series of classes in each subject side by side and working through the strands." At the end of the first year there is a community or educational project. From then on there are regular productions right through to the end of the degree; "we operate as a rep, doing 12 productions a year". While there is a fully equipped television studio on the site, the course has to share it with the rest of the college and has in fact, limited access to it.

In the third year the voice and movement classes are done in relation to specific productions and textual studies are replaced by an exploration of some aspect of theatre and a particular role that the student finds interesting. Many of the students leave at the end of the third year, perhaps coming back at a later date to do the final year. It is the first three years that are accredited by the NCDT.

The fourth year (which is the Honours year) consists of a practical project or dissertation, some taught classes on text and performance, and a specialist acting study which may be devised (it varies from year to year and is project based). "We see a distinction between the process of professional training and the potential for actors who are interested in this to go on for a further year. It is an add-on, for more reflective work."

The main written work is the Actor's Journal, which is similar to a diary. "We are interested in the concept of the reflective practitioner, an actor who understands acting, who understands him or herself, and who understand who their art relates to the larger crafts that feed them. It's about getting people to think to do". All other written work is always in support of the project they are working on at the time. For example, they might be asked to do an appreciation or evaluation of a play from a particular character's point of view.

In the last year there are careers days, professional presentations and so on. At the end of the course is a showcase presentation in Edinburgh, which is mainly attended by Scottish professionals. They also put on a production in the Edinburgh Fringe Festival every year, which gives another opportunity for the students work to be seen. When they have relocated to the Gateway, they will increase the number of productions shown.

3 or 4 Year BA (Hons) Stage Management and Theatre Arts
The course comprises a programme of professional productions, theatre productions, workshops and projects alongside skills-based subjects. The first two years are spent within the production departments studying stage and production management, budgeting and scheduling, set and costume design, lighting, sound, wardrobe management and computer box office operations. In the third year students are allocated a major production role, for example, stage or production manager, set, costume, lighting or sound designer, audience services manager or senior technician. Students may work in more than one of the production departments. Also required is the preparation of a special study. Students undertake a placement in a professional theatre. In the fourth year students work with other students in mounting productions. They also undertake a major independent study, and study text in performance and the politics of theatre provision.

If you are resident in Scotland and want a grant then you have to apply and be rejected by the two Scottish schools (Queen Margaret's and RSAMD) before you can apply for other schools, hence the relatively high proportions of Scots on the course. Having applied for the two, there has to be a suspicion that if you were offered a place by both schools then you would choose RSAMD. But this may be changing. There is a world of difference between the rather subdued department I first visited in 1989 and the one I saw nearly 10 years later. Now it is thriving, dynamic and lively. A further boost will come when the new building is up and running in 1999. The students I spoke to had enjoyed the course and enjoyed being in Edinburgh, although they were less enthusiastic about their fellow students at Queen Margaret's "I went to the student bar once and thought, it's not for me". Generally they intended to stay in Scotland for at least a few years before moving down to London (if they moved at all), regardless of where they had originally come from. There is a very dynamic Scottish theatre scene, and Scotland itself has become very fashionable for television and film productions, especially since Braveheart and Trainspotting to name but two. As one student pointed out "it's easier to be a big fish in a little pond". Another student pointed out that having the fringe festival on the doorstep made it possible to meet London based directors and show them your work away from the standard show case production. Definitely a school on the up.

Redroofs Theatre School

Littlewick Green, Maidenhead, Berks SL6 3QY
Tel: 01628 822982 Fax: 01628 822461

Founder and Director: June Rose

2 Year Student Course
1 Year Post Graduate Course

Fees:
All Courses: £1,450 per term, £5,800 per annum
40 weeks per year
Audition fee: £20

The Maidenhead area is about 40 minutes by train or car directly to the west of Central London. Most of the students find accommodation in Maidenhead, the large town a few miles away. Redroofs Theatre School consists of a stage school up to 16 year olds based in Maidenhead and a student section for 16 years and over based at Littlewick Green a few miles away from Maidenhead. Littlewick Green is a very picturesque village surrounding around a large area of open land. The theatre school building used to be Ivor Novello's home. Ivor Novello wrote musical comedies such as "Careless Rapture" and the World War I song "Keep the home fires burning". He built the theatre there, a delightful miniature seating 42 in red, plush seats. Students work in the rooms of the main house, and there are a few purpose built studios as well. There is no canteen (and no shops nearby to buy food) although there is a vending machine for hot drinks and soup, and a microwave oven for the students use. The school runs the Redroofs Theatre Company at the Novello Theatre in Sunninghill, near Ascot, some 7 miles away. This is a professional children's theatre company which provides students the opportunity to take part in professional work while on the course. The school is also a theatrical agency.

Auditions

200-300 audition for 20 places on the two year course. Applicants are required to prepare a song (a taped accompaniment may be used) and two contrasting speeches, one from Shakespeare or other classical verse play and one from a contemporary play. Neither speech is to be longer than four minutes. Those with previous dance training are also required to prepare a short dance in either tap, ballet or modern to taped music. Those who do not have previous dance training may be tested for their dance aptitude. Applicants are idividually seen and inter-viewed by the principal. Unlike other drama schools Redroofs accepts 16 year olds, and many have come from their stage school in Maidenhead. There is no maximum age - "the oldest is 23 at the moment". The one year course is open to those over 18 who have had previous professional experience, a degree or diploma in Drama or Dance, or two years study at another drama school.

2 Year Student Course

The first year is a mixture of classes and productions in the Little Theatre at the school. Students study dance and music, singing, voice and speech, film and television, acting and supplementary workshops and lectures. These may include theatre history, design (scenic and costume), radio technique, cold reading and other aspects of the theatre. Students can be entered for the exams of the Royal Academy of Dancing and the Imperial Society of Teachers of Dancing. The approach is always pragmatic. "We are very middle of the road, it's not for punks. We want normal kids wanting to make a living in commercial theatre." The second year is called 'The Repertory Year'. During this year students become part of the professional company at the Novello Theatre in Sunninghill. There they play small parts, are understudies and take 'walk-on' roles as required. Each production runs for two to three months, and there may be one or two performances a day. In addition, students are expected to learn and use practical stage management skills such as sound operating, lighting, set rigging and so on. While working at the theatre students are considered to be 'apprentices' and receive fees to cover their travel costs and other expenses. When not in productions or required for rehearsal classes take place at the school together with rehearsals for their own student productions. Final productions are put on at the Novello Theatre. They do not produce a show case production on the grounds that all students can be taken on by the school's own theatrical agency and therefore do not need to attract other agents. Many are put forward for, and get, professional work during their time at the school.
Television and radio work has increased and uses a television studio nearby. Ms Rose's daughter runs a television production company and students sometimes work for that.

1 Year Course

The one year course is simply the second year of the two year course and not a separate course on it's own. As this is the 'Repertory Year' it may not be suitable for those who want to concentrate on developing technique rather than gaining performance experience.

The school is in a beautiful setting, and offers the opportunity to gain considerable professional-level experience of theatre, and in particular, children's theatre. Because the agency actively seeks work for students many graduate having already worked professionally, for example on training films. The students I met were a disparate group. Some had come straight from the stage school and were in their late teens, while others were older. Perhaps it was a bad day for them, but they were full of complaints about the school. The repertory year got the most flak. The work was much harder than expected, especially over the Christmas period when there had frequently been two shows a day and hardly any time off. The commitments of two performances daily meant that sometimes there was little time for their own classes, and they felt that they were being short changed. Having said that, it was also clear that some of them had had unrealistic expectations; the prospectus makes it quite clear how the repertory year works, that it will be demanding and that students will be playing minor roles at best. Another felt that the course was in fact a musical theatre course and not an acting course. "Had I known that there was going to be so much dancing and singing I wouldn't have come - I hate musical theatre!" The prospectus does not make it clear how much time will be spent on each discipline, but does put acting last on the list of classes. Finally they drew my attention to the first paragraph of the regulations: "Students are accepted subject to the understanding that, in the event of terminating their course, for whatever reason, the Fees for the full Course are payable". (My underlining.)

Richmond Drama School

Parkshot Centre, Parkshot, Richmond, Surrey TW9 2RE
Tel: 0181 940 0170 ext. 325   Fax: 0181 332 6560

Director: David Whitworth

1 Year Acting Course

Fees:
£2,025 per annum (non EU students pay £2,700) plus registration fee of £200.
Audition fee: £15

Richmond is one of the most desirable areas to live outside Central London.
There are good road, tube and rail connections, it's on the Thames, there's Richmond and the Old Deer Park, Kew Gardens, a good shopping centre with plenty of pubs and restaurants, and two theatres. Richmond Theatre is often the last stop of plays about to transfer into the West End and the Orange Tree is one of the most interesting fringe theatres in the country. All these attractions are only a few minutes walk from the school. The school has a separate building in the grounds of an Adult Education centre. They have two main rooms for teaching and rehearsals plus a student common room, kitchen and other offices. Other facilities on site include a 100 seat theatre, canteen and gym. There are other classes going on both day and evening as part of the Adult Education programme which students can choose to sign up for.

Auditions
Applicants are asked to prepare two pieces, one by Shakespeare and one from a modern play. After performing their pieces there is an interview with the director of the school, and they may also be asked to sight read. Several hundred apply for 24 places.

1 Year Acting Course
The course runs for one year and aims to provide a comprehensive training in acting. Classes cover the essential three disciplines of acting, voice and movement studied in modules of study, rehearsal and performance of text, voice, radio, dance and exercise, improvisation and devising. The training is classically based with a lot of work on Shakespeare, although most theatre styles are covered including musical theatre. There are many one-to-one tutorials as well as group work. From the day the course starts students are involved in rehearsals for a public performance. There are seven workshop productions and three ma-

jor productions each year, all performed in the theatre. Since I last visited there is more emphasis on the preparation for work with seminars and classes. For example, each week students present audition speeches, either new or well rehearsed, which are marked by their fellow students as well as the tutor. This seems an interesting way to build up a good selection of audition speeches.

The course simply describes itself as an acting course, with no further specification. Some students use it as a foundation course before applying to university or a further drama school course elsewhere. For others it is seen as a post graduate course. Over the years it has become, in terms of the students, more of a post graduate/mature student course. (Presumably the potential foundation level applicants are taking free BTEC Performing Arts courses). The students I saw were in their mid twenties and upwards. They felt that they were getting an excellent training; one student was a mainstream drama school drop out. The school hardly advertises at all so the majority of the students had heard about it from former students, which has to be a good sign. It is also incredibly good value for money; one evening course charges twice the amount for half the hours. Given that cost and time are major parts of the equation for most people when it comes to choosing a course, personally speaking I'd rather do this course full time for a year than struggle with a job and do the acting in the evenings and the weekends over two years.

Rose Bruford College

Lamorbey Park, Sidcup, Kent DA15 9DF
Tel: 0181 300 3024 Fax: 0181 308 0542
email: admiss@bruford.ac.uk

Member of the Conterence of Drama Schools

Principal: Robert Ely, Head of Acting: Sue Colgrave (see post script)

* **3 Year BA (Hons) Acting**
  3 Year BA (Hons) Actor Musician
  3 Year BA (Hons) Directing
* **3 Year BA (Hons) Stage Management**

Fees:
Degree courses: Mandatory grants, £7,000 per annum for overseas/others
Audition fee: £15 Some bursaries are available

The college is split between two sites, Lamorbey Park and Greenwich campuses. Lamorbey Park is in Sidcup, an area to the south of London. Rail links to central London are quite good and accommodation is relatively cheap and easy to find. The college is based a beautiful old building surrounded by parkland and over looking a lake, although the students work in a range of pre-fab and modern buildings. Facilities include a newly constructed 320 seat theatre-in-the-round, a studio theatre, good library, canteen, rehearsal rooms and workshops. The Greenwich campus (which I would consider to be in Deptford rather than the more salubrious and up-market Greenwich) is a large and rather depressing building with many rehearsal studios, canteen, offices and performance studio. The acting courses are based here, while wardrobe and the technical students are based in Lamorbey Park, but both sites are used. They aim to be based entirely at Lamorbey Park in the future.

The College has been established since 1950 and originally offered teacher training as well as actor training - at one time all drama teachers seemed to have graduated from Rose Bruford. It pioneered teaching community theatre and Theatre in Education (TIE), and was the first vocational degree in acting in the UK.

Auditions
About 1000 to 1200 applicants for 60-75 places including about 15 actor musicians. The audition consists of several rounds, all held on the same day. Two speeches are required, one classical and one contemporary selected from a guideline sheet. 20-25 applicants perform their pieces to a panel of three. Usually at least half are go through to the next round with voice and movement tutors.

They are required to sing a song. A second selection is then made, and about two-thirds will go on to an interview. Those applying for the actor musician course are usually seen in two big groups "we start with 50 bodies and end up with, say, 10". Minimum age is 18, no maximum. Most are in the 19-21 range with quite a few older students in their 30s and 40s.

3 Year BA (Hons) Acting

"It's important to note that it is a vocational training that happens to offer a degree, and the degree is implicit in the work. It is not degree worthy because there is an element of written work, because the consciousness of the development of the actor is part of the course. We go through the basic skills of training the voice, the body, the intellect and the acting craft through traditional text and through self-generated work. The intended outcome is that students will develop and find their own nameable methodology, not just one they happen to do, but that they can actually name it."

The first year is a foundation year, introducing the skills and methods that are required for the rest of the course and the profession. Acting, voice and singing, movement and study are developed through the year, with classes such as creating a character, improvisation, and acting methodology. At the end of each term there are performances or presentations for the staff only. The second year continues to develop skills while the presentations centre upon particular theatre genres such as clowning and commedia, naturalistic theatre, ensemble playing and so on. During the second year career classes start, continuing until the show case production at the end of the course. The third year is one of public performances. Television and radio work are introduced in concentrated blocks of time "so that nothing else gets in the way of it".

Written work is a requirement. Students write an essay each term, and a final written dissertation which is an independent self-chosen study of about 6,000 words. "We believe that anybody in vocational training needs to be able to express themselves, not just with their body but also with their brain. They have to be conscious of what they are doing"

3 Year BA (Hons) Actor Musician

The actor musician course is designed for the actor with musical skills who wishes to work as a member of companies that make extensive use of music. Much of the training and the ethos of the course is the same as the acting course, but with additional work on the musical aspects. Skill classes include instrumental and vocal techniques, composition, arrangement, devising and musical direction skills. In the second year there is a placement as Musical Director. In the third year students work on productions, some of which use music, such as a musical or play with music, while others are devised. These are produced in a variety of venues.

3 Year BA (Hons) Directing
The directing course is made up of three elements: classes and projects taken alongside actors, designers and technical artists, learning about and experiencing their skills, methods and ways of working; classes and projects especially designed for the director, offering a range of interpretative and technical skills; and exercises and projects in direction, graduated from observation, through assistant directorship to independent production projects.

3 Year BA (Hons) Stage Management
The course aims to produce the best stage managers, by developing every individual student to the point where they cope with innovation in text, in styles of performance and in production methods. The first year is a foundation in stage management and technical skills; an analysis of design and interpretation skills; and classes and projects providing essential information exploring aspects of professional theatre. In the second year classes continue, but workshops and projects are increasingly complex. The third year is professional and both prepares students for vocational practice and builds up their professional portfolio. Work consists of major projects, a placement and a specialist technical option.

Rose Bruford has a long established course which has more than doubled in size in terms of intake in the last eight years. This undoubtedly has an effect on the quality of the training that the students experience. One commented that he thought the actor musicians were luckier because they got the same course as the actors plus all the musical side. He also felt that the actor musicians got more attention. There were other grumbles: going between the two sites was a pain and took up time in the day that could be better used on something else. "We're doing our final productions and we have to go to down to wardrobe for fittings [at Lamorbey Park] and it takes ages. You could just do without it." It was complicated by the fact that many of them had done their first year based in Sidcup and therefore had their accommodation there, so they might do the journey several times in a day. However, they preferred being at the London site rather than at Sidcup. Other niggles were that there were too many on the course and that you were left to your own devices too much.

Post script: I interviewed Sue Colgrave, the head of acting. During the summer of 1998 she and another member of staff were suspended by the principal for what seemed fairly minor disciplinary offences. Staff and students wrote letters of protest and support. At the time of writing the situation is unresolved.

Royal Academy of Dramatic Art

18-22 Chenies Street, London WC1E 7EX
Tel: 0171 636 7076 Fax: 0171 323 3865
E-mail: enquiries@rada.ac.uk Website: http://www.rada.ac.uk

Member of the Conference of Drama Schools

Principal: Nicholas Barter

* **3 Year Acting Course**
* **2 Year Technical Theatre and Stage Management Course**
  1 year (4 term) Specialist Technical Courses in:
  Scenic Art. Scenic Construction. Stage Electrics. Wardrobe.
  Property Making

Fees:
Acting and Stage Management Courses: £8595 per annum
1 Year Specialist Courses: £11,460 each
Scholarships: Two or three each year. The amounts are not fixed but may be as much as the total fees - no award towards maintenance. The school actively helps applicants who are awarded places to fund raise and claims "up to now we have not actually lost a student who has achieved a place".
Hours: 45+ hours a week rising to 65 hours (including performances).
36 weeks per year
Audition fee: £30, additional $75 for New York Auditions. Preliminary Auditions in: Belfast, London, Manchester, Newcastle, Nottingham and New York. Recall auditions mainly take place at RADA, but may be later in the day for the regional auditions. New York preliminary auditions are always followed by recalls on the same day. All workshops take place at RADA.

RADA is situated in Central London. It is within walking distance of a wide range of amenities including shops and restaurants, the University of London, French's Theatre Bookshop, the British Museum, Channel 4 Head office, Oxford Street and Covent Garden to name but a few attractions. The school was founded in 1904 and moved to Gower Street in the following year. The Gower Street site was a warren of rehearsal rooms, and two theatres. In 1990 the Academy acquired buildings in Chenies Street, just across the road from the Gower Street building. By chance part of this building had been used by a television company and came complete with special floors in many of the studio spaces. In 1996 RADA received a lottery grant of £4,000,000 for the refurbishment of the Gower Street site. At the moment, the actors are based in the refurbished Chenies

Street which has numerous large and airy studios and a wonderful library. A new building was bought in Kennington Park which currently houses the technical and stage management courses, as well as other rehearsal rooms and studios. When work is completed in the year 2000, the Gower Street site will house the refurbished George Bernard Shaw Theatre, plus a new 'State of the Art' 204 seat theatre and other studio spaces. The plans certainly look wonderful, and should make RADA the best equipped drama school in the country. Students can live locally in student accommodation (one hostel is next door) arranged through RADA; priority is given to first and final year students. There is also a subsidised student canteen serving a good range of hot and cold food; some students eat all their meals there.

Auditions
About 1500 apply for 32 places. For the preliminary audition applicants must prepare two pieces of their own choosing, neither to exceed three minutes. One of the pieces must by Shakespeare or other Elizabethan or Jacobean playwright. The other can be by any other playwright and must be in clear contrast to the first piece. Only one piece can be a direct address to the audience, such as a speech by chorus or narrator. The pieces are shown to a panel consisting of two professional actors or directors. About 200-250 are recalled. The recall consists of the pieces again, plus an unaccompanied song, some direction of the pieces and a longer interview. The panel this time consists of about six people, including the principal and vice-principal. About 100-120 are asked to come to do a workshop at RADA. The workshops are all-day auditions from 9.00am - 6.00pm, in groups of 14-16. Applicants take classes in movement, voice, improvisation, scene study with a professional actor and one and a half hours in small groups working on audition speeches. At the end of the day they all come together and everybody watches one of the speeches that the candidate has worked on. Sometimes people are asked in for another recall. This is more likely to happen when the applicant did a workshop in November or December, and they want to remind themselves when they start making offers in June. Offers are occasionally made from March onwards, but most are made in the summer to those on the waiting list. There are no fixed age limits but it would be unusual for a student to be accepted under 18 or over 30. Most students are in their early 20s. About one third are graduates. A handful are overseas students but "we train British actors".

3 Year Acting Course
The first year is entirely classwork based laying the foundations in voice, movement (Laban based), dialect, phonetics and speech. At the start of the course each student is assigned their own voice teacher and singing teacher who stays

with them throughout the course. Students have individual lessons in singing and Alexander technique. The first term consists of acting exercises, which are applied to realist 19th century texts in the second term. The third term applies Stanislavski's methods to Shakespeare. All exercises are shown in-house to staff only. Also at the end of the first year is a period dance demonstration in costume.

In the second year outside directors are introduced for scene study blocks. During the year other skills and techniques are taught such as radio, microphone technique, technical skills, playwriting. Television is taught on a weekly basis in term five, building up a show tape of scenes for each student. When the television facilities are fully developed by 2000 "we will have very beautiful television studios. I think we will have to increase our media training because more and more work is going to be in television at the early stages of their careers." At the end of the year there is a public performance, which might be a devised or workshop piece.

The third year is production based, with classes one morning and one afternoon a week. Each actor will do four productions over the Autumn and Spring terms. In the summer term is the 'Tree Evening', named after the founder, which is a presentation for agents, casting directors etc. held at RADA on four evenings. There is one more final production. The last four weeks of term are spent in voluntary workshops because "so many of them are going off and meeting agents, auditioning and interviewing that it is impossible to hold together a proper curriculum."

2 Year Technical Theatre and Stage Management Diploma Course

The purpose of the course is to train students for careers in theatre and related fields, such as television, video, conference and exhibition work. The first year is spent in classes and workshops and covers the disciplines of lighting, sound, design and scenic art, scenic construction, property making, wardrobe, stagecraft and stage management, plus administrative skills. It is a hands-on course, working in every production department. In the second year the students work on the Academy's seventeen or so productions throughout the year alongside professional directors and designers in a wide range of responsibility. Also during the second year each student spends between four and six weeks on an attachment to a professional theatre or organisation relevant to the career they wish to pursue.

Specialist Diplomas

Up to three students each year are accepted for each of the Specialist Technical Diploma courses in Scenic Art, Scenic Construction, Stage Electrics, Wardrobe and Property Making. All courses include extensive practical experience.

If you have only heard of one drama school then the chances are that it is RADA. For this reason alone it is special as it is able to pick the absolute cream of students for the course, which in turn inevitably leads to the highest of standards. It is the only school which offers continuity of one to one teaching throughout the course in voice and singing. It is the only school that really can draw agents in their droves to the final year shows. When the building work is done it will be the best equipped drama school in the country (if not in the world). One student told me that her father (a drama teacher) had burst into tears of joy when she was offered a place. So you might expect the students to be a bit arrogant and condescending. Not a bit of it; you couldn't meet a nicer bunch of people. Those I met were quiet, considered and, above all, mature. (It must be very irritating when auditioning to be told that the school thinks you need to mature a little - we all feel quite mature enough. But the RADA students I met really did seem mature, even the ones who had come straight from school and after three years were still only just 21.) They said that the weaknesses were not enough career advice early enough because many were made offers by agents and directors at the start of the third year. I was also interested that they were the only students who mentioned that they felt they had been "knocked down in the first year then built up in the second and third years". Everyone agreed that they had been very depressed at the end of the first year "but we're very happy now". Strengths were good tutors, excellent singing and voice work, lots of classical theatre (two students said that their life long ambition was to work for the RSC) and "snob value". If you are serious about a career as an actor, particularly a theatre actor, then RADA has to remain first choice.

Royal Scottish Academy of Music and Drama

100 Renfrew Street, Glasgow G2 3DB
Tel: 0141 332 4101 Fax: 0141 332 8901
email: registry@rsamd.ac.uk   Web site: http://www.rsamd.ac.uk

Member of the Conference of Drama Schools

Principal: Philip Ledger, Director of the School of Drama: Vladimir Mirodan

*   **3 Year BA Acting**
*   **3 Year BA Stage Management Studies**
     1 Year MDra Acting
     1 Year MDra Directing
BA Contemporary Theatre p164

Fees:
3 Year courses: Mandatory awards, £8520 per annum for overseas/other
1 Year MDra Acting: £3900, £9510 overseas/other
1 Year MDra Directing: £9510
Audition fee: £35 for one course, £50 for two courses. Auditions in: Glasgow, London, Manchester and occasionally Belfast. Auditions overseas: Norway, Seattle, New York, Boston, Toronto, Montreal, Chicago.

Glasgow is on the East coast of Scotland about an hour by train or road from the smaller, more refined Edinburgh and five hours from London on the train. It is built on a grid system which makes it easy to find your way around the city centre and once out of the suburbs is surrounded by spectacular scenery. From being a by-word for inner city decay the city has regenerated itself to become a vibrant and lively city and is one of the most exciting cities to live in in the UK. Glasgow was the European City of Culture for 1990 and European City of Architecture and Design for 1999. The Theatre Royal is across the road from the school, Scottish Television is a few doors down, and BBC Scotland, eleven other theatres (including the internationally known Citizens Theatre), Glasgow Film Theatre, Royal Scottish National Orchestra and various art galleries are all nearby. Accomodation is not difficult to find, and the Academy has a number of flats reserved in managed accomodation five minutes away. Priority is given to first year students whose homes are a long distance from Glasgow.
RSAMD is said to be the best equipped drama school in Europe (although it will have competition from RADA when their work is finished) and the facilities are amazing, with a 350 seat theatre, a 100 seat studio theatre, concert hall television studio, sound broadcast studio and numerous large rehearsal and movement

rooms, often with their own video equipment for instant playback of class work. (None of the students I spoke to could remember actually using them in class, and in the class I sat in on, the equipment was shoved into a corner behind some broken furniture). As with Guildhall and the Welsh College of Music and Drama, the drama department is a small percentage of the school as a whole but one hardly notices the music and singing departments at all.

Auditions
600 applicants for 20 places. The audition takes a whole day in three phases. 60 applicants start by performing two speeches of their choice, one modern and one Shakespeare, to a panel made up of one member of the teaching staff and one outside professional actor. About half are asked to stay onto the second phase. They are seen for about 20 minutes by a panel of five or six, including the heads of department, the principal and at least one outside professional. During this time they perform one of the speeches, choose a short piece to sight read, are given some simple voice and ear exercises to test rhythm, pitch, etc. and have an interview. On average five or six will be asked to stay for the final phase. During the next two hours or so they will take part in a group workshop, including acting exercises and improvisation, learn a simple song and perform it both solo and with the group. Finally there is usually a group interview (which is seen as a chance for the students to ask questions) although they may have further individual interviews instead. Of these applicants, normally one will be offered a firm place, two or three will be put in the 'pool' and the rest will be rejected. The pool is a waiting list to compare applicants from one audition day to the next. The minimum age is 18; there is no maximum - approximately a quarter are over 21 and a 54 year old has graduated recently. However their 'ideal' age is 20-21. They particularly like graduates from university courses (not necessarily drama).

3 Year BA Acting
"This is a solidly Stanislavski based course." There are no essays throughout the course, although there are occasional written tests on technical subjects. The first year is described as being the Year of the Actor. Students concentrate on Stanislavski exercises and scene study. Running in parallel with this is "a famously strong" voice department. There may be as many as ten different voice and speech strands per year, including dialects, singing, verse work and radio. They are proud of their radio work, which is taught in part by a producer from BBC Scotland, and have won a Carleton Hobbs prize four out of the last five years. Movement is based on Lecoq and Alexander technique. Dance includes period and tap, and students also study fencing. As well as technical classes there is a critical studies course. This is a programme of theatre going with reviewing, historical research, discussion of ideas following "it widens the horizons".

The second year is the Year of the Play. Students start with a project on Brecht "which challenges the whole Stanislavski approach, which throws them!" The next acting projects cover a classical verse play or restoration play and contemporary material. The end of year project is a Shakespeare play which usually tours abroad, often in France or Holland. This tends to be performed in non-conventional spaces, such as outdoors. Technical classes continue and, from the second year onwards, students with serious singing potential have the opportunity to train with teachers from the opera school. The third year is the Year of the Audience. "We produce more than the National Theatre." All performances are in the school's main theatres and are open to the general public. 64,000 people come into the Academy each year to watch productions, including plays, recitals and concerts. Critics are invited in from The Scotsman and other newspapers so that the students start to be professionally reviewed. The school claims that every professional in Scotland comes at least once to a production. "We have one or two little tricks up our sleeves...for example, we have a number of prizes to award each year, and we ask casting directors, television producers and directors to be the jury." At least one production is taken to the Edinburgh Festival each year. The Showcase production for agents, casting directors, and directors takes place at the beginning of February "to give the chance to be seen in four more productions". It is produced in Glasgow, Manchester and London.

Preparation for entry to the profession starts in the second year with lectures and help with speeches. A top casting director acts as a consultant and "contributes massively to their professional preparation." Of the 21 graduating the year I visited, 17 had already got agents and one "had nineteen agents after him, it was extraordinary. There's a great vogue for Scottish actors, every one is looking for the next Euan MacGregor, the next Robert Carlyle, we're riding on the crest of the wave."

The school has always had regular exchanges with international theatre schools and this has continued. There are now formal agreements with three major conservatoires in France for individual students to visit for period of six weeks to three months. They re also developing the same agreements with conservatoires in New York, Warsaw and Bucharest. The outreach programme sends groups of students on tour to a variety of theatre schools and drama festivals including Lyons, Agen, Amsterdam, California. "British training has the best training, by far the best theatre - and I say this as a foreigner - but none the less there are other ways of working. We are training theatre people, they should be able to draw on different traditions. Stagnation is challenged by this."

MDra (Acting)

The course "is designed for people who already know enough about their own strengths or weaknesses. They must have significant previous experience or training in drama and want to do high level acting work which is problem solving based. It is not a course designed primarily to enable graduates from university enter the acting profession." There is a maximum of 12 places on the course, of whom 7-8 are full time and the remainder studying part time. Part time students take blocks of work as and when they can over a five year period. "I'm very proud of this course. It is very closely run with the profession, and was developed with in-put from every single artistic director in Scotland, Equity...". There are three main blocks covering television and radio, theatre and career management. Within the blocks are 40 weeks worth of units, so students select 30 weeks from the various options. These include two five week blocks of television, a six week radio block, a six week block rehearsing and then taking a production to the Edinburgh Festival, a three week career management block and so on. One block develops a one man show.

MDra Directing

"I believe directors should be properly trained. We're not going down the road of putting ten people in a room and talking about directing. It is all productions with professional actors - I can not tell you how expensive it is being for us. There is lots of one to one, lots of placements." There are places for a maximum of three directors. The students work very little with the acting students except as assistant director on a few shows and on scenes with second year students. Prior to coming here Vladimir Mirodan set up the directors courses at Rose Bruford and Middlesex University.

3 Year BA Stage Management Studies

This is a practical course offering study and practice over the full range of Stage Management duties in a variety of situations. All students study a range of technical skills in the areas of workshop, paintshop, lighting, sound, props, wardrobe, design and general stagecraft. In addition students may choose to specialise in various aspects of design: set, lighting and sound. There is the opportunity for secondment to a professional theatre company in order to develop further specialist technical or design skills.

RSAMD has a great deal going for it in terms of facilities, teaching staff, location and professional opportunities. I left the interview with the new director, Vladimir Mirodan, fired with enthusiasm, he is so full of ideas for the courses. I was therefore surprised that the students I spoke to were a rather lack lustre bunch, who had no particular comments about the course, good, bad or indifferent. Scottish actors who want grants have to apply for and be turned down by RSAMD and Queen Margarets before auditioning elsewhere. An actor who had a place on both courses would probably choose RSAMD pm the grounds of prestige alone. Other reasons could be the international outlook, a charismatic and dynamic principal, and a method approach to actor training.

The School of the Science of Acting

67-83 Seven Sisters Road, London N7 6BU
Tel: 0171 272 0027 Fax: 0171 272 0026

Principal: Sam Kogan

2 Year Acting Course
1 Year Acting Course
2 Year Evening Acting Course
3 Year Directing Course
2 Year Evening, 3rd Year Full Time Directing Course
Short courses

Fees:
2 Year and 1 Year Acting Course: £7,580 per annum
2 Year Evening Acting Course: £3,200 per annum
3 Year Directing Course: £7580 per annum
2 year Evening 3rd year Daytime Directing Course: Years 1&2, £3860 per annum, Year 3, £7580 per annum. Intensive evening course:£1080 . 2 Week Workshop course: £425. 2 Week Summer school: £295. 10 Week Directing course £995. Science of Acting Seminars: Free
44 weeks per year. 45 hours per week for day time courses, 18 hours for the evening course.
Audition fees: Acting Courses: £20, Directing Courses: £25
50% discount on all audition fees if you attend a Science of Acting Seminar.

Holloway is a run down area of London, just to the north of the centre. As an area where many immigrants have settled, the shops and restaurants reflect the cosmopolitan residents. Almost every culture seems represented from the Ethiopian restaurant to the Bagel shop, to the more usual Indian and Chinese restaurants. The School of the Science of Acting is based on the top floor of a large building just off the main road. The rooms are large, light and airy. One has been fitted out as a small studio theatre where they mount all their productions. The school was founded seven years ago by Sam Kogan. He trained in Russia, at the Moscow Institute of Theatre Arts (now the Russian Academy of Theatre Arts) and came to the west in 1973. He started to teach acting here but found that the English versions of Stanislavski's work had been badly translated and edited. Many of the teachers who used Stanislavski's methods were, apparently, basing their knowledge on a shortened and badly translated small section of his work. He started to develop his own ideas, which have become 'the science of acting' classes.

Auditions

Applicants are asked to prepare a speech from Shakespeare, a fable, a piece of modern poetry or prose and a song or dance, with no piece to last longer than two minutes. They are seen on a one to one basis by the principal. "In auditions we look at the problems that students have and decided what we can do to help them and how long it will take. Sometimes with some of them you can see that it is going to take much longer." At the moment between 6-10 people are taken on each year, with places for 12-5 available.

All courses

The school is very small, with about 20 full time students in total, so many of the years do classes together. Also, a large proportion come as acting students, then decide to become directors as well so stay for a further year or two. Every day starts with Hatha yoga and finishes with a mediation session. In between comes science of acting classes, voice, singing, dance (jazz, tap, ballroom, classical and historical), stage combat, mime, improvisation, the history of art, music and theatre, microphone and TV technique, sight reading, theatre-in-education, acrobatics, circus skills and commedia dell'arte. The last three subjects mean that "when actors leave here they're much better with props than other actors. You'll see unicycles, stilts lying around, it's another way of overcoming fear". All the acting classes are done in front of the camera. "They have to watch themselves so many times a week which accelerates the learning process. They can review their acting piece and check it against the comments the tutor gave. In this way, they can see if the comments are relevant."

The Science of Acting itself is a psychological approach to acting, derived from Stanislavski. It claims to be "the only school which tells you what was right and what was wrong and why you did not act as well as you could. We also tell you how to correct your mistakes. To be a good actor who have to have a skill. Not the skill to pretend, but the skill to think whatever you want. If you can do this then you have total freedom."

There is very little on getting work once you have left school. Agents, directors and casting directors are asked to shows but few come (indeed, few could physically come; when I saw the studio theatre there were only 12 seats for the audience). Sam Kogan says "If you can act well, then you can look after yourself. I look at my past students and I see that those who were dedicated do well. Of course we invite people to shows, but unless you can act, nothing matters. Other drama schools organises a showcase, spend five or ten thousand pounds and then can say 'we wash our hands of you'. Our students leave here, they know that they can act, and that's more that any other student from any other school can say. That's why we get so many students who have already studied at other schools. They come because they know they can't act."

Initially I was very impressed with the school. Sam Kogan explained the Science of Acting to me, and I found myself nodding in agreement with everything he said. Then the students were as enthusiastic and full of energy as Sam Kogan himself, and thought the courses were great. And so many of the students had been to other drama schools - RADA, Central, ALRA for example - and felt that here they were being really taught how to act. And it's certainly true that in many schools the teaching of acting (rather than skills and techniques) is surprisingly rare. The principal of another school, for example, told me "We don't actually teach acting skills, we allow students to explore their own creativity whilst working on texts". So I left feeling very positive about the Science of Acting.

Now I am less sure. The explanation of the Science of Acting which had seemed so logical at the time seemed incomprehensible when played back on the tape. Yes, of course being a better actor is desirable, and I am sure that working through a method such as the Science of Acting will make one more adept. But acting is about more than that, it is also about getting work as an actor, about being 'out there'. It can be easy to think that there is some magic that will turn you into a good actor, that there is some secret that everybody else knows. I became worried that, for all their enthusiasm, the students on the course were looking for that secret. To have done one three year course, and then to come and do another two or three years (and many stay for four) seemed indicative of a particular type of actor. I'd love to come here, because I enjoy acting classes and these ones sound good, but there has to be a point when one stops going to class and becomes a professional. On the other hand of course, it may just be true that Sam Kogan has found the secret of acting.

If you are intrigued there are free seminars throughout the year on 'The Science of Acting'. Attendance gives you a 50% discount on the cost of auditions. There are also other short courses, some held during the evenings.

Webber Douglas Academy of Dramatic Art

Chanticleer Theatre, 30 Clareville Street, London SW7 5AP
Tel: 0171 370 4154 Fax: 0171 373 5639

Member of the Conference of Drama Schools

Principal: Raphael Jago

*   **3 Year (8 Terms) Acting Diploma**
*   **2 Year Acting Diploma**
*   **1 Year Post Graduate Diploma**

Fees:
3 Year and 2 Year Courses: £8097 per annum, 1 Year Course: £8478
Two scholarships available for existing students on the 3 and 2 Year courses.
Audition fees and locations: London £25, Los Angeles £30, New York $65

South Kensington is just to the west of Knightsbridge (with the famous Harrods department store and other smart shops) and the school is in walking distance of three of the major museums in London and the trendy Brompton Road and Fulham Road shopping areas. Only the wealthiest of students will be able to afford to live near the school, but it is easily accessible by tube and bus from other areas of London. The school is situated in a prime bit of real estate. It is in the middle of a normal terrace of houses and is a higgledy piggledy warren of rehearsal rooms and studios, and the Chanticleer Theatre. They use additional rehearsal rooms nearby. They have been looking for new premises for some years now, but a move to more space means a move out of a very good location. "It's very central, it's very safe, it's right on top of the West End, and it has access to a large pool of people - and accessibility is everything to agents and directors, they don't like having their time wasted and they don't like going over the river".
Webber Douglas was founded in 1926, originally as a school of singing. One of the teachers was brought in to develop the acting potential of the singers and by the end of the Second World War the training of actors had become the main focus. The current principal was appointed in 1966.
The school looked at the degree option and decided it was not for them. "We decided we'd prefer to stay with the economic problems and not take on the academic problems and the demands they make in terms of superstructure."

Auditions
900 applicants in total. 11 places on 1 year course, average age early to mid 20s. 16 places on 2 year course, average age early to mid 20s, 30 places on 3 year

course (24 in autumn, 6 in summer) average age 18-21. They aim for a 50:50 male/female ratio "but it depends on who auditions". Applicants are required to prepare two contrasting speeches, one Shakespeare and one modern (after the mid 19th century), neither to exceed three minutes. They recommend that one should be comedy, and some movement should be included in at least one speech. The preliminary audition consists of speeches and an interview. About 10% are recalled. At the recall, applicants do the speeches again, plus a song "to find out how they pitch their voices and it does sometimes tell you a fair bit about their personalities". They are then interviewed by a panel of four, usually the principal and three outsiders who work in the profession, often directors.

The 3,2 and 1 Year Acting Diplomas

"As a school we don't have any particular philosophy of acting, although certain members of the staff do. Hopefully working with a whole string of directors with very different backgrounds they get used to responding to different people, different attitudes, different value systems. One of the keys is flexibility as they may move from Whitehall farce to Shakespeare to a musical to a gritty modern comedy." There is a tremendous emphasis on skills in the first year, concentrating on voice, dance, singing and movement. Singing and voice have always been central to the school and individual classes are given in these subjects to allow the actors to develop at their own rate, and in the areas of most benefit to them. In the second year they add television, tap, radio, period dance and other specialist skills plus more rehearsals. "The classical is one of our strengths and always has been, even though the market for classical actors is quite small. Its great virtue is that you can play a dual career, whereas if you have never had the experience of doing the classics it can be a bit daunting." There are 'threads' throughout the course, so the classical theatre thread starts in the first year and continues to the end of the second year, and a musical theatre thread starts in the second and ends in a musical production in the third year. Everyone starts the threads, but not everyone stays with them through to the end "it's horses for courses really".

Television is done in a series of workshops in the second year and looks at how the market works as well as how to act in front of the camera. "It's as much mental perception as it is getting used to standing on your mark and not doing things in the right order." The school does a lot of work on 'marketing' the students, working on speeches, interviews, auditions, photographs and so on. The final year (two terms) is spent in public productions and an agent showcase, all shown at the Chanticleer Theatre. There are also 'extra' productions, such as a Shakespeare at Cliveden for the National Trust, which is cast across the courses as "not everyone can cope vocally in the open air with a difficult text".

The two year course does the same course as three year course, but over fewer terms. The first year is virtually the same, the middle three terms are cut to two "they don't need as much space to develop" and there is one less term of productions.

The one year course is different, in that it is seen as "an 'add-on' course, as in 'there's something wrong with the way I approach text, I'll add it on', or 'there's something wrong with my voice, I'll add it on'. You can not unwind and then rewind up in one year, but you can in two years."

Webber Douglas is a small school which has pragmatically decided to concentrate on one thing - actors. It has not diversified into other courses, nor has it taken the degree route. It does what it knows well and efficiently. Students appeared to be very 'commercial' types, presumably because it looks at employability and uses outside professionals at audition. They struck me as being a very confident group of people, who said they had enjoyed the course. I saw a large group together and interestingly, if one said one thing it was immediately contradicted by another. I thought this was in part to do with a competitive spirit rather than radically different experiences. They thought the support given by the school in looking for work was exceptional. "I know they don't do anything like as much at other drama schools" was a universally acceptable comment.

Mr Jago has been principal for over 30 years, and has made Webber a force to be reckoned with as well as promoting drama schools as a whole through the Conference of Drama Schools. Webber remains a good, established, small drama school, used to playing to its strengths.

The Welsh College of Music and Drama

Castle Grounds, Cathays Park, Cardiff, Wales CF1 3ER
Tel: 01222 371440 Fax: 01222 237639
email: Drama.admission@wcmd.ac.uk

Member of the Conference of Drama Schools

Principal: Edmond Fivet, Head of Acting: David Bond

*   **3 Year BA (Hons) Theatre Studies: Acting**
*   **3 Year BA (Hons) Theatre Studies: Stage Management**
*   **1 Year Advanced Diploma: Acting**
*   **1 Year Advanced Diploma: Stage Management**

Fees:
3 Year Courses: Mandatory Grants, £6,800 per annum overseas/other
1 Year Courses: £3200
35 weeks per year
Audition fee: £25

Cardiff is the capital city of Wales and is about two hours due east from London by train or car. The town is on the coast surrounded by beautiful countryside and mountains. Over the last ten years Cardiff has been a focus of urban regeneration money and has been extensively redeveloped. Theatre, television, film and television companies based in Cardiff include Welsh National Opera, BBC Wales, HTV Wales, S4C (Channel 4 for Wales), the Sherman repertory theatre, the Welsh National Film Theatre and several touring theatre companies. Bristol, another regional centre of employment for actors, is just the other side of the Severn bridge. The cost of living is low, the quality of life high. As a result many actors choose to make Cardiff their base, especially if they are Welsh speakers. The school is a few minutes walk from the city centre in an area that also houses the town hall and other civic offices (including the traffic wardens base, so watch out if you come by car as there is no obvious place to buy a parking ticket - the nearest is the central library - and hundreds of wardens going backwards and forwards). As you would imagine facilities are good, and have been recently refurbished. They include two theatres, a recital hall, fully equipped radio studio, library and huge restaurant, coffee shop and bar. Rehearsal rooms and studios are large, plentiful and well lit. The only thing lacking are television studios (they use a local FE college).

Auditions

Applicants are seen in groups of 30-35 and are asked to prepare two contrasting speeches, one from an Elizabethan or Jacobean play, the other from a modern or contemporary play. Neither speech should be longer than two minutes. The audition starts with a 45 minute physical warm-up then a 45 minute vocal warm-up. Then the speeches are performed to a panel consisting of the acting tutors. Usually between five and ten applicants are asked to stay for the afternoon session. This includes sessions in singing, improvisation and direction on the two speeches. Applicants may also be asked to sight read and to write a short piece on an aspect of theatre that appeals to them. About 700 people apply for 16 places on the 3 year course, 12 on the one year course. The minimum age is 18, but they prefer people in their mid 20s. The average age is early 20s. There is about a 40:60 male/female ratio. Usually about 20% are Welsh. Foreign students are welcomed "for the mix".

3 Year BA (Hons) Theatre Studies: Acting

"We work to produce an actor who uses his/her total resources as a human being in the creation and communication of a role. Training is concerned with the wholeness and uniqueness of the individual rather than simply the function which he/she is to fulfil." The course has five components: acting projects, voice, movement, theatre studies and acting studies. Practical and academic work are integrated. Students are assessed in performance, research projects, individual presentations and course work. There are no formal written examinations but at the end of the first and second years students are assessed on the following: essay, oral, lecture demonstration or creative project (two each year and students can choose the order in which they take these options).

The first year is seen as a year of personal discovery. Class work consists of voice, speech, singing, dance, Alexander technique and stage combat. There are three acting projects which might include building a character, ensemble work, devised piece, naturalism, epic theatre, ritual or experimental theatre. All performances are to tutors and year group only.

The second year builds on the first. Acting projects include restoration, musical theatre, and Shakespeare. Students also start to study radio; the school is proud of having won the BBC Carleton Hobbs radio competition for the last two years running. Television is taken as a four week block during this year using nearby facilities. Projects are viewed by staff and the other students.

The third year concentrates on public performance. Final year productions are usually directed by guest directors. Each year there are usually 14 productions and each actor will perform in at least four full productions at the school's theatres or on tour plus the Showcase production for agents, casting directors and directors. This is performed in Cardiff, London and Manchester "we have a lot of Northern based actors". Four times a year the college takes small scale productions on tour to Hungary as part of a British Council exchange programme. Students whose first or second language is Welsh tour a Welsh language production annually. There are Theatre in Education projects and students take productions to the National Student Drama Festival and the Edinburgh Festival where the school has a regular fringe venue.

Physical skills classes continue in the third year alongside a series of vocational classes which cover the information and skills needed to find employment, such as audition and interview technique, presentation, CVs and agents.

1 Year Advanced Diploma: Acting

The one year course should not be considered to be the three year course rolled into one, although it shares the same philosophy and objectives. The first term covers the same classes in physical skills as the first year of the three year course: voice, speech, singing, dance, Alexander technique and stage combat plus acting studies and theatre studies such as improvisation. These classes continue for the next two terms as students prepare for two main stage productions and their showcase, which they share with the three year students. They also share the same programme of professional classes throughout the year.

3 Year BA (Hons) Theatre Studies: Stage Management

"The course is designed to cover all aspects of stage management and technical theatre training to ensure that students are properly equipped to meet the current demands of an industry which is becoming increasingly diversified and seeking to establish new levels of competence."

In the first two terms students follow a course of basic classes which cover: stage management and production organisation, technical studies and stagecraft. From the second term onwards students are introduce to production work supported by class work and projects. The level of responsibility increases during the second and third years. Each student will have been in charge of a production at least once. Productions take place in either of the schools own theatres, on tour locally and abroad in Hungary or at the Edinburgh Fringe Festival and National Student Drama Festival. They also manage productions for the music department. Students have the opportunity to take short professional work placements during the second and third years.

1 Year Advanced Diploma: Stage Management

This course is for those with some previous experience. Areas of study include: the work of touring and company stage managers, stage lighting, sound for theatre, prop making, stage craft, health and safety in the theatre. Students participate in a wide range of productions mounted by both the drama and music departments.

The drama department at the Welsh College is a small part of the school as a whole, as at Guildhall and RSAMD. It seems self contained within the building, and is not dominated by the music department. The students could have complained about the changes at the top (Michael Gaunt, from Guildford School of Acting, had taken over as head of the drama department only to have the job vanish after less than a year), but there seemed to have been no problems caused by having a different head of the course in each of their years at the school - which must show a good continuity of staff and efficient organisation. For the most part they enjoyed being in Cardiff and felt no hurry to move to London (although one or two could not wait to get away). "There's plenty of work here, and I'd rather be a big fish in a little pond, certainly at first". When I last came Paul Clements had been in charge (now at Mountview) and there was a very caring and supportive atmosphere. I am sure that will not change, but I think Dave Bond could bring in a harder, perhaps more demanding, edge to the acting training. For example, when I spoke to him just as he had taken over he said "you could, if crafty, avoid writing an essay throughout - but I'm going to stop that". He also aimed to change the direction of the course slightly, to make it less university like and more actor centred. "We want to provide the actor with tools in the kitbag and to understand why they are doing it". I think the change will be all to the good.

University Degree Courses

The University of Wales, Aberystwyth

Old College, King Street, Aberystwyth SY23 2AX
Tel: 01970 622021 Fax: 01970 627410
e-mail: undergraduate-admissions@aber.ac.uk Web: http://www.aber.ac.uk

BA (Hons) Drama

"The course has been carefully designed to ensure a balance of academic and practical experience and a steady development of intellectual, performative and technical skills for our students."

Year 1: In the first year you study a number of introductory modules, combining textual analysis and theatre history, as well as all skills of practical work - design, technical aspects and performance.

Year 2: Takes a closer look at the theatrical event, starting with a core of analytical modules - including textual and performing analysis, European drama and Shakespeare. You then study a series of modules which explore theatre design and production, including acting, directing, lighting, sound, set and costume design.

Year 3: The third year begins with an intensive semester of practical work, where analytical and practical skills are brought together and tested creatively through full-scale production work. This experience informs and greatly enhances your approach to the following optional modules, such as theatre in education, American drama, creative writing, contemporary British and Irish drama. As a student of Theatre Studies, you can expect to be assessed through formal essays and written examination, as well as through extended essays, seminar presentation, group project and performance work.

Also available: Drama is available for study with Art, Art History, Education, English, Film and Television Studies, French, Geography, German, Information and Library Studies, Irish, Italian, Pure Mathematics, Spanish, Welsh, Welsh History.

Barnsley College

Old Mill Lane Site, Church Street, Barnsley S70 2AX
Tel: 01226 730191/216216 Fax: 01226 216166
e-mail: l.kirk@barnsley.ac.uk

BA (Hons) Combined Studies (Performing Arts)

"The course incorporates and encourages new and exciting contemporary approaches in the variety of performance and production design elements which it offers. Its focus is practical activity underpinned by a solid understanding of theatre in a historical context, with an emphasis on group work. The main areas cover the development of individual and group performance skills and the study of production practices and performance processes. There are four core units: Performance, Performance Contexts, Production and Technology, together with additional units of movement and vocal skills, offering a balance of practical and theoretical aspects. The course allows a degree of specialism at levels 2 and 3 but there is encouragement for students to develop as multi-skilled practitioners in the industry."

Year 1: Introduces the student to range of theatre practices, building a foundation of practical performance and production skills and understanding.

Year 2: Develops increased responsibility for the application of these skills within various performance contexts, and understanding of the significance of all elements - visual and audible - in the creation of theatre. In Year 2 a range of electives is offered, including circus skills, acting for camera, dance techniques and musical theatre.

Year 3: The final year sees continued development and realisation of these skills in a professional context.

A variety of assessment methods is used, including continuous assessment of performance and production skills, performance assessment, written work and oral examination. Students are required to keep a working log. There are no formal examinations.

Entry: EE/8 points. Places available: 15.

The Queen's University of Belfast

Belfast BT7 1NN
Tel: 01232 245133 Fax: 01232 247895
e-mail: admissions@qub.ac.uk Web: http://www.qub.ac.uk

BA (Minor Honours) Drama

"Drama is one of the oldest and most enduring of all art forms. It is, of course, entertainment, but it is also a unique way for human beings to act out and to understand the great issues that affect us all. The theatre provides a crucial space in society where we can take time to pause, reflect and, through the enriching impact of performance, to renew ourselves.

The course content consists of three principal strands. Students will be introduced to the variety and range of theatre through the study of individual texts. These texts will be taught by staff from across a number of schools in the College of Humanities, including the School of Greek, Roman and Semitic Studies, the School of English and the School of Modern Languages. The course will also enable students to situate these individual plays in a historical and theoretical context through classes on the development of drama across the ages. Finally, students will also have the opportunity of gaining invaluable experience in the various skills of practical theatre-making."

Entry: BCC

Bolton Institute

Deane Road, Bolton BL3 5AB
Tel: 01204 528851 Fax: 01204 399075
e-mail: enquiries@bolton.ac.uk Web: http://www,bolton.ac.uk

BA (Hons) Theatre Studies

"Theatre Studies is an ideal subject for those with an interest in drama. It is not intended as an acting qualification as such (although our students have had successes in the National Student Drama Festival). It is a course which offers insight into theatre through theory and practice and provides the student with important transferable skills including the ability to communicate, to organise, to work as a member of a team and to bring together elements of the arts, technology, marketing and literature. There are links between the study of contemporary drama and opportunities to act and direct. The course involves workshops, practical and theoretical exploration of productions, writing and video techniques in the theatre. Modules include theatre studies (introductory course, theatre in education and production), modern dramatic theory, TV drama, creative writing, Shakespeare, morality and Greek tragedy, literature and film."

Entry: 2 A Levels including Theatre Studies, or evidence of substantial experience of theatre.

Also available: Theatre Studies can also be studied as a joint or minor subject.

University College, Bretton Hall

West Bretton, Wakefield, West Yorkshire WF4 4LG
Tel: 01924 830261   Fax: 01924 830521
e-mail: bretton@mailhost.bretton.ac.uk   Web: http://www.bretton.ac.uk

BA (Hons) Theatre (Acting)
BA (Hons) Theatre (Acting: Devised Performance)
"This programme is for you if you want to act and yet are not content just to have a director tell you what to do. Our focus is upon the thinking, creative actor who wants to develop a 'toolbox' of skills and understanding that will stand them in good stead for a career in the theatre. You can focus your studies on work from texts, or on the processes of devising and improvisation. We will encourage you to question your fundamental assumptions about acting and theatre, while at the same time developing good actor's habits of discipline and study. Almost all of the work is practical, drawing upon your creativity as well as your developing skills. The focus is on the interpretative work of the actor but based on improvisational process leading to fully developed performance. There are opportunities throughout the three years to be involved in a variety of programme and non-programme productions and to work with students from Music, Dance and Design programmes. We look at as broad a range of theatre as is possible and use visiting directors and theatre visits to create contacts for you with the reality of the business. You will need an appetite for very hard work, confidence and humility in equal measure, and a willingness to play your part in a dynamic team activity. We study acting by making theatre in all its diversity. Depending on the chosen pathway, emphasis can be placed either on the actor in the formal theatre setting or on applied performance for client-specific purposes."
Year 1: Approaches to Acting; Solo Storytelling; Narrative Acting; Improvisation v. textual study; Theorists and practitioners; Solo movement piece; Solo character; Field study; The Mike Leigh project; Contemporary theatre project; Applied performance.
Year 2: Skills workshops; Comedy; Mime presentation; Lazzi; Mask theatre projects; Classical theatre platform performance; Linked research essay; Field study; Classical theatre project; Client-based theatre.
Year 3: Small cast plays festival; Dissertation; platform performance; Either: Directing a play, or Playwrighting, or Acting research project; Preparation for the business; Final showcase productions; Theatre for specific contexts.
Entry: BC grades at A Level.

BA (Hons) Theatre Design
The programme has been developed to meet the needs of designers for the theatre and emphasises, therefore, the role of creative design and its realisation for

performance. It embraces the four key areas of concern for the theatre designer: space and staging; light; costume; and sound. These are explored and investigated through practical projects and workshops. The study of core skills develops from a foundation level in Year One, where all disciplines are studied by all students to an equivalent level, through to increasing specialisation in Year Two. It is, however, the practical application of these skills for performance, and as performance, that forms the basis of the programme. This creative practice is challenged and supported throughout by the close study and analysis of the work of key design movements and practitioners."

Entry: BC grades at A Level.

BA (Hons) Theatre Studies

"The programme is for those students who have a fascination for drama and theatre in the widest possible context. The professional model addressed is that normally known in this country as "literacy management" and in continental Europe as "dramaturgy". The course provides students with the opportunity to examine drama from a critical perspective. Drama is explored within an intensive scholastic context and you will develop conceptual, analytical and organisational skills within an academically rigorous framework.

While some modules are taught through the practical medium, the programme is not concerned with actor training. Practical classes have the intention of informing theoretical understanding of the complex inter-relationship between drama, theatre and society. Opportunities will be provided for students to work alongside professional directors, designers and choreographers, preparing productions with performers, designers and managers. Emphasis therefore, will be placed on the application of dramaturgical skills.

We expect a high level of self-motivated, self-disciplined study from you, supported by our advice, encouragement and task setting. We seek to provide an academic and practical environment and models of scholarship, criticism and practice that will enable you to make your own investigations in a spirit of rigour, academic credibility and imagination."

Year 1: Interrogating texts; interrogating contexts; Understanding events; Exploring performance; Exploring dramaturgy; Presentation.

Year 2: Interrogating cultures; Interrogating politics; Exploring roles; The performance; The post-performance; Management.

Year 3: Research project; Dissertation; Dramaturgical project.

Entry: BC grades at A Level.

BA (Hons) Theatre and Arts Education

"This exciting and innovative three years joint honours programme enables students to realise their creative potential in theatre, alongside the study of key aspects of arts education. The theatre component enables students to gain an understanding of and experience in the use of theatrical and dramatic conventions in order to facilitate work in the community, in arts centre, in schools, in museums, and in the application of dramatherapy."

Year 1: Theatre: Drama and community; Developmental drama; Dramatisation of issues; Individual practical projects.

Year 2: Theatre: Solo and ensemble; Representation and fact; Improvisation and devising; Applied drama; Aspects of theatre.

Year 3: Theatre: Shakespeare in performance; Trends in 20th century drama.

BA (Hons) Performance Management

"The programme focuses on the theory and practice of management in the context of the performing arts. You will specialise in Theatre, Music, Dance or Media Arts Management whilst undertaking a broad range of study in areas such as Stage Management, Administration, Front of House, Publicity and Marketing, Production Management and Rehearsal Practice procedures. You will also engage in a wide range of practical drama activities in order to experience issues of performance management from the perspective of the performer. The course is essentially practical and you will have enormous scope to practice the skills of production management in real situations."

Entry: BC grades at A Level

University of Brighton

Mithras House, Lewes Road, Brighton BN2 4AT
Tel: 01273 600900 Fax: 01273 642825
e-mail: admissions@brighton.ac.uk Web: http://www.brighton.ac.uk

BA (Hons) Theatre with Visual Practice

"This course involves the study of theatre and visual art practice supported by critical and historical studies. Students are encouraged to make original work in both disciplines, focusing on the territory of contemporary live art practice and the cross-fertilisation between theatre and visual art."

Year 1: Students are introduced to practical and theoretical vocabulary in performance and visual art, making work individually and in groups. In the summer term students participate in final year degree shows and present visual work.

Year 2: Develops core study towards a professional conception of audience and communication. Students stage public performances and/or exhibitions both in and outside the university. They undertake a professional placement period and complete an elective subject of their choice.

Year 3: Concentrates on preparation of the final presentations and completion of a research essay. Final year students can choose to combine their theatre practice and visual practice into an integrated assessment.
Entry: offers follow interview and portfolio inspection

University of Bristol

Senate House, Tyndall Avenue, Bristol BS8 1TH
Tel: 0117 928 9000 Fax: 0117 925 1424
e-mail: admissions@bristol.ac.uk Web: http://www.bris.ac.uk

BA(Hons) Drama

"The Drama Department approaches theatre, film and television across the three years of the curriculum in a comprehensive and broadly based way, regarding them as much more than branches of literature. Plays and films are studied in the light of their historical background and the cultural conditions of their production and presentation. You will receive a solid grounding in the technical and craft aspects of theatre and video, to enable you to explore creative and aesthetic questions through productions, classes and workshops.
The programme is designed to enable you to broaden your knowledge through a series of units which develop the subject through all three years, such as Approaches to Theatre and Film Studies; and to deepen your understanding of specific areas of interest in related seminar-based and practical project units. All first-year units are mandatory. In the second and third years, you will choose from a range of options, some of which will result in public performance or video production. Number limits on project units mean you may not be able to take your first choice."
Entry: BCC. Interview will include practical workshop.
Also available: BA Joint Honours in Drama and English, French, German, Italian and Spanish.

Brunel University

Uxbridge, Middlesex UB8 3PH
Tel: 01895 274000 Fax: 01895 232806
e-mail: Courses@brunel.ac.uk Web: http://www.brunel.ac.uk

BA (Hons) Drama Studies

"Drama Studies at Brunel has a strong practical emphasis. Your theoretical, critical and historical work will focus primarily on the 20th century, and much of it will deal with current practice. You will be introduced to a diverse range of practices and you will be encouraged to develop an independent approach. You will investigate the entire spectrum of live performance, including mainstream text-based work, music theatre, popular theatre, and experimental performance. The key skill areas covered are: performing, directing/devising, and writing for performance; although this does not exclude other skills (design and lighting design, for example). All curriculum work is underpinned by theory."

Year 1: The core programme focuses on performing, including character-based work (including improvisation and text), and work on ensemble body-based approaches to performance. There is a weekly programme of training invoice and movement.

Year 2: Concentrates on divers text-based work, examining a range of radical approaches to rehearsal and performance in the 20th century. This leads to presentations by specially formed companies, in which you can select acting, devising or directing (or some combination of these) for assessment.

Year 3: In a year-long independent project, you select an aspect of performance for advanced practical and/or critical investigation. A series of options throughout the three levels supplements this core practical work. Currently these include, critical studies in several areas, laboratory theatre, music theatre, community projects, and placement with a range of arts organisations.

Entry: 18 points.

Also available: BA (Joint Hons) Modern Drama Studies is offered with American Studies, English, Film/TV, History, Music. Entry: 16 points.

Trinity College, Carmarthen
Carmarthen SA31 3EP
Tel: 01267 676767 Fax: 01267 676766

BA (Hons) Theatre Studies

"The course unites theoretical and practical work and is designed: to stimulate critical thought about the nature of Drama and the development of the Theatre; to develop an appreciation of a wide range of dramatic literature, especially from the standpoint of production; to encourage, through individual and group experience, the integration of theory and practice in a range of Theatre Arts; to ensure that the students' skills and experience of acting, directing and other aspects of stage performance are developed; to lead to the students' own productions being staged before audiences, either as full-scale college productions or in a studio setting."

Part 1: In the first year there are four modules: An Introduction to Modern Drama and Theatre 1 and 2; Performance (2 modules); Textual Analysis (2 modules).

Part 2: In the second and third years, twelve units are offered, which fall into five groups: Movements in Modern European Theatre; Playhouse and Production; Design and Production; Perspectives on Performance; Perspectives on Directing.

BA (Hon) Theatre Design & Production

"This single honours course combines a wide range of academic, creative, conceptual and practical skills within theatre design and its associated crafts. Students taking the course are encouraged to develop the necessary skills, confidence and qualifications to make a career in theatre as lighting designers, propmakers, costume designers or scenic artists. Knowledge and expertise developed in diverse areas of the course aim to assist students to work, after graduation, as collaborative theatre artists."

Also available: Technical Theatre Arts (Part 1 option only with BA Humanities). This part one course has been designed to provide students with a firm foundation both in the methodology of visual communication and in certain key aspects of technical theatre and stagecraft. It provides a crucial grounding for all Theatre Studies students and its wide range of transferable skills constitutes a sound investment for Humanities students in general.

The Central School of Speech and Drama

Swiss Cottage Site, Embassy Theatre, 64 Eton Avenue, London NW3 3HY
Tel: 0171 722 8183 Fax: 0171 722 4182

BA (Hons) Drama and Education

see also p39 for BA Acting and BA (Hons) Theatre Practice, p168 for BA (Hons) World Theatre with the South Bank University

"This course is intended for students who are interested in the practical applications of drama, particularly in school/college, continuing and community education. Students will be involved practically in creating drama, transposing it to the television medium, discovering how it is used in education, training and the community, and studying the work of writers, directors, designers and actors in this and other societies."

Year 1: Students work on improvisation, and on a media and a playtext project. Drama texts are studied within the context of their relevant society. Students will be introduced to drama in schools/colleges and youth culture, and will study voice, movement and theatre technologies.

Year 2: Begins with a directed production. Students subsequently address certain genres or dramatic historical period and also undertake a collaborative project. Study of the arts in society and its assessment, and a major placement comprise the education strand.

Year 3: A student-initiated final year where individuals pursue their specialist interests. Students undertake a dissertation, a practical project and a further major placement. The final education unit allows the student to formulate a philosophy concerning drama in a school/college, continuing or community environment.
Entry: 2 Arts related A Level passes or equivalent.

University of Central Lancashire
Preston PR1 2HE
Tel: 01772 201201 Fax: 10772 892935
e-mail: enquiries@uclan.ac.uk Web: http://www.ucaln.ac.uk

BA Combined Honours Drama (Joint or Minor)
"The subject focuses on the dramatic text in performance and the course considers such topics as the development of the theatre, the process involved in the realisation of the text into performance, the role of the director. In addition to specialised drama modules, students will also take some drama-based English modules. These will be at local theatres."
Suggested combinations: English, American Studies, History, History and Theory of Art, Design History.
Entry: A pass in A Level English.

Cheltenham & Gloucester College of Higher Education
PO Box 220, The Park, Cheltenham, Gloucestershire GL50 2QF
Tel: 01242 532700 Fax: 01242 256759
e-mail: admissions@chelt.ac.uk

BA (Hons) Performance Arts
"Performance Arts offers a wide range of opportunities for the study of contemporary performance practices and time-based media. You will be encouraged to take an innovative approach to the live arts, developing your individual performance practice through modules which focus on different areas: performance skills, movement and dance work, script writing, design, sound, lighting, large scale production work and theatre in the community.
An important feature of Performance Arts is its involvement with the professional arts and performance world and its emphasis on enabling students to relate their practice to contemporary culture. Modules include 20th Century Cultural Studies as well as arts management and administration. Performance Arts works closely with arts organisations and theatres in the area and there are

many opportunities to present your work at these professional venues and to undertake work placements."

Year 1: Introduction to Performance; Contemporary Performance Practice; Time Based Media Arts; Arts in a Social Context.

Year 2: Contemporary Performance (dance/writing option); Time Based Media Arts; Devised Theatre; 20th Century Cultural Studies.

Year 3: Interactive Arts; Women & Performance; Performance Production; Site Specific Performance; Interdisciplinary Arts.

Performance Arts can be studied as a Major, Joint or Minor subject.

Entry: Selection is by interview. A Level in Theatre Studies or Art or a BTEC in Performing Arts.

University College Chester

Cheyney Road, Chester CH1 4BJ
Tel: 01244 375444 Fax: 01244 373379
e-mail: B.Reg@Chester.ac.uk Web: http://www.Chester.ac.uk

BA(Hons) Drama and Theatre Studies

"The work of the Department is focused on contemporary theatre in both their 'pure' and 'applied' forms. We operate in the belief that the best performance fuses the demonstration of craft with intellectual enquiry."

Year 1: You will explore the means of making theatre from the perspective of the actor/devisor via courses in interpretation and devising, thus honing and extending skills gained within A Level Theatre Studies or BTEC Performing Arts. This study will be supported by a further module in Theatre Design and Technology exploring design and its constituent elements such as sound and light.

Year 2: Your practical explorations will be reinforced by further critical reflection. A study of presentation and representation will encourage you to ask searching questions about 'what' and 'why' contemporary performers choose to perform. Applied drama and theatre will shift your focus into the broader arena of the social applications of drama in spheres such as the health service, education, museums and personnel training. An intensive course in performance theory concludes the core course and you are able to make choices concerning your remaining study pathway. Initially this allows you to elect an extended period of work-based learning or you may seek to join the Department production company for a period of performance practice working alongside Year 3 students in the public domain.

Year 3: You are able to create your own route from options such as Writing for Performance or Research and Production for performance. On the other hand,

you may wish to pursue a subject of your own choice within a formal dissertation or follow taught courses in contemporary theatre or representing gender.
Entry: CC/12 points with C in Drama plus drama workshop experience.
Also available: Drama and Theatre Studies can be combined with Art, Biology, Computer Science and Information Systems, English Literature, French, German, Geography, History, Mathematics, Physical Education and Sports Science, Psychology, Theology. BEd Primary Teaching with Drama.

Coventry University
Priory Street, Coventry CV1 5FB
Tel: 01203 631313 Fax: 01203 838638

BA (Hons) Theatre and Professional Practice
"The Theatre and Professional Practice course encourages you to develop skills, knowledge and creativity through the practical and academic study of the craft, history and work environment of the actor or theatre artist. Modules focus on the study of performance, performance-related skills, the professional life of a theatre artist and the underpinning knowledge and theory. Studies include voice, movement and acting skills and traditions, devising and creating performance, personal and company administration, staging performance, and historical, cultural and analytical studies."
Also available: BTEC National Diploma in Performing Arts; HND Theatre Practice.

Cumbria College of Art and Design
Brampton Road, Carlisle CA3 9AY
Tel: 01228 400300 Fax: 01228 514491
e-mail: q@cumbriacad.ac.uk Web: http://cumbriacad.ac.uk

BA (Joint Honours) Performance Studies
"The Performance Studies pathway is a practical exploration of the craft of performance for the theatre. The course aims to develop understanding of performance processes and contexts and, in doing so, focuses on performance primarily through activities in drama. Students' experience across the range of performing arts activity (music, dance, drama, design) will be relevant to these aims. This course is designed for those who wish to continue their studies in theatre and performance into higher education and who may see the theatre and performance as a potential career. The Performance Studies pathway is production driven: the course team believe that the best way to learn about performance and theatre is through the act of performance itself."

Year 1: Studies in year one are divided into one single and two half modules. The single module is concerned with the development of performance skills such as voice and speech, movement and rehearsal techniques. This is a highly practical module where there are at least two major performance projects, one student-devised and one text-based. The first of the two half modules explores stage technology including sound, lighting and general stagecraft. During the remaining half module students explore the various theoretical approaches to theatre and performance.

Year 2: Is divided into two modules. During Comparative Studies in Theatre students explore the theory and practices of differing theatre traditions and approaches. This module does not take a Eurocentric approach but instead explores theatre from across the world. Performance Projects A gives students the opportunity to work in teams in the development and production of a range of performance projects, with students taking on a range of production roles form director and actor to designer and administrator. It is envisaged that theses productions would be toured regionally.

Year 3: Studies consist of one double module. Performance Projects B. Within this module students are required, either individually or in teams, to write, produce and perform a substantial piece of theatre. The exact nature of the projects and the roles undertaken by any individual team member are negotiated with course staff.

Entry: There will be an audition at which students will be invited to present performance pieces related to their own interest in performance theatre.

Performance Studies can be studied with one of the following: Film Studies, Literary Studies, Visual Arts, Heritage Management.

Dartington College of Arts

Totnes, Devon TQ9 6EJ
Tel: 01803 862224 Fax: 01803 863569
e-mail registry@dartington.ac.uk Web: http://www.dartington.ac.uk

BA (Hons) Theatre

"This is a 3 year full-time programme for contemporary theatre makers. From the beginning of your third week you will work collaboratively within small companies and begin experiencing and constructing the culture of ensemble theatre practice."

Year 1: is taught and directed by staff and visiting artists, but includes regular theatre Labs for sharing and discussing work. It provides you with a rich and intensive introduction which includes: development of a range of skills using the body as your primary source material; visual choreographic and textual skills for composition; opportunities to talk and write about theatre with special reference to twentieth century performance, collaboration, multi-cultural performance and the relationships between theatre and society. You work with students from all subjects on Cultural Theories exploring issues of importance to arts practitioners.

Year 2: is a year of development both personally and as a company member with intensive workshops on collaborative group work and devising methods in theatre making. Theoretical investigations include dramaturgy, manifestos and motivations, methods of research, and systems of written and visual documentation. Links between theory, practice, and public contexts for performance are emphasised throughout. In the second semester performance and composition work is developed for specific locations and audiences. This project work also addresses the organisation and management of a touring company. Two practical electives allow you to choose specific skills and projects. Theoretical electives engage with contemporary cultural and critical debates.

Year 3: includes a considerable amount of choice and independence, which enables you to round off your studies. You must complete six modules during the year including at least one Final Practical Study, Contextual Enquiry and Written Research Project.

Entry: BB

De Montfort University Bedford

Landsdowne Road, Bedford MK40 2BZ
Tel: 01234 351966
Web: http://www.dmu.ac.uk

BA/BSc Hons (joint/combined) Dance and Drama in Contemporary Culture
"The degree is founded on the principle of exploring the interdisciplinary nature of theatre and dance as they relate to their social and cultural contexts. This necessarily involves developing an understanding of the relationship of form and content to social context, together with an investigation of the politics of performance and representation which includes gender, class, ethnicity and sexuality. This approach informs an interrogation of a range of aspects of contemporary performance in theatre and dance such as the devising process, approaches to choreography, multimedia in performance, authorship, ownership and writing for performance."

All students take core courses in years one and two which investigate the theoretical underpinning of contemporary performance and provide a foundation for the Special Study which is an individual dissertation presented in year three. The core theoretical modules are expressly designed to promote progression and

intellectual coherence. These may include: Dance Technique and Choreography, Devising Theatre, Reconstruction Workshop in Dance, Production Workshop in Theatre, Film Studies, TV Drama, Dance on Film and TV.
Entry: Minimum of two A Levels. 10/12 points.

De Montfort University Leicester
The Gateway, Leicester LE1 9BH
Tel: 01234 351966

BA Hons (joint or combined) Performing Arts
"The portfolio of Performing Arts modules offers a variety of disciplines, embracing Contemporary dance, music and music technology, theatre and performance, both in theory and in practice. Students put together a selection of module choices which matches their needs. You may select either joint honours in two subjects or combined honours in three subjects from the following: American Studies, Education, German, International Relations, South East Asian Studies, Sports History & Culture."
Entry: BCC

BA (Hons) Theatre
"Theatre teaching at DMU is challenging, international and contemporary and is led by a team which includes theatre critics, researchers and theatre makers. The department is strongly committed to exploratory, innovatory approaches as well as providing a thorough background in each discipline. The emphasis is on education rather than training so that the degrees are intellectually as well as practically challenging and provide a foundation for a variety of careers in theatre and arts-related subjects.
The specialist single honours route in Theatre is taught through a series of theatre modules. Teaching focuses on 20th century theatre, on contemporary approaches to history and explores the cross-overs between theatre and other art forms including dance, music and the visual arts. Students engage with the making of performance in theatre and non-theatre spaces and take part in ensemble work for public performance as well as making work which is self-devised and composed. The ability to work as a member of a team, to manage, budget, publicise and tour theatre projects is an essential part of the learning process, as is the ability to analyse and place the work within an intellectual context. As well as practical work students choose from additional modules which offer further practice based learning and theoretical and historical approaches."
Entry: BCC

University of Derby

Kedlestone Road, Derby DE22 1GB
Tel: 01322 622222 Fax: 01322 294861
e-mail: J.Bains@derby.ac.uk Web: http://www.derby.ac.uk/

BA (Hons) Performing and Media Arts

"We offer an exciting opportunity with a specialist Performing and Media Arts full-time honours degree operating within the Modular Degree Scheme. This programme draws primarily on Theatre Studies, Dance, Music and Writing but has potential for other related areas. Students choose two main subject pathways from the four named above. As you progress through the programme you will be able to concentrate on a particular art form. You will still continue with your second choice pathway whilst referring to related developments in others. The programme has a strong practical bias."
Entry: 12 A Level points.

University of East Anglia

Norwich NR4 7TJ
Tel: 01603 593113 Fax: 01603 507719
e-mail: env.admiss.@uea.ac.uk Web: http://uea.ac.uk/env

BA (Hons) Drama

"This programme allows you to combine a strong practical emphasis with the study of the theory, history and social significance of drama. This work is complemented by detailed study of dramatic literature, and aspects of visual and technical design. You will participate in a major production each year as well as undertaking a wide variety of project work; and there is also the opportunity for you to study on placement with professional companies."
Year 1: Introduces the study of drama through texts, practical classes and lectures covering the media of theatre, film and television.
Years 2 and 3: You take on the study of dramatic theory, critical practice and theatre history, culminating in a dissertation and an individual performance project. Course work and the assessment of performances constitute a large part of the final assessment.
Entry: BBB/BBC.
Also Available: BA English Literature and Drama.

Edge Hill University College

St Helens Road, Ormskirk, Lancashire L39 4QP
Tel: 01695 575171 Fax: 01695 579997
Web: http://www.ehche.ac.uk

BA (Hons) Drama

"This drama programme aims to provide a wider access to the study of drama and theatre by offering a range of modules that reflects the experience of performance in our contemporary culture, an understanding of performance heritage and an opportunity to explore the possibilities of performance as it continues to develop in the modern world. The first year modules allow you to look at the nature of performance as we experience it in our culture. In the second year you will learn from the heritage of theatre and drama (in terms of performance theory and skills) and have an opportunity to undertake a full-scale, modern theatrical production. In the third year you will be involved in either a piece of ensemble theatre or the production of a piece of drama for television. You will explore political and issue-based theatre and the culture theory underpinning the performing arts. You will also have the opportunity to look at significant makers of contemporary theatre and drama and work in the fields of arts and disability."
Modules could include:
Year 1: Performance and Contemporary Culture (core); The Artist and Society; Drama; Theatre Criticism.
Year 2: The foundations of the Modern Theatre (core); Directing; Production in Classical Tradition; Creative Research; Performance - the World Perspective; The British Theatre Heritage; Women and Performance.
Year 3: Ensemble and Theatre Production (core); The Theatre and Disability (core); Performance and Culture Theory; Television Drama (core); Creating and Managing an Arts Project: Creative research; Contemporary Practitioners; Disability and Creativity; Stagecraft.
Entry: CC
Also available: Drama can be studied as a Major, Joint or Minor programme.

University of Exeter

Northcote House, The Queen's Drive, Exeter EX4 4QJ
Tel: 01392 263035 Fax: 01392 264580
e-mail: L.G.Buchanan@exeter.ac.uk Web: http://www.exeter.ac.uk/drama

BA (Hons) Drama

"The programme aims to develop an understanding of performance skills alongside a critical and imaginative engagement where the social, historical and cultural contexts of theatre are central. The programme encourages this both as a subject of study and as a practical experience through performance and community-based activities. The studio-based processes of study also equip students with abilities to communicate effectively, to pursue creative analysis and to initiate and organise complex individual and group projects.

Drama at Exeter is taught largely through studio sessions. That is to say that the subject is practised at the same time as it is learned. The relationship between theory and practice is central to the discipline. The degree is composed of a series of modules, all of which lay emphasis on the social nature of theatre. Many, but not all, of these modules conclude with a presentation, open to other Drama students and staff, to the University at large, or to the general public. In the early stages of the programme the emphasis is on group collaborative work. As the student moves through the degree this group work becomes the basis for the development of individual interests and skills. Throughout the programme students get an equal opportunity to act, to direct and to write or otherwise create dramatic events."

Year 1: Modules in semester 1: Acting and Not Acting: the dialectics of performance (a studio-based module), and Pre-Texts and Contexts of Drama (a seminar-based module) aimed at introducing students to a critical and theoretical vocabulary of theatre. The second semester concentrates on a performance-orientated module rooted in research through practice and theory.

Year 2: Two modules offer two core explorations: Theatrical Interpretation (twentieth-century practitioners) and Textual Interpretation (directed towards the performed interpretation of a given playtext.) The other work over the two semesters is represented by a series of options chosen form the generic titles of Theatre Practice 1 and Theatre Research 1.

Year 3: Modules offer options ranging from Theatre Practice and Theatre Research to the Practical Essay (a piece of original dramatic work, created and seen through to a performance by each student and accompanied by a portfolio of commentary), and the possibility to develop individual research on a chosen topic, presented in the form of a Dissertation.

Entry: 22-24 points. Short interview with studio sessions involves an overnight stay in Exeter. Invitations to attend are sent out from early December to mid-February.

Also available: Drama combined with English (3 years), or with German or Spanish (4 years - the third year being spent in the appropriate country).

University of Glamorgan

Prifysgol Morgannwg, Pontypridd, Mid Glamorgan CF37 1DL
Tel: 01443 480480 Fax: 01443 4802199
Web: http://www.Glam.AC.UK/Home.HTML

BA (Hons) Theatre and Media Drama

"This subject will provide you with a foundation in contemporary theatre analysis and practice and give you the chance to sample and develop range of performance and production skills in theatre and media drama. There are good opportunities for critical and creative work in drama in film, television, radio and theatre. Specialist work included textual study, film theory, theatre and media production, scriptwriting, acting, directing and arts administration."

Years 1 and 2: You must study three modules in each year from the areas of Performance, Direction and Production. You will study one module in each of Textural Studies and Cultural Studies and choose five options. The options are in areas such as: Scriptwriting; Contemporary Television Drama; American, European and Alternative Cinema.

Year 3: You must study four specialist modules in one subject chosen from: Acting; Directing; Theatre Production; Arts Administration. You must complete the compulsory module Elizabethan and Jacobean Drama and choose five options.

Entry: BC, including a literature or theatre/media-based subject.

Goldsmiths College, University of London

New Cross, London SE14 6NW
Tel: 0171 919 7414 Fax: 0171 919 7413
e-mail: drama@gold.ac.uk Web: www.goldsmiths.ac.uk

BA (Hons) English and Theatre Arts

"This degree provides a study of English Literature and Theatre Arts and examines interdisciplinary connections between the two disciplines. The Theatre Arts component offers you the opportunity to explore the theory and practice of performance, as it is produced in a range of media. We have completely revised this part of the degree to reflect fully the diversity and excitement of the subject as it enters the new Millennium."

Theatre Arts: The Theatre Arts component follows a specified pathway. In the first year, you learn how to analyse the performance event by taking a course on Analytical Vocabularies. You also take either Technical Theatre (looking at technical and design elements) or Performing Bodies (studying modes of physical performance). After this you choose those pathway courses which have the most productive relationship with the English courses you have chosen, whilst developing a specific knowledge of Drama.

The pathway for the second and third years is currently under revision.

Entry: BBC with Grade B in English

BA (Hons) Drama and Theatre Arts

"Drama at Goldsmiths has traditionally placed a major and distinctive emphasis on performance and production work throughout its undergraduate degrees. This emphasis on production, together with a stimulating atmosphere created by staff with diverse research interests, and the College's location in the heart of London's performance culture, means we can offer a syllabus at the cutting edge of the disciplines of drama and performance. The programme leads you through a range of material which will include, at the least, the acquisition of basic technical skills, physical investigation of, and reflection upon, modes of performance; close analysis of both performance and written text; learning how to study the intercultural history of the theatre; an understanding of how performance affects audiences, and an ability to define what 'performance' actually is.

In addition to a broad knowledge of the basic general areas mentioned above, this degree gives you a chance to develop a specialist focus. This focus should involve both a distinct area of knowledge and a specific practice, thus you might study and then produce a piece of 'physical theatre'; you might learn the basic issues and techniques of theatre administration; theoretical administration; theoretical definition of 'community theatre'; you might analyse and then write a radio drama; investigate the history of melodrama, and then stage its possible relationship to the video camera."

Entry: BBC

University of Hertfordshire

College Lane, Hatfield, Herts AL10 9AB

Tel: 01707 284000

Web: http://www.herts.ac.uk

BA (Hons) Performing Arts

"This innovative degree is designed for those wishing to take up employment or develop their interest in the performing arts and allied areas. The course enables you to develop potential and skill in all areas of dance, drama, musical theatre and music whilst specialising in one form. At each level of the course arts management and sponsorship are taught. On graduation, you will have had experience of organising performance tours at a sufficiently high level to equip you for a professional career. At Level 3 of the course there is the opportunity for major or overseas performance tours. Groups studying this course have toured in

Europe and the United States. You develop a range of core skills including planned performance skills for main house and small scale productions, community productions and touring productions both nationally and overseas."
Entry: A Level points 8. Also available: HND Performing Arts (2 years).

University of Huddersfield

Queensgate, Huddersfield HD1 3DH
Tel: 01484 422288
e-mail: prospectus@hud.ac.uk Web: http://www.hud.ac.uk

BA (Hons) Theatre Studies

"Huddersfield has developed a challenging and exciting range of modules which aim to address the personal, academic and professional needs of today's students and of relevant professions. A rich diversity of programmes, all of which integrate studio-based practical and theoretical methods of study, offers students the flexibility needed to identify and pursue a course which matches their aspirations. After a compulsory foundation year which explores performance, production and study skills through an introduction to the wide range of available study areas, students are invited to specialise in or combine modules from, Performance Analysis, Social, Historical and Cultural Contexts of Theatre, Practical Performance Studies, Theatre Research, Performance Practice in Social, Health, Education and Community Contexts."
Year 1: (Foundation) Play and Performance Analysis; Social Context of Theatre; Study Skills; Approaches to Acting; Theatre Design and Technology; Devising; Script into Performance; Information Technology.
Years 2 and 3: (Advanced) Modules currently include: Ritual: the Physical Performer; 17th Century Theatre; 19th Century Theatre; Music Theatre; Brecht; Issue Plays; Contemporary Playwrights; Carnival and Street Theatre; Performance Art; Drama in Community Contexts.
Entry: A Levels must include Theatre Studies or English. Evidence of practical interest in drama. Also: Theatre Studies combined with Media or Music.

University of Hull

Hull HU6 7RX
Tel: 01482 466210 Fax: 01482 465936
e-mail: admissions@admin.hull.ac.uk Web: http://www.hull.ac.uk

BA (Hons) Drama

"This programme concentrates on the study of drama in all its aspects - literary, historical, aesthetic and presentational - with an equal stress on formal teaching and practical work. An introductory survey of theatre forms and conventions and the sources of dramatic inspiration leads on to a close study of the theatre. This comprises a series of modules, from a list of 40-50, covering many aspects of European, American and Oriental theatre history and dramatic literature. These allow you to explore your chosen subjects in greater depth through seminar discussion.

Available options will vary from year to year but currently range from Classical Theatre, through Shakespeare and Renaissance theatre to the work of individual dramatists such as Ibsen or Brecht, and the contemporary theatre in Britain, France, Germany and America. Other options are purely practical in nature and cover all areas of design, technical theatre and the media, as well as performance. A proportion of modules may be taken in another department."

Entry: BBB-BCC. One A Level should be among the following subjects: English, Classical Studies, History, Art or Art History, Music, Theatre Studies.

Also available: Joint Honours in Drama with American Studies, English, French, German, Italian, Music, Theology.

University of Kent at Canterbury

The Registry, Canterbury, Kent CT2 7NZ
Tel: 01227 764000
e-mail: admissions @ukc.ac.uk   Web: http://ukc.ac.uk

BA (Hons) Drama and Theatre Studies

"Theatre is a collaborative process: the production of a play requires the coming together of different arts and crafts, technical and managerial skills and intellectual knowledge. At Kent we offer a broad-based study of that process with practical courses which cover a wide range of those theatre arts and crafts, and intellectual courses which cover the cultural history of the theatre, techniques of play analysis and theories of representation. Our objective at Kent is to enable you to develop your intellectual and creative talents - equally and in tandem."

Part 1 (Year 1): Modules serve to introduce you to range of historical, theoretical and dramatic approaches to the study of drama and theatre in both theory and practice. Particular attention is paid in theatre practice modules to enabling you to use all the technical and studio facilities of the Department in a safe and creative way. Students taking the Single Honours degree will take six units of drama and theatre study; the remaining units will be drawn from a Faculty-wide list of courses. **Part 2 (Years 2, 3,4):** Consists of seven modules (24 units) taken over the three years of Part 2. This programme consists of equal amounts of practical and intellectual study of the theatre.

Year 2: you take a four-unit Theatre Practice module - Introduction to Performance or Community Celebration plus two-unit Dramatic Studies modules. These are chosen from a list which currently includes: The Origins of European Drama; Drama and Society in the Age of Shakespeare; European Tragedy; Theatre and the 'Woman Question' 1880-1918; Farce; British Drama ad Theatre 1860-1940; Contemporary British Theatre: 1950 to the present.

Year 3: you take a four-unit Theory And Practice module. This is chosen from a list which currently includes: The Theory and Practice of Performance; Gender Theory and Theoretical Practice; Playwriting; Theatre Systems and their Funding; Modern European Theatre and Scenography: Theatre and Practice, plus two further two-unit Dramatic Studies as listed above. Subject to the approval of the Drama Board you may apply to spend your third year in Amsterdam, Bologna, Dublin, Munich, or other approved centres. You will be required to take a course in the relevant language before beginning the year abroad.

Year 4: 'Four at Kent'. In this year you will take just one specialism module valued at eight units, and which lasts the whole year. Theses are intensive practice-based modules and for many serve as preparation for future careers in theses specialist areas. You will spend the full working week on the module which has a term of intensive tuition and small project work before moving to a series of major creative projects. The current 'Four at Kent' list includes Devising: Design for Performance; Directing and Radio Production.

Entry: 24 points at A Level.

Also available: Drama can be studied as a three year joint honours degree with: Classical and Archaeological Studies, Comparative Literary Studies, Computing, English and American Literature, European Studies, Film Studies, French, German, History, History and Theory of Art, Italian, Philosophy, Spanish, Theology and Religious Studies. It can also be studied as a component of the Visual and Performed Arts degree programme

King Alfred's University College Winchester

Winchester SO22 4NR
Tel: 01962 841515 Fax: 01962 842280
Web: http//www.wkac.ac.uk

BA (Hons) Drama, Theatre and Television Studies

"This unique programme offers the chance to work in both theory and practice, with a focus on community drama and documentary television. Drama studies will involve you directly in the communication and analysis of values, ideas and information in the world of entertainment and other social contexts. The emphasis is on the state of the art in the contemporary world, and you will explore this through practical creative experience, both by making dramatic presentations and by thinking, discussing and writing about your own work and the work of others. A particular hallmark of the course is interdisciplinary study, combining drama with music and dance, and investigation of the relationship of the present to the past."

Year 1: Conducted mostly in-house. The first semester introduces the theory and practice of live performance narrative, improvisation, imaging and seminar presentation, plus video work: filming, editing and storyboarding. Semester two examines the development of theatre and cinema in other cultures, and their relationship to politics and social change.

Year 2: is divided between a semester of community drama and one of documentary television. In each case, the focus is on small group project work, undertaken in conjunction with the local community. In some cases, students undertake performances or make programmes themselves; in others, they act as facilitators so that communities can engage in self-representation.

Year 3: Sees students devising a project of their own choosing, with particular relevance to their intended career. in addition, there are taught modules in reading theatre, film and television, where issues of contemporary theory are tackled. A dissertation is also required.

Entry: 20-24 points

BA (Combined Hons) Drama Studies is also available. It does not teach acting but will guide you towards full appreciation of the skills involved in communicating through drama.

Lancaster University

Lancaster LA1 4YW
Tel: 01524 65201 Fax: 01524 846243
Web: http://www.lancs.ac.uk

BA (Hons) Theatre Studies

"This innovative and energetic department offers you a unique opportunity to explore the relationship between practice and theory within Contemporary Theatre through a creative 'hands on' approach to the subject. All our students engage with theoretical and critical issues through participation in workshops, performances and the regular attendance of professional productions. These activities are central to our academic process. Although we do not provide preparation specifically for a career in theatre, our approach includes a degree of training in theatre techniques and performance skills. There are a wide range of practical projects including work with local community groups, hospices, prisons, senior citizens, and those with special needs."

Year 1: This introduction to Theatre Studies is designed to equip students with a knowledge of different approaches to the production and analysis of performance. The course includes one staff led and two student initiated production projects. Assessment is one third (essays), project work one third (presentations/ demonstrations),, and practical exam one third.

Year 2: Up to four courses in Theatre Studies. Performance Analysis 1 and Theatrecrafts are required courses for major students. Theatrecrafts consists of two options chosen from: Acting, Directing, Devising, Playwriting, Lighting and Sound, Design, Physical Theatre and Dance, Popular Performance, Video Making, Stage Production. Other courses : Major modern theatre innovators, Performance analysis, Avant gard theatre, Radical theatre, Modern European playwriting, Applied theatre practice, Special subject. An American exchange at the University of Colorado is available.

Year 3: Three of four courses from Theatre Studies chosen from: Applied theatre practice, theatrecrafts (two further options), Television drama, Gender and politics in performance, Theatre and drama in the community, Performing Shakespeare, Performance and power, Modern experimental performance, Body performance, Contemporary performance in Europe, theatre administration.

Entry: BBC

Also available: BA (Hons) French Studies and Theatre Studies (BCC including French B)), BA (Hons) Spanish Studies and Theatre Studies(BCC including Spanish B), BA (Hons) Theatre Studies and English (BBC including English B and normally a GCSE foreign language). Theatre Studies is also taught as part of the BA (Hons) Creative Arts, along with Art, Creative Writing and Music. (BCC. A Level Theatre Studies an advantage. You will also need to show experience and practical ability in theatre skills).

Liverpool Hope University College

Hope Park, Liverpool L16 9JD
Tel: 0151 291 3000 Fax: 0151 291 3100
Web: http://www.livhope.ac.uk

BA (Hons) Drama & Theatre Studies

"The subject aims to provide you with relevant skills, knowledge and experience in theatre, in the academic disciplines of Drama and Theatre Studies and in areas of independent work and professional interpersonal relations. As you progress, you will be able to concentrate on areas of specialisation in order to play to your strengths or to focus what you learn towards your own individual goals."

Year 1: The two compulsory modules in Year 1 will introduce you to answers to the question 'What is theatre?'. In the first module, students will undertake practical workshops and seminars to explore the dramatic presentation of narrative, before moving on to a group research project in the second module. This project will focus on the challenges of staging a text from a previous period for a contemporary audience. Through these modules, you will develop your academic and relevant interpersonal skills and an appreciation of the practical aspects of the subject.

Years 2 and 3: At this level a range of optional modules clustered under general headings is offered. You may select options in order to develop your own particular areas of interest and related practical, academic and personal skills. You will take responsibility for what you learn and work independently of tutors, often in collaboration with other students.

Semester 3: Practical Skills modules (such as Acting or Technical Theatre) as well as Critical Skills modules(such as Introduction to Film Studies or Shakespeare: Performance and Practice.)

Semester 4: You will be encouraged to develop your work independently. You can undertake an Independent Project, or may wish to explore ways of producing theatre through one of the modules in Modes of Production (such as Theatre Making).

Semester 5: Advanced Practical Skills modules (such as Physical Theatre); Advanced Critical Courses.

Semester 6: Drama with a Purpose (such as Political Theatre and Theatre in Education). You may also negotiate and Independent Learning Module or undertake a Directed Performance module.

Also available: Drama and Theatre Studies can be combined with American Studies, Art, Business and Community Enterprise, English, European Studies, Geography, History, Human & Applied Biology, Information Technology, Mathematics, Music, Psychology, Sport, Recreation & PE, Theology & Religious Studies, creating either a BA or BSc.

The Liverpool Institute for Performing Arts

Mount Street, Liverpool L1 9HF
Tel: 0151 330 3000 Fax: 0151 330 3131
e-mail: reception@lipa.ac.uk Web: www.lipa.ac.uk

BA (Hons) Degree in Performing Arts

"The distinctive feature of this degree is the Core Programme which takes up 50% of your time. The other half of the programme is the six specialist routes: Acting, Music, Dance, Performance Design, Enterprise Management and Community Arts."

Core Programme: Provides you with a firm base upon which you can build your specialist skills.

Year 1: You will gain skills in communication, team work, organisational and self management skills and develop skills in an art form other than your own. You will also learn how to operate the technical hardware of performing arts - lighting, sound, video and computer based systems. Finally, you will complete a Collaborative Performance Project, working with students form other disciplines.

Year 2: A further major collaborative project will develop technical and cross-art form skills. You will spend some time away from the University working with fellow professionals.

Year 3:
Designed to finalise your preparation for work, with modules in business and theoretical areas as well as a major performance related project.

Acting Route

Year 1: This is a foundation year in which you will work toward freeing and discovering your expressive capabilities. Acting classes will cover improvisation, scene study, textual analysis and practical play study and preparation. Voice, speech and movement occupy half the class hours and we will approach texts both through speech and song. In your second semester, you will work on y our first major Collaborative Performance Project. Additionally, the core syllabus will provide basic analytical, technological and communication skills.

Year 2: Is a year for applying and extending the skills learned in the first year, through work on increasingly demanding material. You will be encouraged throughout the year to explore beyond your immediate strengths to make bolder decisions within your work. You can choose between a number of options for concentrated study including Comedy, Screen and Radio Acting, Creating narrative Performance and Musical Theatre. Additionally, you will perform in a Shakespeare production and a major Performance Project.

Year 3: You will be applying skills developed over the first two years in a simulated professional experience in producing, directing, acting and/or writing. In semester five, you will take a leading part in organising and performing in the LIPA Festival. In semester six, you will prepare a showcase for agents. A strong emphasis on professional preparation will help to ensure that you are ready to make the transition from a learning to a professional environment.

Assessment is done through course work - by assessment of your practical, oral and written work.

Entry: For the Acting Route, it is normally expected that you demonstrate ability in more than one performance skill.

Liverpool John Moores University

Roscoe Court, 4 Rodney Street, Liverpool L1 2TZ
Tel: 0151 231 5090/5091 Fax: 0151 231 3194
email: Recruitment@livjm.ac.uk

BA/BA(Hons) Drama

"Our aim is to develop an understanding of drama as a creative, physical and intellectual discipline. The Drama programme focuses on a practical approach informed by theory, with a range of modules covering the performative, technical and crafting elements of drama emphasising group work and ensemble practice. Theoretical modules embrace aspects of contemporary theatre, explorations into theatre history and praxis, the significance of drama as a social art form, and its role in global culture. Production work is both in-house and in a variety of venues around the city. Specialist opportunities exist for independent study and work placements."

Year 1: Core Modules: Theatre in Perspectives, Improvisation and Ensemble, Performance Theory, Performance Skills, Devising and Performance, Contemporary Theatre; Option: Anatomy of Theatre; Electives: The Teller and the Tale, Stage to Screen.

Year 2: Core modules: Experimental Theatre, Theatre in Perspective, Text and Production, Context and Production, Contemporary Theatre; Options: Physical Theatre, Technical Theatre; Electives: TV Drama Production, Writing for Screen, Writing for Stage.

Year 3: Core: Directing in Practice, Contemporary Theatre, Production in Practice/Application of Drama; Options: e.g. Musical Theatre, Queer Theatre, Avant Garde Theatre, New Writing. Independent Study and Work Placements.

Entry: 18 points including Theatre Studies Grade B and successful audition.

Also available: BA (Hons) Theatre Studies, a joint honours course where drama is studied as a major or minor subject with e.g. Imaginative Writing or Screen Studies.

Loughborough University

Loughborough, Leics LE11 3TU
Tel: 01509 222498/9 Fax: 01509 223905
email: Prospectus-Enquiries@lboro.ac.uk Web: http://www.lboro.ac.uk

BA (Hons) Drama

"This programme combines the theory and practice of drama. The two approaches are seen not merely as complementary but as indivisible in the study of a performance art. The main teaching mode is of linked seminar discussion and practical workshop sessions which explore play texts, theoretical writings, performance traditions and techniques, and examine the theatre's role and function in society throughout history. European and American theatre as well as British theatre are studied. Technical theatre (lighting, sound, costume), radio and television drama, and playwriting are also available as areas in which you may specialise."

Year 1: Compulsory modules: Theatre Studies (practical), Theatre Studies (theoretical), Theatre Studies (historical), Theatre Studies (technical). Optional modules: chosen from a range of modules within or without the Department.

Years 2 and 3: In each year students take compulsory modules: Theatre Practice and Group Project. In addition they may take optional modules in: 20th Century British Drama, Playwriting and Dramaturgy, Technical Theatre (Advanced), Staging and the Renaissance, Shakespeare Conference Project, Costume Design, Gender, Devising and Performance, 19th Century British Drama, 19th Century European Drama, 20th Century American Drama, Representing Performance, Gender Culture and Presentation), Caryl Churchill, Form (Agency, Politics), Television Studies Scenography, theatre Funding in the UK, Theatre in Education, Costume Design, Scenography, Individual Topic, Lighting Design, theatre in Education, Dissertation.

All modules are assessed by 100% coursework. A feature of the Drama programme is that there are no formal sit-down written examinations. Most modules are assessed by written assignment, project, practical work, seminar paper, or a combination of these.

Entry: 22 points at A Level

Also available: Drama is available as a minor subject with English and is also offered as part of BA (Hons) Drama with English.

The University of Manchester

Oxford Road, Manchester M13 9PL
Tel: 0161 275 2077
Web: http://www.man.ac.uk

BA (Hons) Drama

"The BA (Hons) in Drama is concerned with the study of drama in performance as well as on the printed page, and our courses address the various conditions that inspire dramatic production. They also explore technical and performance aspects of drama."

Year 1: Is a foundation course which introduces the subject through the study of contrasting texts, ideas about the function of drama in society, and a practical exploration of performance approaches.

Years 2 and 3: There are core-courses in aspects of film and of dramaturgy, but you also choose from a wide range of courses offered as optional areas of study. The particular choice may change from year to year, but all have elements of history, theory and performance applications.

Also available: BA (Hons) Drama and Screen Studies is broadly similar but the programme allows for specialisation in the drama and methodologies of cinema and television. It is possible to transfer onto this course after the first year of Single honours Drama. BA (Hons) joint degree in Drama with English has a more theoretical emphasis, with two-thirds of courses taken from the Drama programme and one-third from the English Department. The four year BA (Hons) Double Honours in English and Drama is studied on a half and half basis during the first two years, with the third year following the Drama programme, and the fourth year solely the English programme.

Entry: BBC with a B grade in English Literature or Language is required for the Drama and Drama and Screen Studies degrees, with BTEC in Performing Arts considered. BBB is the normal requirement for Joint and Double honours, including the subject to be studied with Drama.

Middlesex University

Whitehart Lane, London N17 8HR
Tel: 0181 362 5000 Fax: 0181 362 5649
e-mail: admissions@mdx.ac.uk Web: http//www.mdx.ac.uk

BA (Hons) Drama and Theatre Studies

"A study of modern drama and theatre allowing more extensive practical exploration of a wider range of material than major and minor joint honours programmes."

Year 1: Semester one: Drama introductory, Technical Theatre Introductory. Semester two: Theatre Production 1 and 2, (Theatre Context - optional).

Year 2: Semester one: Modern Drama in Theory and Practice 1 (Realism and Naturalism). Semester two: Modern Drama in Theory and Practice 2 (The Theatre of Personal Experience), plus between 40 and 80 credit points from : Applied Technical Skills 1, Practical Technical Skills 1, Vocal Skills, Voice, Acting, Environmental Theatre, Directing Skills, Interpretative Processes, Theatre Technology, Shakespeare and His Contemporaries in Performance, Storytelling and the Oral Tradition, Contemporary Television Drama, Dance Proposition.

Year 3: Semester one: Modern Drama in theory and Practice 3 (The Theatre of Social Experience). Semester two: Contemporary Theatre, plus between 40 and 80 credit points from the same range of modules offered in Year 2 as well as Comedy, Approaches to Physical Theatre, The Director and the Stage, Theatre Arts Internship, 4 Drama Proposition Modules.

BA (Hons) Performing Arts: Drama

"This programme allows study of aspects of one performing art (dance, drama or music) in depth, while developing skills in the other two. Students study and create material for performance, perform, act as audience and critics, study the performance environment and integrate theses experiences with growing understanding and sensitivity."

Modules include: Communications, Popular Contemporary Arts, First Year Performance, Interdisciplinary Performance, TV Production, Writing for Performance, Mask Work, Solo Performance, Theatre Links, theatre in Education, Opera, The Musical, Vocal Performance, Intercultural and Historical Studies, Performing Arts and the Critic, Performing arts: Interpretations and Issues, Interdisciplinary Environmental Performance, Special Exercise, African-American and African Theatres, Black British and Caribbean Theatres.

Drama options: Directing for Performing Arts Students, Clown.

Entry: Performance qualifications are normally expected and applicants should have substantial performance experience, particularly in their chosen specialism. Audition and interview.

Nene University College of Northampton

Park Campus, Broughton Green Road, Northampton NN2 7AL
Tel: 01604 735500 Fax: 01604 720636

BA (Hons) Performance Studies

"Performance Studies aims to facilitate a degree-level understanding of the variety of forms of performance. Through an engagement with theories and practice of performance students will develop skills in creation, presentation, reception and analysis. These skills will enable students to take an informed critical perspective both on their own work and that of others and will be fostered through a combination of teaching and learning strategies. Working individually and as part of a group, participants are encouraged to question their notions of what constitutes a performance and are challenged to extend themselves both academically and practically." The course is undergoing a process of restructuring but is currently structured as described:

Year 1: Is a foundation year which involves all students in studying dance, drama, and music together with complementary studies in stage technology and design. This work will culminate in a devised performance in the latter part of the year. Assessment will be through both practical and written assignments as well as continuous assessment. This foundation year must be completed successfully for students to pass on the second year.

Year 2: Students will commence Honours work by choosing two of the available options in each of the first two terms. Options will include specialist topic in different areas of performance which will involve the possibility of studying dance, drama and music separately as well as in combination. in the third term there will be a choice of performance projects allowing the further development of specialist studies.

Year 3: Students will choose from available options to build on work undertaken previously. Students will demonstrate the ability to work on their own initiative by undertaking dissertation research in a topic of their choice.

Entry: Students will need to demonstrate evidence of previous study or experience in the area of dance, drama and music.

Newman College of Higher Education

Bartley Green, Birmingham B32 3NT
Tel: 0121 476 1181 Fax: 0121 476 1196
Web: http://www.newman.ac.uk

BA (Joint Honours) Expressive English (with Drama)

"The course offers opportunities to those who have a particular interest in drama to explore this area further. You will study language, drama, poetry, and prose fiction but the emphasis of the course is on the practical applications of English. The study of language has an emphasis on areas such as the description of spoken language, language acquisition and development, the linguistic analysis of written texts, and the social context of language performance. The first phase concentrates on developing students' creative and academic faculties through a dramatic analysis and interpretation of literary text; the second phase explores the collaborative nature of the arts through the production of an interdisciplinary multimedia performance; and the third focuses on the major developments in 20th century theatre, with an emphasis on movements such as Expressionism and Epic theatre, and key practitioners who have contributed to modern theatre, such as Brecht, Stanislavski and Grotowski. In these areas you will consider not only texts but how they can be interpreted dramatically."

Year 1: Modules : Introductions to Literary Studies, Language Studies and Drama and Theatre Arts.

Year 2: Modules: An Interdisciplinary Study of the Visual and Performing Arts, The Language of Spoken and Written Text, Language and Society, Literature and Film.

Year 3: Modules: Expressive English , Contemporary Women Writers, Critical Approaches, Afro/Asian/Caribbean/Black, British Writers, Irish Drama, American Literary and Film Studies.

Entry: CC. Drama experience is desirable but not essential.

University of North London

166-220 Holloway Road, London N7 8DB
Tel: 0171 753 3355
e-mail: admissions@unl.ac.uk Web: http://www.unl.ac.uk

BA (Hons) Performing Arts

"This new BA (Hons) in Performing Arts, run in collaboration with the Holborn Centre for Performing Arts (Kingsway College), will provide a distinctive professionally-oriented course aimed at producing theoretically informed and technically proficient graduates. Students choose a specialism from a range which includes acting, dance, technical and administrative skills."

Year 1: Compulsory methodological modules will be taken alongside daily dance and theatre skills classes over two semesters. Core modules are Text and Performance (double module); Theatre Skills or Dance Movement Skills 1 and 2; IT and Performing Arts. Students are also strongly advised to take Analysing Performances; Sociology of Performances; Text and Production.

Years 2/3: Core theoretical and practical modules continue. Daily classes will continue throughout the three semesters of Advanced Level with the final semester being devoted entirely to the Practical Performance modules in Dance or Drama. Core modules include: Dance Techniques; Theatre Production; Improvisation; Choreography; Dance Production. Optional modules include Directing; 20th Century Theatre Practices; Alternative Forms in Performance; Stanislavsky; Shakespeare and Renaissance; Placement; Interdisciplinary Performance; Videodance; Design for Performance.

Entry: 2 A Levels with Grade C or above in one of English, Theatre Studies, Film Studies, Media Studies, Dance or Drama. Applicants will be asked to attend an audition, which will consist of a group workshop and/or solo piece or interview. Students with prior academic or work-based qualifications may be exempt from specific parts of the course on an individual basis. Applicants who feel they may be eligible should contact the Admissions Office.

University of Northumbria

Ellison Place, Newcastle upon Tyne NE1 8ST
Tel: 0191 232 6002 Fax: 0191 227 4017
Web: www.unn.ac.uk

BA (Hons) Drama

"This course involves the study of drama and theatre with the aim of promoting access to the arts for all sections of the community. The programme provides performance based courses which are responsive to changing patterns of cultural engagement and encourages innovative practice to supply knowledge and understanding of the role of drama in society. The community focus of this degree permits you to apply the skills learnt in a number of areas but may have particular significance in the caring professions and education."

Year 1: Improvisation and devising, Approaches to performance, Arts, society and culture, Guidance, Basic skills, Textual analysis and realisation, In house production.

Year 2: Approaches to interactive theatre, Interactive theatre production, Basic skills, Arts, society and culture, Popular theatre skills, Popular theatre production. There is an exchange programme with a university in Canada for students wishing to spend their second year of study abroad.

Year 3: Performance in context, Profession practice, Dissemination of practice, Arts , society and culture, Dissertation. In Years 2 and 3 there is also the possibility of undertaking a placement either in this country or abroad.

Work throughout the course is continuously assessed. Theory is assessed via seminar presentation and written assignments. The final year dissertation of between 10,000 and 12,000 words, completed with supervision, requires you to document and evaluate your practice.

Entry: We normally interview all suitable applicants to this course. The interview is a full day event which includes participation in a staff led workshop, an individual audition piece, and a written exercise.

University of Plymouth

Drake Circus, Plymouth PL4 8AA
Tel: 01752 232232 Fax: 01752 232141
e-mail: ncrocker@plymouth.ac.uk Web: http://www.plym.ac.uk/

BA (Hons) Theatre and Performance Studies

"Theatre and Performance Studies is about creativity, analysis and practical performance. While it explores work in theatre; dance; ritual; circus and community arts, its essence lies in evaluating the relationship between performer and audience."

Year 1: elements of performance - this foundation year introduces you to the skills, techniques and understanding with which to create and analyse successful performance. Stage 1 looks at the practice of improvisation, performance theory and textual analysis, directing and stagecraft.

Year 2: structures of performance - you will explore the practical, aesthetic and cultural structures which form and inform contemporary performance. It is at this stage that large scale productions are realised. Options include physical theatre; political theatre; avant garde/experimental theatre; contemporary dance;

community arts; mask and puppetry; theatre and performance criticism, and South American and African theatre.

Year 3: issues in performance - you will pursue your individual concerns and research in contemporary performance practice and theory. This comprises performances, presentations, cross-cultural studies and, for single honours students, a dissertation.

Also available: As part of the Combined Arts Programme, Theatre and Performance Studies can be studied as a major or option with any of the following subjects. At the end of Stage 1 you can choose whether you follow a route leading to a combined or single honours degree. American Studies, Art History, Cultural Practice, Education Studies, English, French, Heritage and Landscape, History, Media Arts, Modern Languages, Music, Spanish, Visual Arts.

Queen Margaret College
Edinburgh EH12 8TS
Tel: 0131 317 3000 Fax: 0131 317 3256
e-mail: admissions@qmed.ac.uk Web: www.qmed.ac.uk

BA/BA(Hons) Drama & Theatre Arts
BA/BA(Hons) Acting see p96
"This course examines the practice of theatre from a number of angles - practical, textual, historical, theoretical, critical and structural - and in the context of rehearsal, physical exploration and creative development. It explores the ways in which the changing forms of theatre and the pressures of society have influenced the development of drama into its present diversity. The course develops a broad view of the differing conditions and contemporary forms of theatre and is aimed at those who wish to develop a sound understanding of theatre processes without having to commit themselves exclusively to vocational training. It is not an acting course."

Years 1 and 2: You will study the practicalities of staging, and the challenges faced by the actor, stage manager, writer, director and other key players. Meanwhile, you will learn about the social and economic contexts of key periods in the development of theatre, how plays are written and directed and contemporary ideas of the role of theatre.

Years 3 and 4: You will carry out a detailed study of contemporary theatre in Scotland, the UK, Europe and beyond. You will also undertake advanced studies of play structure, critical ideas and theories, arts policy and performance studies. At least a third of the time will be spent following your specialist study which may be, as available, one of directing, writing, community theatre, arts administration or literary management. You will work with other honours students in small theatre company activity. You will also undertake a major, independent study and study text in performance and the politics of theatre provision.

Entry: BCC

Also available: Theatre Studies can be studied as part of a Joint Degree with a range of subjects from Business, Arts, Science and Humanities.

Queen Mary and Westfield College

University of London, London E1 4NS
Tel: 0171 975 5555 Fax: 0171 975 5500
Web: www.qmw.ac.uk

BA (Hons) English and Drama

"The Drama component of this joint honours degree seeks to engage students in the study and practice of performance. The course combines practical and theoretical study in a wide range of interconnected areas, which provide students with a variety of approaches to drama as an active and dynamic subject. Students are introduced to a study of drama which locates performance within its political, cultural and historical context. Particular emphasis is given to the role and function of performance in settings outside traditional theatre spaces and the application of drama in social institutions such as schools, prisons, hospitals etc. Non-English language theatre forms an important part of the focus of the studies in the second and third years.

Year 1: Students are introduced to theories of performance and the key critical practices of twentieth century theatre. Questions are raised about the issues involved in historical and theoretical study of drama.

Years 2 and 3: Amongst a variety of options courses offer opportunities to study playtexts, historical periods, the theatre of other countries, and the performance of race, sexuality and gender. Students are encouraged to develop their own individual and group projects focusing on the uses and application of drama, as well as experimenting with new theatrical strategies, forms and practices. Final year students are required to undertake a research project in consultation with their adviser.

Entry: 26 points at A Level. Deferred entry will be considered.

Also available: Drama can be taken as a joint honours degree with Hispanic Studies, French, Russian or German.

The University of Reading

Whiteknights, PO Box 217, Reading RG6 6AH
Tel: 0118 931 8618 Fax: 0118 931 8924
e-mail: ug-prospectus@rdg.ac.uk Web: www.rdg.ac.uk

BA (Hons) Film & Drama

"After the First university Examination you will follow core units of critical study approaches to ways in which film and drama have been closely related historically or to concerns which they share and to areas of study considered fundamental to understanding contemporary film and drama culture. These units involve studies in modernism in European film and dram, studies in US cinema and British theatre and studies in alternative forms in film and drama. Alongside these units, you are involved in practical work designed to provide extended experience in drama production and in film/video, together with an option to pursue work in either film/video or drama. You also undertake, in the third year, an independent project, which may take the form of a dissertation, drama production, film or video, or some combination of these."
Entry: BBC. At least one from English Literature, Theatre Studies or Film Studies preferred but not required.
Also available: Film & Drama may be combined with English, German or Italian.

The University College of Ripon & York St John

York Campus, Lord Mayor's Walk, York YO31 7EX
Tel: 01904 612512 Fax: 01765 600516
Web: http://www.ucrysj.ac.uk

BA/BSc(Hons) Film, TV, Literature & Theatre Studies

"A theoretical 'core' module underpins practical activity throughout the degree, thus production modules are supported by continuous examination of theories, concepts and critical positions. Each core module addresses a central theme, for example the relationship between author, text and audience, culture and community, or 're-presenting reality'. Production modules running concurrently realise these themes in workshops, production exercises and fully staged theatre productions or video pieces for television. Theoretical work and production activity includes:

Film: Introduction to feature film production, Theories of Film, Narrativity, Authorship and Genre, Hollywood and Cinema, British Cinema. There are limited opportunities for 16mm film production.

Television: Forms and conventions in TV production. Studio and location shooting skills, Making television drama. Making television documentaries, Independent production.

Literature: Study of the process of writing using the work of chosen novelists, poets, dramatists, playwrights, screenwriters. The relationship between author and audience, the adaptation of texts from one mode of production to another.

Theatre: Forms and conventions in theatre production, devising techniques, contemporary theatre, experimental theatre, theatre and gender, theatre and protest.

While we are not a training school you can expect to gain some key skills in producing, directing, production planning and management, performing and writing. there are also opportunities to gain expertise in related skills such as lighting and sound, set design and construction, psc and TV studio operation, TV graphics, analogue and digital video post-production, stage and studio management, producing treatments and storyboards.

Features: A four week work placement during Year 2 with a regional, national or international organisation. An internship programme during Year 3 (usually ten weeks) with a professional company. Academic exchanges, currently with universities in the Netherlands, Denmark, Portugal, Germany, Finland. In the US exchanges are made in New Hampshire and Wisconsin.

Roehampton Institute London

Senate House, Roehampton Lane, London SW15 5PU
Tel: 0181 392 3000 Fax: 0181 392 3229
Web: www.roehampton.ac.uk

BA(Hons) Drama and Theatre Studies

"The Drama & Theatre Studies programme focuses on the art of performance through both practical and theoretical study. We actively encourage intellectual curiosity and creativity, helping you to articulate your ideas in writing, speech and performance. You will critically analyse plays, performers and audiences, build confidence in presentation skills and develop specific performance techniques. However this programme is not designed for those wishing to pursue acting careers."

Foundation Level: You will be introduced to some of the key debates and issues in Drama and Theatre Studies.

Honours Level: You may choose from a wide range of options including: Community Drama, Mask & Physical Theatre, Writing for the Theatre, Representing Women, Theatre & the American Dream, Socialist Theatre in Britain, Tragedy & Terror, Comedy, Modernism & the Avant Garde, and Approaches to Directing. You may also undertake a research project or dissertation at this level. Entry: 16-20 points from at least 2 A Levels.

Also available: Drama and Theatre Studies can also be taken as part of a Combined Honours programme with a choice of about thirty different subjects.

Royal Holloway, University of London
Egham, Surrey TW20 OEX
Tel: 01784 434455 Fax: 01784 437520
e-mail liaison-office@rhbnc.ac.uk

BA (Hons) Drama and Theatre Studies

"Our degree programmes are grounded in the belief that practical engagement with dramatic texts is a vital tool for imaginative and analytical development. All courses contain a blend of both practical and conceptual work so that theory and practice are integrated throughout our degrees. The seminar/workshop is the main forum for teaching and learning, supplemented by lectures from members of staff, visiting academics and theatre professionals."

Productions arise out of academic work. Every Single Honours student has an opportunity to spend one term working exclusively on a major production project which results in two performances of related material.

The degree is divided into courses which are usually assessed continuously or as they are completed and which all contribute to the final degree.

Year 1: The first year courses - Elements of Performance, Reading the Text, Critical Theories and Practical Skills - are compulsory and form an introductory course designed to introduce the theoretical and practical aspects of the study of performance, and to develop all the necessary skills.

Years 2 and 3: A wide range of choice is available. You select your own pathway through such topics as Modern British, French, American, Australian, Eastern and Central European Drama, Noh Theatre, Greek Theatre, Chinese Theatre, Renaissance Drama, Shakespeare in Performance, Popular Performance, Expressionism, Naturalism, Feminism, Cultural Theory, Theatre Anthropology, Playwrighting and Devising, Drama Therapy, the Director and the Stage, Movement Studies, Dance Drama, Set and Costume Design, Lighting and Sound.

Also available: Joint degree courses are available with Classical Studies, Music, English, English Language and French. For the Drama component of the joint degrees you take introductory courses in the first year which are designed to lay

a foundation in all the theoretical and practical aspects of the study of perform-ance. Second and final year courses are then chosen from the same selection as Single honours students.
Entry: BBC

Royal Scottish Academy of Music and Drama
100 Renfrew Street, Glasgow G2 3DB
Tel: 0141 332 4101 Fax: 0141 332 8901
e-mail: registry@rsmad.ac.uk Web: http://www.rsmad.ac.uk

BA /BA(Hons) Contemporary Theatre Practice
BA Acting, BA Stage Management Studies, Mdra (Acting) and Mdra (Direct-ing) see page111
"The course is designed to provide practical, creative experience and theoretical understanding of a variety of uses of drama, using devising as its main approach to performance. It is not suitable for those wishing to focus solely on acting as a career. The practical and performance-led activities inform and develop the theorising skills of students, enabling them to become independent theatre mak-ers. Students are required to engage creatively and systematically with their learning experience and record their conclusions in the form of log-books, re-flective journals, videos and essays. The Honours year will provide, for those selected, specialist training in the following areas: Devisor/Performer; Devisor/Director (includes professional placement); Devisor/Educator (professional place-ment).
Entry: English or Theatre Studies required.

University College of St Martin
Bowerham Road, Lancaster LA1 3JD
Tel: 01524 384384 Fax: 01524 384385
Web: www.ucsm.ac.uk

BA (Hons) Performing Arts
"The course offers depth of study, equal amounts of performance and theory, opportunities for researching personal interests, areas which draw the perform-ing arts together, strong links between performance theory and practice, good organisation, and promotes progress in personal skills and techniques."
Year 1: You will study all three Performing Arts subjects. Your main specialism has two modules and there are modules to help you develop a variety of skills within the subject area.

For Drama Specialists: Four double modules are taken, two in Year 2 and two double modules in Year 3. Performance and Production; Theatre as Social Comment; Studies in Theatre and Performance; Drama and Myth.

Core Studies: Whatever your main specialism, you also take the following cross-arts double modules, as listed below:

Year 2: Core Studies - The Performing Arts in Context (double module) considers performance as a phenomenon conditioned by and influencing society. Conceptual frameworks for the critical analysis and creation of performance (e.g. cultural materialism, feminism, psychoanalysis, post-modernity) are also explored.

Year 3: Core Studies - The Performing Arts in Practice (double module) explores the value of the Performing Arts for the community (community outreach, therapy) and for the performer (motivation, therapy, personal identity, stress management). Arts management and ethical issues are also investigated.

Integrated Arts Project: This double module provides opportunities for students to engage in individual research and experimentation into aspects of arts integration. However, students may opt to write an individual dissertation, which considers similar issues and concerns.

Entry: CC (with an A Level or BTEC in music, drama, dance, theatre studies or performing art being an advantage).

Also available: BA (Hons) Drama is a Modular Studies Degree Joint Subject in which you will study performance work as a combined degree with another subject. BA (Hons) Drama with QTS may also be offered, subject to validation.

St Mary's University College

Waldergrave Road, Twickenham, Middlesex TW1 4SX
Tel: 0181 240 4029

BA (Hons) Drama and Theatre Studies

Year 1: Students follow Foundation courses in improvisational projects, voice and movement, designed to increase awareness of self, of the group and of the social context in which theatre takes place. Additional courses aim to explore the basic elements of a play, investigate different theatre spaces and actor/audience relationships, and introduce students to the work of major 20th century theatrical innovators. Students are encouraged to test out their ideas both in practice and in seminar discussion. since the year is intended to offer both individual study and the ability to work collaboratively, productions are specifically mounted to enhance and examine collective experience.

Year 2: Introduces students to Critical Theory. In addition, students follow a course in Art & Techniques of Theatre and Television, with opportunities to work on practical projects in acting, costume design, make-up, masks, set design, stage lighting, stage management or television production. Other modules available include Shakespeare in Performance, British Television Drama, British Naturalism, Theatre of Commitment and Expressionistic Theatre.

Year 3: There are opportunities to develop experience in directing for theatre or television, in play writing, play devising and dramatic criticism. There is also a wide variety of modules which enable students to pursue areas of particular interest. These include Avant Garde Theatre, Popular Theatre, Gender & Sexual Politics in Contemporary Theatre, Farce, Tragedy, American Drama 1920-60, Chekhov, Stanislavsky and Meyerhold. An additional option in the form of a supervised dissertation allows an opportunity for original research on a topic of the student's own choice.

Entry: CC

Also available: Drama can be studied as part of BA Combined Honours with Classical Studies, Education Studies, English, Geography, Heritage Administration, Irish Studies, Management Studies, Media Arts, Sociology, Sport Rehabilitation, Sport Science, Theology and Religious Studies.

The University of Salford

Salford, Greater Manchester M5 4WT
Tel: 0161 295 5000 Fax: 0161 295 5999
Web: http://www.salford.ac.uk

BA (Hons) Performing Arts

"This course focuses on the development of creative performance skills to a professional level and draws on the department's expertise in theatre and TV performance and physical theatre. The course offers certain modules available on the Media and Performance degree (TV Acting, Presenting, TV Comedy and Radio Drama) but its main emphasis is on live theatre performance and its associated practical skills - acting, improvisation, voice, dance, movement and singing. Other modules include Physical Theatre Techniques, Devised Theatre, and there are options in Scriptwriting, Theatre Directing, Stand-up Comedy and Live Art. Theoretical lecture-based modules examine cultural and critical perspectives on performance. In Year 3 students create a range of scripted and devised theatre performances."

Entry: 2 A Levels.

BA (Hons) Media and Performance

The course will be of interest to actors, presenters and directors who wish to obtain challenging positions in future developments of the performing arts and media industries. This course allows students to integrate elements of the University's strengths in dramatic performance and media production. The course emphasises multi-skilling with students acquiring video techniques as well as performance skills for theatre, television and radio. Theory modules cover historical and cultural approaches to the analysis of media and performance. Group project work provides a practical focus with students working to produce theatre and radio performances and video drama productions.

During the second and third years students can choose between a wide range of optional modules which suit their interests and career aspirations. Practical Performance options include: Acting for Television, Radio and Theatre, TV Presenting, TV Comedy, Stand-up Comedy, Physical Theatre. Production-based options include: TV Directing, Scriptwriting, Producing, Camera, Sound and Editing. Lecture-based Critical Theory options include: Action Movies, Visual Culture, European Media, print Journalism, Modern British theatre, British TV Drama, Avant Garde Theatre and Shakespeare in Performance."

Entry: 2 A Levels. Applicants with talent but without the formal entry requirements are encouraged to apply. All students must demonstrate at interview/audition a strong performance ability and interest in TV/radio production.

Also available: 2 year HND Media Performance.

University College Scarborough

Filey Road, Scarborough YO11 3AZ
Tel: 01723 362392 Fax: 01723 370815
e-mail: external@ucscarb.ac.uk Web: www.ucscarb.ac.uk

BA (Hons) Theatre Studies

"Theatre has its life in performance, not simply on the written page. To fully appreciate the nature of that life requires critical understanding. It also requires direct and personal experience of the process of performance itself. The Theatre Studies programme is designed to offer students a a rich variety of learning experiences which lead to a long-lasting and informed appreciation of modern and contemporary theatre. The unifying focus is the twentieth century, its diverse and controversial practices, its challenging forms of staging, its thinkers and practitioners, its innovations and its orthodoxies."

Year 1: A foundation year in which students are introduced to essential principles in theatre study and practice and the experience of group-based theatre projects.

Year 2: Students have increased options for specialisation in modules such as Political Theatre, Children's theatre or the production-based Applied theatrecrafts.

Year 3: Provides opportunity for independent study and self-directed theatre work, as well as further specialisation in modules such as Writing for Theatre, Beckett in Performance and Modern Theatre Practice.

The National Student Drama Festival also has its permanent home in Scarborough and is run in association with the University. If you are interested in a career in theatre the Festival represents unrivalled opportunities for you to become directly involved in this major national event.

Entry: 2 A Levels, one of which should be appropriate to Theatre Studies. 10-12 points.

The South Bank University

Southwark Campus, 103 Borough Road, London SE1 OAA
Tel: 0171 928 8989 Fax: 0171 815 8155
e-mail: enrol@sbu.ac.uk Web: http://www.sbu.ac.uk

BA (Hons) World Theatre

"This field is offered in partnership with the Central School of Speech and Drama. You will be able to enjoy the benefits of membership of both colleges and the opportunity to study World Theatre in a major multi-cultural centre of theatre diversity and excellence. Theatre as an integral part of society is examined by employing examples of theatre practice form a variety of cultures that demonstrate the diversity and commonality of theatrical expression.

The course enables you to compare theatre traditions and to understand, by analysis of cultural conventions, varying concepts of performance, text, staging, design etc. that characterise different theatrical forms. You will become familiar with theatre in its many forms, for example, as political, religious or social events, and you will examine the methodologies and practice of theatre makers in a number of specific case studies. the field aims to develop your critical and analytical skills of interpretation and review but also offers elements of practice based work intended to further understanding through practical experience."

Entry: CC with one A Level preferably in English, Theatre Studies or Performing Arts.

Staffordshire University

College Road, Stoke-on-Trent ST4 2DE
Tel: 01782 292752 Fax: 01782 745422
e-mail: prospectus@staffs.ac.uk Web: http://www.staffs.ac.uk/welcome.html

BA (Hons) Drama and Theatre Arts

"This exciting new award offers you the opportunity to integrate the development of personal, practical and performance skills with a study of the theatre's theoretical, historical, social and technical disciplines. Study modules will stress

the links between theory and practice and emphasis will be placed on active involvement in production work; community projects and innovation as well as developing a critical, analytical and conceptual context for performance. Assessment methods will foster and encourage individual initiative and teamwork, professional and interpersonal skills, as well as creativity and flexibility allied to a level of critical analytical skills appropriate to a graduate."
Entry: CC

University of Sunderland

Edinburgh Building, Chester Road, Sunderland SR1 3SD
Tel: 0191 515 3000 Fax: 0191 515 3805
e-mail: student-helpline@sunderland.ac.uk Web: http://www.sunderland.ac.uk

BA (Hons) Performance Arts Studies

"This interdisciplinary programme offers the study of more than one art form. Choose from modules in Dance, Drama, Music or Performance and Visual Culture. Choose one main and one subsidiary subject; study two art forms equally; or keep your options broad initially, narrowing your focus later. Each arts discipline provides opportunities for creative exploration and expression, subject knowledge and application, analytical study and personal transferable skills."
Years 1 and 2: The Arts in Context, plus four options from at lest two of the following disciplines: Dance, Drama, Music, Performance and Visual Culture. Plus an elective or one further option module. In Year 2 you can study in the USA at one of several universities, for one semester or a full year.
Year 3: The Integrated Arts Project is a core module if you have studied three art forms in Years 1 and 2; for others it is optional. If you take a main subject or two subjects in equal amounts your subject leader(s) will designate a core subject module. An elective is still possible.
Entry: Students with non-standard entry qualifications may be accepted, subject to interview.

University of Sussex

Sussex House, Falmer, Brighton BN1 9RH
Tel: 01273 678416 Fax: 01273 678545
e-mail: UG.Admissions@sussex.ac.uk Web: http://www.sussex.ac.uk

BA (Hons) European Drama with French, German or Italian

"This degree gives you the opportunity to explore, in a practical way through workshops, the theories introduced and discussed in lectures and seminars. You have the chance to develop your own creative writing, although we do not give you professional training in acting, directing or stage management. You spend Year 3 studying theatre in France, Germany or Italy, or in a work placement."

Year 1: Theories of Drama; Theatre and Society: European Drama from the Greeks to 1900; School Courses (studied in the School of European Studies.)

Year 2: Modern and Post-modern Drama; Writing for the Theatre; School Courses.

Year 3: Year Abroad

Year 4: French, German or Italian Special Author, and Special Subject; Group project; School Courses. If your language is French, work in the final year is conducted in French, with a course devoted to the study of a French playwright (probably Moliere) and a course on Modern French Theatre. If you opt for German language, you follow a course on Bruchner, followed by Post-war Drama in German-speaking Countries. If Italian is your language, you study special author - Pirandello, followed by Italian Theatre and Society.

Entry: BBB. A/AS Level in appropriate language.

Swansea Institute of Higher Education

Mount Pleasant, Swansea SA1 6ED
Tel: 01792 481000 Fax: 01792 481085
e-mail: enquiry@sihe.ac.uk Web: http://www.sihe.ac.uk

BA(Hons) English Studies and Drama and Media Studies

Drama and Media Studies: "Considers the related fields of theatre, film and television, concentrating on the study of film and television products and on "plays" and "playwrights". There are opportunities to explore practical drama. You will see the development of theatre form its earliest beginnings and be able to explore fill and television products and understand them better."

Entry: 2 A Levels. Mature students without A Levels may also be considered.

University College Warrington

Padgate Campus, Crab Lane, Warrington WA2 ODB
Tel: 01925 494494 Fax: 01925 494289
e-mail: registry.he@warr.ac.uk Web: http://www.warr.ac.uk

BA (Joint Honours) Performing Arts with Business Management and IT

"Whether you are a performer yourself, hope to be a manager in any business that needs effective communications, or want to apply your love of the Performing Arts in social or community contexts, you will find that we can give you the education, experience and business skills you need."

Modules currently offered:

Year 1: Performance and Staging Skills: You will work on two stage productions for public performance, developing your understanding of the practical skills needed both to perform in and to provide technical support for an ensemble company. First-year productions are designed to involve all members of the class, from the least to the most experienced technicians and performers.

Performance Forms and Conventions: Given in the form of lectures and small-group seminars, this is a survey of the history and theory of live performance. it is intended to develop your personal philosophy about what the performing arts are "for": their value and function in society. There are also options in Community, Communications or Cultural Studies.

Year 2: Touring Productions: Small groups of students identify target audiences and devise performances appropriate to their needs. You will take these performances on tour to appropriate local venues. The you will evaluate, revise and repeat them to develop your audience awareness, y our flexibility and your efficiency in managing the touring process.

Arts and Entertainment: This is a study of contemporary Arts Management: the funding, politics, management and marketing of the arts in Britain today.

Year 3: Independent Production: You can work alone or in a group to develop a piece of performance work that can make an entertaining but useful (and financially-viable) contribution to the community outside the campus. You will be expected to manage your won company, raising funds, booking venues, negotiating contracts etc., all along professional lines.

You will also make a choice of academic options which currently include: Community Arts, Performance and Therapy, Access and Marketing the Arts, Theatrical innovators of the Early 20th Century, Contemporary Alternative Performance, Music & Audiences and topics in Community and Communication Studies.

Entry: 12 points at A Level. We positively welcome application from mature students.

The University of Warwick

Coventry CV4 7AL

Tel: 01203 523523 Fax: 01203 461606

e-mail: ugadmission@admin.warwick.ac.uk Web: http://www.warwick.ac.uk

BA (Hons) Theatre and Performance Studies

"The degree allows students to emphasise a practical or an analytic, historically based approach to Theatre Studies, with emphasis placed on the study of the modern period. Students are introduced to a wide range of modern theatre practice and are encouraged to build their own critical and creative responses to contemporary performance. At the same time, a solid grounding is offered in the discipline of European theatre history so that judgements may be made in the context of historical development and change."

Year 1: Course 1: (Core) Society, Stage and Text - the first part of a two year course examining the interaction between society, stage and text in historical periods of major importance in the development of the theatre from Ancient Greece to the late 18th century. Course 2: (Core) Approaches to Modernism - the first part of a two year course exploring the impact of modernist ideas in the theatre at the turn of the century. The work of directors, designers, performers and playwrights is examined in lectures and seminars. Course 3: (Core) Contemporary Theatre and its Context - begins exploring a wide range of contemporary performance, which involves an extensive programme of theatre visits. Contemporary British playwrights are discussed and the current economic and organisational framework of the theatre in the UK is looked at. Course 4: (Core) Aspects of Practice: Performance, Media, Theatre in the Community - introduction to contrasting approaches to practical work, addressing key issues of practice. Introduction to technical equipment of a modern performance studio.

Year 2: Courses 1 and 2 are a seminar-based continuation of the first year. Courses 3 and 4 (Optional) Performance and Text - a studio-based course exploring the relationship between live performance and written text, in the context of contemporary experimental theatre; Theatre in the Community - a course which explores the theory and practice of modern community-based theatre. Student production companies are formed to devise original programmes in a variety of different locations; Video and the Culture of the Moving Image - students create and present their own practical video projects and will also analyse and discuss theories around moving image culture; Marketing Theatre - introduces the management philosophy of arts marketing and gives students an opportunity to work on a specific project within a local arts organisation; an Option from a wide variety offered.

Year 3: Concentrates almost exclusively on developments in the theory and practice in 20th Century theatre. Course 1: (Core) theatre and ideology - examines some of the crucial lines of debate which have emerged in the modern theatre in Europe and the USA. Courses 2, 3 and 4 (Options) may include: Women in the Theatre; Staging Shakespeare from 1960 to the Present Day; Structure; Language and Symbol; Ancient Drama on the Modern Stage; or a studio-based Practical Option, Presentation and Performance, or Marketing Theatre. A Research Option and further Practical Options are available.

Entry: BBB with an A Level pass in English Literature, History or Theatre Studies. Two AS Levels may be offered in place of a third A Level.

Westhill College of Higher Education

Weobley Park Road, Selly Oak, Birmingham B29 6LL
Tel: 0121 472 7245 Fax: 0121 415 5399
Web: http://www.westhill.ac.uk

BA (Hons) Humanities, Creative Arts

"Students select three from the four subject strands: Art and Design; Dance;
Drama; Music. All students follow the compulsory interdisciplinary strand for
the first two years. The Creative Arts degree is designed for students who have
an interest in, and a commitment to, the art and who wish to develop both their
creative and critical skills. We recognise that you are unlikely to be equally strong
in all strands, so the course is designed, at least in the first year, to take account
of individual differences, providing introductions which will enable you to work
at your own level."

The Drama Strand: will appeal both to those interested in Drama as Performance and Drama as Literature, since it contains close study of texts from the
history of Western drama, with performance and the development of a range of
theatre skills. Students will be encouraged to develop their own talents and
work to the highest standards both academically and practically. As part of the
interdisciplinary strand you will undertake a negotiated placement related to
your subject studies.

Entry: 2 A Levels

University of the West of England

Frenchay Campus, Coldharbour Lane, Bristol BS16 1QY
Tel: 0117 965 6261 Fax: 0117 976 3804
Web: http://www.uwe.ac.uk

BA (Joint Hons) Drama and English

"As far as Drama is concerned; this joint honours degree offers a balanced pack-
age of practical, contextual and theoretical approaches to the study of theatre.
The main focus of the programme is on nineteenth and twentieth century British, European and American drama, although there are opportunities to widen
the scope further. Practical workshops, text analysis and theatre history are all
part of the student experience. The degree should interest students who wish
both to explore theatre, and to use theatre as a means of exploration while at the
same time studying the more traditional discipline of English Literature."

Year 1: You take four foundation modules during your first year of study - two in
Drama and two in English. The modules in drama are: The Language of Theatre; and Introduction to Theatre Studies.

Years 2 and 3: You take two modules in each subject, each year. Drama: You choose from the following: Revolutions in the European Theatre; Twentieth Century American Drama; Nineteenth Century Theatre; Shakespeare and the Modern Age; Epic and Ensemble Drama; the short dissertation. The latter consists of an independent project of 8,000 words and is completed in Year 3.
Entry: BBC. English or Theatre Studies, Grade B.
Also available: BA (Hons) Drama and Cultural and Media Studies is similar in structure (Entry: BBC) Also BA (Hons) Drama and History (Entry: BCC) These combined degrees offer an opportunity to study in the United States during the second year, either in Virginia or Pennsylvania.
The half award in Drama is also offered in a wide range of possible combinations outside the Department of humanities: with Accounting, Education, Geography, Languages, Marketing, Mathematics, Politics, Psychology, Sociology and Statistics. 16-22 A Level points. These joint programmes do not offer work/study abroad.

University College Worcester
Henwick Grove, Worcester WR2 6AJ
Tel: 01905 855000 Fax: 01905 855132
Web: http//www.worc.ac.uk/

BA (Hons) Drama
"Drama combines the skills of performer and observer, reader and critic, producing a student with a sound understanding at both practical and theoretical levels."
Year 1: You will be introduced to basic concepts through a variety of practical and theoretical approaches. The texts you will study are chosen to represent a range of authors, contexts, forms and conventions. In practical work, you will explore movement and improvisation, with work on posture and gesture, spatial awareness and group sensitivity; and you will study theatre performance through theatre visits, videos and films.
Years 2 and 3: Core skills will be developed further. Optional modules include improvisation for performance, production of a theatre text, Shakespeare and Renaissance drama, feminist drama, naturalism, theatre between the wars, postwar British theatre, Irish theatre and documentary drama. You can also do a dissertation topic in Drama, which if you wish can have a practical emphasis.
Also available: Drama can be studied through Major, Joint and Minor pathways in the Undergraduate Modular Scheme. Excluded combinations are Drama and Education Studies, European Studies, Geography, Health Studies, Heritage Studies or Sports Studies.

Centres offering BTEC awards in Performing Arts

LEA	Centre	Award
Avon	City of Bath College, Bath	NC, ND
	City of Bristol College, Bristol	NC, ND
	Filton College, Bristol	NC, ND, HNC, HND
	Weston College, Weston-super-Mare	NC, ND
Barking	Dagenham Priory Comp Sch, Dagenham	NC, ND
	Barking College, Romford	NC, ND, HNC, HND
Barnet	Barnet College, Barnet	NC, ND
Barnsley	Barnsley College, Barnsley	NC, ND
Bedfordshire	Bedford College, Bedford	NC, ND, HNC, HND
	Luton VIth Form College, Luton	NC, ND
Belfast Area	Belfast Inst of F & HE, Belfast	NC, ND, HNC, HND
Berkshire	Newbury College, Newbury	NC, ND
	Reading Coll of Arts & Design, Reading	NC, ND
	East Berkshire College, Slough	NC, ND
Bexley	Bexley College, Belvedere	NC, ND
Birmingham	Sutton Coldfield FE Coll, Sutton Coldfield	NC, ND
Bolton	Bolton College, Bolton	NC, ND
Bradford	Bradford & Ilkley Comm College, Bradford	NC, ND
Brent	College of NW London, London	NC, ND
Bromley	Orpington Coll of FE, Orpington	NC, ND
Bucks	Amersham & Wycombe Coll, Amersham	NC, ND, HNC, HND
	The Cressex School, High Wycombe	NC, ND
	Stantonbury Campus, Milton Keynes	NC, ND
Bury	Bury College, Bury	NC, ND
Calderdale	Calderdale College, Halifax	NC, ND
Cambs	Cambridge Regional College, Cambridge	NC, ND
	Peterborough Regional Coll, Peterborough	NC, ND
	Isle College, Wisbech	NC, ND
Camden/West	Kingsway College, London	NC, ND
	Westminster College, London	NC, ND
	North Westinster School, London	NC, ND
	Pimlico School, London	NC, ND
Cheshire	West Cheshire College, Chester	NC, ND
	South Cheshire College, Crewe	NC, ND
	Halton College, Widnes	NC, ND
City London	Tower Hamlets College, London	NC, ND
	Mulberry School for Girls, London	NC, ND
Cleveland	Stockland & Billingham C of FE, Billingham	NC, ND
	Teeside Tertiary College, Middlesbrough	NC, ND
	Redcar & Cleveland College, Redcar	NC, ND
Clwyd	Llandrillo College, Colwyn Bay	NC, ND
	NE Wales Inst of HE, Wrexham	NC, ND
	Yale College, Wrexham	NC, ND
Cornwall	Penwith College, Penzance	NC, ND
	Cornwall College, Redruth	NC, ND
	St Austell College, St Austell	NC, ND
Coventry	Hereward Coll of FE, Coventry	NC, ND

	Coventry University, Coventry	NC, ND
	Tile Hill College of FE, Coventry	NC, ND
Croydon	Brit Perf Arts and Tech Sch, Croydon	NC, ND
	Croydon College, College	NC, ND
Cumbria	Morton Comp School, Carlisle	NC, ND
	Cumbria College of Art & Design, Carlisle	NC, ND
	Caldew School, Carlisle	NC, ND
	Ulverston Victoria High School, Ulverston	NC, ND
Derbyshire	Chesterfield College, Chesterfield	NC, ND
	N Derbyshire Tertiary Coll, Chesterfield	NC, ND
	Derby Tertiary Coll: Wilmorton, Derby	NC, ND
	SE Derbyshire College, Ilkeston	NC, ND
Devon	North Devon College, Barnstaple	NC, ND
	Exeter College, Exeter	NC, ND
	Plymouth College of FE, Plymouth	NC, ND
	South Devon College, Torquay	NC, ND
	University of Plymouth, Plymouth	HNC,HND
Doncaster	Doncaster College, Doncaster	NC, ND
	Adwick School, Doncaster	NC, ND
	Don Valley High School, Doncaster	NC, ND
Dorset	Bournmouth & Poole Coll of FE, Poole	NC, ND
	Weymouth College, Weymouth	NC, ND
Dudley	Dudley College of Tech, Dudley	NC, ND
	Halesowen College, Halesowen	NC, ND
Durham	New College Durham, Durham	NC, ND
Dyfed	Coleg Ceredigion, Aberystwyth	NC, ND
	Pembrokeshire College, Haverfordwest	NC, ND
	Carmarthenshire Coll of Tech & Art, Llanelli	NC, ND
Ealing	Ealing Tertiary College, London	NC, ND
East Sussex	Brighton College of Technology, Brighton	NC, ND
	Eastbourne Coll of Arts & Tech, Eastbourne	NC, ND
	Lewes Tertiary College, Lewes	NC, ND
Enfield	Enfield College, Enfield	NC, ND
Essex	Basildon College, Basildon	NC, ND
	Braintree College, Braintree	NC, ND
	Rainsford High School, Chelmsford	NC, ND
	Colchester Institute, Colchester	NC, ND
	Palmer's College, Grays	NC, ND
	Harlow College, Harlow	NC, ND
	Epping Forest College, Loughton	NC, ND
	SE Essex Coll of Arts & Tech, Southend	NC, ND
Gateshead	Gateshead College, Gateshead	NC, ND
Glouces	National Star Centre Coll of FE, Cheltenham	NC, ND
	Glos College of Arts & Tech, Cheltenham	NC, ND
	Cirencester College, Cirencester	NC, ND
Greenwich	Plumstead Manor/Negus, London	NC, ND
	John Roan School, London	NC, ND
Gwent	Ebbv Vale Senior Comp School, Ebbv Vale	NC, ND
	St Alban's RC Comp School, Pontypool	NC, ND
	Gwent Tertiary College, Pontypool	NC, ND
Gwynedd	Coleg Menai, Bangor	NC, ND
	Coleg Meirion Dwyfor, Dolgellau	NC, ND

Hackney	Hackney Community Centre, London	NC, ND
	City & Islington College, London	NC, ND
H'smith/Fulham	Holland Park School, London	NC, ND
	H'smith & W London Coll, London	NC, ND
Hampshire	Cricklade College, Andover	NC, ND
	Queen Mary's College, Basingstoke	NC, ND
	Eastleigh College, Eastleigh	NC, ND
	Fareham College, Fareham	NC, ND
	S Downs College, Waterlooville	NC, ND
Haringey	College of NE London, London	NC, ND
Harrow	Stanmore College, Stanmore	NC, ND
Havering	Havering Coll of F & HE, Hornchurch	NC, ND
Hereford/Worc	NE Worcs College, Bromsgrove	NC, ND
	Royal National Coll for the Blind, Hereford	NC, ND
	Kidderminster College, Kidderminster	NC, ND, HNC, HND
	Worcs College of Tech, Worcester	NC, ND
Hertfordshire	N Herts College, Hitchin	NC, ND
	Oaklands College, St Albans	NC, ND
	Hertford Regional Coll, Ware	NC, ND
	W Herts College, Watford	NC, ND
Hillingdon	Uxbridge College, Uxbridge	NC, ND
Hounslow	Brentford School for Girls, Brentford	NC, ND
	West Thames College, Isleworth	NC, ND
Humberside	Grimsby College, Grimsby	NC, ND
	Hull College, Hull	NC, ND
	Wyke VIth Form College, Hull	NC, ND
	North Lindsey College, Scunthorpe	NC, ND
Isle of Wight	Medina High School, Newport	NC, ND
Kent	The North School, Ashford	NC, ND
	Thanet College, Broadstairs	NC, ND
	Canterbury College, Canterbury	NC, ND
	Mid Kent Coll of H & FE, Chatham	NC, ND
	NW Kent College, Dartford	NC, ND
	South Kent College, Folkestone	NC, ND
	Southlands Comm Comp Sch, New Romney	NC, ND
	Chapter School, Rochester	NC, ND
	Sittingbourne Comm Coll, Sittingbourne	NC, ND
	West Kent College, Tonbridge	NC, ND
Kirklees	Dewsbury College, Dewsbury	NC, ND
	Huddersfield Tech College, Huddersfield	NC, ND
Knowsley	Knowsley Community College, Roby	NC, ND
Lambeth	Lambeth College, London	NC, ND
Lancashire	Accrington & Rossendale Coll, Accrington	NC, ND
	Blackpool & the Fylde College, Blackpool	NC, ND
	Burnley College, Burnley	NC, ND
	Nelson and Colne College, Nelson	NC, ND
	Preston College, Preston	NC, ND
	Skelmersdale College, Skelmersdale	NC, ND
Leeds	Park Lane College, Leeds	NC, ND
	Intake High School, Leeds	NC, ND
	Thomas Danby College, Leeds	NC, ND

Leicestershire	Charles Keene Coll of FE, Leicester	NC, ND, HNC, HND
	De Montfort University, Leicester	HNC, HND
	Guthlaxton College, Leicester	NC, ND
	Lutterworth Grammar School, Lutterworth	NC, ND
	Melton Mowbray FE Coll, Melton Mowbray	NC, ND
Lewisham	Lewisham College, London	NC, ND
Lincolnshire	Boston College, Boston	NC, ND
	Grantham College, Grantham	NC, ND
Liverpool	Liverpool Community College, Liverpool	NC, ND
	De La Salle School, Liverpool	NC, ND
	Liverpool Theatre School, Liverpool	NC, ND
Manchester	Shena Simon College, Manchester	NC, ND
	City College, Manchester	NC, ND
	N Manchester Community Coll, Manchester	NC, ND
Mid Glam	Bridgend College, Bridgend	NC, ND
	Merthyr Tydfil College, Merthyr Tydfil	NC, ND
	Pontypridd College, Pontypridd	NC, ND
	Porthcawl Comp School, Porthcawl	NC, ND
Newcastle	Newcastle College, Newcastle-upon-Tyne	NC, ND
Newham	Newham VIth Form College, London	NC, ND
	St Angela's and St Bonadventure's Centre	NC, ND
Norfolk	Great Yarmouth College, Great Yarmouth	NC, ND
	The College of West Anglian, King's Lynn	NC, ND, HNC, HND
N Tyneside	Tynemouth College, North Shields	NC, ND
	North Tyneside College, Wallsend	NC, ND
N Yorkshire	Harrogate College, Harrogate	NC, ND
	Yorkshire Coast H & FE Coll, Scarborough	NC, ND
	York College of F & HE, York	NC, ND
N Eastern Area	Causeway Inst of F & HE, Coleraine	NC, ND
	E Antrim Inst of F & HE, Newtownabbey	NC, ND
Northants	Daventry Tertiary College, Daventry	NC, ND
	Tresham Institute, Kettering	NC, ND
	Northampton College, Northampton	NC, ND
	Mereway Upper School, Northampton	NC, ND
Northumber	Northumberland College, Ashington	NC, ND
Notts	W Nottinghamshire College, Mansfield	NC, ND
	Newark & Sherwood College, Newark	NC, ND
	Arnold & Carlton College, Nottingham	NC, ND
	New College, Nottingham	NC, ND, HNC, HND
	Sutton Centre, Sutton-in-Ashfield	NC, ND
	N Nottinghamshire College, Worksop	NC, ND
Oldham	The Oldham College, Oldham	NC, ND, HNC, HND
Oxfordshire	Abingdon College, Abingdon	NC, ND
	N Oxfordshire Coll & Sch of Art, Banbury	NC, ND
	The Henley College, Henley-on-Thames	NC, ND
	Oxford College of FE, Oxford	NC, ND
Powys	Coleg Powys, Newtown	NC, ND
Richmond	Richmon Upon Thames Coll, Twickenham	NC, ND
Rochdale	Hopwood Hall College, Middleton	NC, ND
	Oulder Hill Community School, Rochdale	NC, ND
Rotherham	Rotherham Coll of Arts & Tech, Rotherham	NC, ND

Sefton	Southport College, Southport	NC, ND
Sheffield	The Sheffield College, Sheffield	NC, ND
Shropshire	Ludlow College, Ludlow	NC, ND
	Shrewsbury Coll Arts & Tech, Shrewsbury	NC, ND
	Thomas Telford School, Telford	NC, ND
	New College, Telford	NC, ND
Solihull	City Tech Coll, Kingshurst, Birmingham	NC, ND
	The Solihull College, Solihull	NC, ND
Somerset	Bridgwater College, Bridgwater	NC, ND
	Strode College, Street	NC, ND
	Somerset Coll of Arts & Tech, Taunton	NC, ND
	Yeovil College, Yeovil	NC, ND
S Glamorgan	Coleg Glan Hafren, Cardiff	NC, ND
	Cantonian High School, Cardiff	NC, ND
S Tyneside	South Tyneside College, South Shields	NC, ND, HNC, HND
S Eastern Area	N Down & Ards Inst of F & HE, Bangor	NC, ND
Southern Area	Armargh College of FE, Armargh	NC, ND
	Newry & Kilkeel Inst of F & HE, Newry	NC, ND
Southwark	Southwark College, London	NC, ND
St Helens	St Helens College, St Helens	NC, ND
Staffordshire	Burton upon Trent Tech Coll, Burton	NC, ND
	The Blake High School, Cannock	NC, ND
	Cannock Chase Tech Coll, Cannock	NC, ND
	Nether Stowe High School, Lichfield	NC, ND
	Newcastle-under-Lyme College, Newcastle	NC, ND
	Stafford College, Stafford	NC, ND
	Stoke on Trent College, Stoke on Trent	NC, ND, HNC, HND
	Tamworth College, Tamworth	NC, ND
	Queen Elizabeth's Mercian Sch, Tamworth	NC, ND
Stockport	Ridge Danyers College, Stockport	NC, ND
	North Area College, Stockport	NC, ND
Suffolk	Lowestoft College, Lowestoft	NC, ND
	Suffolk College, Ipswich	NC, ND, HNC, HND
	West Suffolk College, Bury St Edmunds	NC, ND
Sunderland	City of Sunderland College, Sunderland	NC, ND
Surrey	NE Surrey College of Tech, Ewell	NC, ND
	Brooklands College, Weybridge	NC, ND
	Woking College, Woking	NC, ND
Tameside	Tameside Coll of Tech, Ashton-under-Lyme	NC, ND
Trafford	South Trafford College, Altrincham	NC, ND
Wakefield	St Wilfrid's Catholic High Sch, Pontefract	NC, ND
	Wakefield College, Wakefield	NC, ND
Walsall	Walsall College of Arts & Tech, Walsall	NC, ND
Waltham For	Waltham Forest College, London	NC, ND
	Leyton VIth Form College, London	NC, ND
Wandsworth	Ernest Bevin College, London	NC, ND
	South Thames College, London	NC, ND
Warwickshire	Warwickshire College, Leamington Spa	NC, ND
	N Warwickshire & Hinkley Coll, Nuneaton	NC, ND
	Rugby College, Rugby	NC, ND
	Stratford-upon-Avon College, Stratford	NC, ND

W Glamorgan	Neath College, Neath	NC, ND
	Afan College, Port Talbot	NC, ND
	Swansea College, Swansea	NC, ND
	Gorseinon College, Swansea	NC, ND
W Sussex	Chichester Arts, Sci & Tech Coll, Chichester	NC, ND
	Crawley College, Crawley	NC, ND
	Northbrook College Sussex, Worthing	NC, ND, HNC, HND
Western Area	North West Inst of F & HE, Londonderry	NC, ND
	Omagh College, Omagh	NC, ND
Wigan	Wigan & Leigh College, Wigan	NC, ND
Wiltshire	Chippenham College, Chippenham	NC, ND
	New College Swindon, Swindon	NC, ND
	Salisbury College, Salisbury	NC, ND, HNC, HND
	Trowbridge Centre, Trowbridge	NC, ND
Wirral	Wirral Metropolitan College, Birkenhead	NC, ND
Wolverhampton	Bilston Community Coll, Wolverhampton	NC, ND
	Wulfrun College, Wolverhampton	NC, ND

Overseas		
Germany	Prince Rupert School, Rintein	NC, ND
Greece	N Avgerinopoulou Centre, Athens	HNC, HND
Ireland	Senior College, Dublin 10	HNC, HND

Useful Addresses

Arts Council of England
14 Great Peter Street, London SW1P 3NQ Tel: 0171 333 0100

Arts Council of Northern Ireland
185 Stranmills Road, Belfast BT9 5DU Tel: 01232 381591

Scottish Arts Council
12 Manor Place, Edinburgh EH3 7DD Tel: 0131 226 605

Arts Council of Wales
9 Museum Place, Cardiff CF 3NX Tel: 01222 394711

British Actors Equity Association
Guild House, Upper St Martin's Lane, London WC2H 9EG Tel: 0171 379 6000

British Council
11 Portland Place, London W1N 4EJ Tel: 0171 930 8466

Conference of Drama Schools
24 Dover Court Road, Dulwich, London SE22 8ST

National Association of Youth Theatres
Unit 1304, The Custard Factory, Gibb Street, Digbeth, Birmingham B9 4AA
Tel: 0121 680 2111

National Council for Drama Training
5 Tavistock Place, London WC1H 9SN Tel: 0171 387 3650

Publications:

Contacts
The Spotlight, 7 Leicester Place, London WC2H 7BP Tel: 0171 437 7631

The Stage Newspaper
47 Bermondsey Street, London SE1 3XT Tel: 0171 403 1818

How to get into Drama School, How to become a Working Actor
The Cheverell Press, Manor Studios, Manningford Abbots, Pewsey SN9 6HS

Scholarships, Bursaries and Charities

The following three scholarships are awarded to students for NCDT accredited courses put forward by drama schools only.

The Mackintosh Foundation Drama School Bursary Scheme

Bursaries are awarded anually to two students, male or female, who have been offered a place of study at a drama school for a course which is accredited by the NCDT. The bursary is for a three year period and covers (in whole, or in part) opayment of the tuition fees, and may also included a contribution towards maintenance.

The Lady Rothermere Award

Bi-annual bursary for actor/actress who is unable to find the necessary financial support for his/her drama studies. Successful candidates are awarded the cost of fees and maintenance for a period of three years.

The Lawrence Olivier Bursary

The Society of West End Theatres offers this annual bursary to help second year drama students who will have financial difficulty in their final year of training.

The following is a list of charities which have in the past given financial assistance to drama school students. You will find their addresses in the Directory of Grant Making Trusts and Charities, which should be in your local library. Many charities are restricted to particular areas, religions, races or other specific associations so it is worth looking through to see which apply to you.

The Laura Ashley Foundation, Norman C Aston Foundation, The Atlantic Foundation, Lawrence Atwell's Charity, Buttle Trus, Carpenter's Company, The Sir John Cass Foundation, The Sir James Colyer-Fergusson Charitable Trust, The Clothworkers' Foundation, Bets and Jim Cooper Bursary Fund, The Henry Cotton Memorial Trust, The Mary Datchelor Trust, D'Oyley Carte Charitable Trust The Ann Driver Trust, The Drapers Guild, Gilbert and Eileen Edgar Foundation Fenton Arts Trust, Alfred Foster Settlement, The Sir Anthony Hopkins Charitable Foundation, The Verity Hudson Award, The Nicholas Hytner Charitable Trust The Idlewild Trust, The Irish Times ESB Irish Theatre Bursary, The Leverhulme Trust, Littler Foundation, Matthews Wrightson Charitable Trust, Mercers Company, The Millington Company, Philological Foundation, Stanley Picker Trust, Mr and Mrs Pye's Charitable Settlement, Royal Victoria Hall Foundation - Lilian Baylis Award, Sedgefield Educational Foundation, Alastair Selway Trust Fund The Sports and Arts Foundation, South Square Trust, Stoll Moss Theatre Foundation, Stoller Charitable Trust, The Truro Fund, Walcott Educational Charity, The Walker Trust, The Thomas Wall Trust, Charles Wallace India Trust, The Garfield Weston Foundation

Glossary

The following are all terms or names which are either included in this book or you might hear at audition.

Accreditation: System by which the National Council for Drama Training (NCDT) assesses drama school courses (not the schools themselves). Accredited courses will have reached certain standards and have certain advantages such as it is usually easier to get grants to go to an accredited course. NCDT courses are marked with a * in the text.

Alexander Technique: A method of body alignment developed by an actor and used by actors to improve posture and free tension physically and vocally. It is one of the most widely accepted 'alternative' treatments.

Brecht, Bertolt: Most successful playwright of the style known as the Theatre of Alienation. The idea was to stimulate political and philosophical thought rather than emotional responses. Author of 'Mother Courage'.

Brook, Peter: Very influential British director who now lives in Paris. His book 'The Empty Space' is essential reading for all actors.

Carlton Hobbs Award: Annual competition open to final year students at Conference of Drama Schools. There are various categories of winners, some of whom are awarded a contract for a year with the BBC Radio Repertory Company.

CDS: see Conference of Drama Schools

Chekhov, Michael: Son of the playwright, he developed Stanislavski's methods. Very influential in America.

Commedia dell'arte: An acting style, often using masks and mannered gestures in the tradition of Harlequin - and Mr. Punch!

Community theatre: Performances devised with and for the community, often based on oral traditions.

Conference of Drama Schools: An organisation set up in the 60s by the main drama schools to promote themselves. They have been extremely unwilling to let anyone else join since then, but recently invited two more drama schools to join, namely Cygnet and Oxford School of Drama. Is it a coincidence that neither school could be described as being competition for the original members?

Discretionary Grants: Grants awarded at the discretion of your LEA, now as rare as hens teeth for all performing arts courses. Note that grants for degree courses at private institutions are discretionary not mandatory (see below).

Equity: The actors union. It used to be a closed shop with a limited quota of newcomers each year, then it allowed graduates from accredited courses to join. Now the closed shop has gone and you do not need an Equity card to act professionally. Numbers are falling so they have relaxed the entry restrictions again and any drama student can now join.

FOH: Front of House

Growtowski, Jerzy: Polish director who has developed the ideas of the Theatre of Cruelty. Nothing to do with violence, but rather total theatre involving music, song and dance as well as words.

Improvisation: Performance without preparation, as seen on "Whose line is it anyway?" At best it frees the actors imagination, at worst it descends to the "now be a tree" school of acting.

Laban, Rudolf: The founding father of the contemporary dance movement.

LEA: Local Education Authority see below

Lecoq, Jacques: Founded of the mime and physical theatre school in Paris which bears his name.

Littlewood, Joan: Director who pioneered ensemble and working class theatre in Britain. Founder of Theatre Workshop, best known for 'O What a Lovely War!'

Local Education Authority: Once the main source of fees, with discretionary and mandatory grants. Cut backs mean that grants are forthcoming from only the richest of boroughs, usually in predominantly rural areas in the south.

Mandatory grants: Awarded to all courses at publicly funded institutions. This does not include degrees at private institutions.

Method: Any system which allows an actor to explore a character following certain steps, and drawing heavily on the actors own experiences. The most famous is that developed by Stanislavski, see below, but there are others. Method acting is the most widely used acting style in the USA and it is particularly good for television and film acting.

NCDT/National Council for Drama Training: The main accreditation body for assessing acting and stage management courses.

RP/ Received Pronunciation: Also known as Standard, BBC or the Queen's English. Taught as an accent at most drama schools.

RSC/Royal Shakespeare Company: Famous acting company, based at Stratford-upon-Avon, Warwickshire and the Barbican in London. Mainly performs Shakespeare, Elizabethan and Jacobean plays and is considered the ultimate name for an actors CV.

The Spotlight: A company providing many acting services, including a directory of actors and actresses and the essential publication, 'Contacts'.

Stanislavski/Stanislavsky: Russian director and founder of the Moscow Arts Theatre who developed a method enabling actors to discover and explore the characters they were playing. He wrote several books, including 'An Actor Prepares' which is essential reading for all actors.

Tai Chi: A martial art which has developed into a series of movements used by actors as a means of teaching physical control and mental concentration. When it is used for exercises strictly speaking it should be called Tai Chi Ch'uan.

TIE/Theatre in Education: Productions for children.

Index

A

Aberystwyth, University of Wales 125
Academy of Live and Recorded Arts 18–20
Advanced Residential Theatre and Television Skillcentre 21–24
ALRA. *See* Academy of Live and Recorded Arts
Arden School of Theatre 25–27
Arts Educational Schools London 28-30
ARTTS. *See* Advanced Residential Theatre and Television Skillcentre

B

Barnsley College 126
Belfast see Queen's University at Belfast
Birmingham School of Speech and Drama 12, 31–33
Bolton Institute 127
Bretton Hall, University College 7, 128–130
Brighton, University of 130–131
Bristol, University of 131
Bristol Old Vic 5, 34- 38
Brunel University 131–132
BTEC awards in Performing Arts 175–180

C

Carmarthen, Trinity College 132–133
Central Lancashire, University of 134
Central School of Speech and Drama 6, 13, 39–41, 133–134
Cheltenham & Gloucester College 134–135
Chester, University College 135–136
Court Theatre Training Company 42–44
Coventry University 136
Cumbria College of Art and Design 136–137
Cygnet Training Theatre Company 45–47

D

Dartington College of Arts 7, 137–138
De Montfort University Bedford 138–139
De Montfort University Leicester 139
Derby, University of 140
Drama Centre London 8, 9, 11, 13, 48–50
Drama Studio London 15, 51–54

E

East 15 Acting School 55–58
East Anglia, University of   140
Edge Hill University College 141
Exeter, Univeristy of 141–142

G

Glamorgan, University of 143
Glossary 183–184
Goldsmiths College, University of London 143–144
GSA see Guildford School of Acting
Guildford School of Acting 59–63
Guildhall School of Music and Drama 6, 11, 64–66

H

Hertfordshire, University of   144–145
Hertfordshire Theatre School 67–69
Huddersfield, University of 145
Hull, University of 145–146

K

Kent at Canterbury, University of 146–147
King Alfred's University College Winchester 147–148

L

LAMDA see London Academy of Music and Dramatic Art
Lancaster University 148–149
LAPA see London Academy of Performing Arts
LISA see London and International School of Acting
Liverpool Hope University College 149–150
Liverpool Institute for Performing Arts 150–151
Liverpool John Moores University 152
London Academy of Music and Dramatic Art 6, 70–74

London Academy of Performing Arts 75–77
London and International School of Acting 80–81
London Centre for Theatre Studies 5, 78–79
Loughborough University 152–153

M

Manchester, University of 153-154
Manchester Metropolitan University 82–84
Middlesex University 154–155
Mountview Conservatoire for the Performing Arts 85–89

N

Nene University College of Northampton 155–156
Newman College of Higher Education 156
North London, University of 157
Northumbria, University of 157–158

O

Oxford School of Drama 90–93

P

Plymouth, Univeristy of 158–159
The Poor School 94–95

Q

Queen Margaret College 96–98, 159–160
Queen Mary and Westfield College 160
Queen's University of Belfast 126–127

R

RADA see Royal Academy of Dramatic Art
Reading, University of 161
Redroofs Theatre School 99–101
Richmond Drama School 102–124
Ripon & York St John, University College of 161–162
Roehampton Institute London 162–163
Rose Bruford College 104–106
Royal Academy of Dramatic Art 6, 7, 9, 13, 107–110
Royal Holloway, University of London 163–164
Royal Scottish Academy of Music and Drama 15, 111–114, 164
RSAMD see Royal Scottish Academy of Music and Drama

S

St Martin, University College of   164-165
St Mary's University College   165-166
Salford, University of   166–167
Scarborough, University College of   167–168
Scholarships, Bursaries and Charities   182
School of the Science of Acting   115–117
South Bank University   168
Staffordshire University   168–169
Sunderland, University of   169
Sussex, University of   169–170
Swansea Institute of Higher Education   170

T

Trinity College Carmarthen see Carmarthen, Trinity College

U

Useful Addresses   181
UWE see West of England, University of

W

Warrington, University College   170–171
Warwick, University of   171–172
Webber Douglas Academy of Dramatic Art   5, 6, 118–120
Welsh College of Music and Drama   10, 121–124
West of England, University of   173–174
Westhill College of Higher Education   173
Worcester, Univeristy College   174

HOW TO BECOME A WORKING ACTOR

* NEW EDITION COMING SPRING 1999 *

It is well known that in the over crowded world of acting most actors spend much of their careers out of work. But there are some actors - and not just the famous ones - who are always in work. How they manage to find work where others fail is the subject of this book. Advice comes from both sides of the table, from directors, producers, casting directors and agents, as well as actors.

Contents include:

Auditions	Castings	Interviews	Agents
Equity	Letters	Speeches	Readings
CVs	Commercials	Voice Overs	Theatre
Film	Television	Radio	Musicals
Photographs	Techniques	....and much, much more	

"In Duncan's handy book there is plenty to keep any young hopeful occupied. Arranged clearly and concisely this well-researched and easily readable book has advice on writing letters, choosing photographs and agents. Mercifully jargon free, this book is a good introduction to the world of the actor. Her advice could put you at least six months ahead of rivals at auditions."

The Stage and Television Today

"How to become a Working Actor" has become essential reading for all actors, whether newcomers to the profession or well established. This new edition contains hard information on subjects as dirverse as Equity membership, getting a part in a commercial or being good at interviews and auditions. From tax, VAT and social security to TV, rep, musicals and one man shows, "How to become a working Actor" covers all aspects of an actor's life.

ISBN:1-872390-14-5   £8.95 pbk   Available Spring 1999

HOW TO GET INTO DRAMA SCHOOL

At up to £30 a time, auditions at drama school aren't cheap so you've got to make the most of your chances. This book shows you how.

Find out:
*   How to choose and prepare good audition speeches
*   Audition and interview techniques
*   What questions to expect - and some good answers
*   What to wear and what to say
*   Which auditions are the cheapest, the most expensive, the best value or even free
*   What each school looks for at audition
*   What to expect when you turn up for audition
*   Which schools want speeches from their list, and which don't want speeches at all
*   What are the odds on being accepted - 10 to 1, or 100 to 1?
*   How to improve your chances before you set foot on the premises

If you are thinking of going to drama school this book is essential reading.

ISBN: 1-872390-01-3   £6.95

Available from bookshops or direct from the publisher (please add £1 towards p&p)

The Cheverell Press
Manor Studios, Manningford Abbots, Pewsey SN9 6HS.